"The third in this pioneering series will roll of some of African contributing. Unmissable." — Geoff Ryman, author, a time Arthur C. Clarke, thr Canadian Sunburst, as well Dick, and James Tiptree Jr., awards.

"The compelling, graceful stories in *AfroSFv3* embrace a generous spectrum of places and peoples, eras and objectives. From sophisticated space operas to gritty cyberpunk streets; from day-after-tomorrow beginnings to far-off futures; from familial closeness to alien vastness, these well-wrought tales, infused with all the sharp, bright, enticing flavors of their African origins, show us the commonality of our species across all racial, ethnic and gender lines. Truly, these writers speak the same science fiction tongue as their like-minded cousins from the rest of the planet, with beautiful accents of their native soil." — Paul Di Filippo, author of *Cosmocopia*, *The Steampunk Trilogy*, and others.

"With stories ranging from mundane science fiction to distant space opera passing from post-colonial bi-opunk and new family ties, the latest book of in the *AfroSF* series shows that inclusivity and multiculturality is the key to the future. As quality storytelling - rooted in every culture and tradition – doesn't belong to a single country or language, these stories prove that the future - as evident as it might sound although not always considered so - does happen everywhere. Excellent reading!" — Francesco Verso, author of *Nexhuman* and editor of *Future Fiction*.

AfroSFv3

Edited by Ivor W. Hartmann

Introduction

Ivor W. Hartmann

It has been six years since the first *AfroSF* anthology was published, and in those years the landscape of African SFF has radically changed for the better.

The African Speculative Fiction Society was founded in 2016 and created and hosts the annual Nommo Awards (funded by Tom Ilube) for African SFF since 2017. The ASFS also created and maintains the most comprehensive database of published African SFF.

We have Mazi Nwonwu and Chinelo Onwualu's *Omenana* magazine dedicated to and publishing African SFF on a regular basis. Ainehi Edoro's *Brittle Paper* magazine though not dedicated to African SFF also regularly publishes it. Likewise African publishers: Jalalda, Chimurenga, Dada, Short Story Day Africa, The Kalahari Review, Black Letter Media, Johannesburg Review of Books, Okada Books, Enkare Review, African Writer, Afreada, umSinsi Press, Bahati Books, Kwani?, Munyori Literary Journal, Afridiaspora, Pan African Publishers, Sub-Saharan Magazine, and Jacana Media, to name a few have embraced African SFF in short stories, novellas, anthologies, and novels.

Nnedi Okorafor has become our undisputed queen, winning the World Fantasy award in 2011, and both the Nebula Award and Hugo Award in 2016. And if there is a king to be it is probably Tade Thompson, winner of two Nommos, Kitschies Golden Tentacle Award, and a finalist for the John W. Campbell Award as well as nominations for the Shirley Jackson Award and the British Science Fiction Award.

What this all amounts to is an unparalleled interest in African SFF both at home and abroad with more and more writers, publishers, and most importantly readers, realising a thirst for homegrown African SFF, for works that address our unique problems and envisions our futures.

This brings me to the focus of *AfroSFv3*. Space, the astronomical wilderness that has enthralled our minds since we first looked up in wonder. We are ineffably drawn to it, and equally terrified by it. We have created endless mythologies, sciences, and even religions, in the quest to understand it. We know more now than ever before and are taking our first real steps. What will become of Africans out there, will we thrive, how will space change us, how will we change it? *AfroSFv3* is going out there, into the great expanse, and with twelve visions of the future we invite you to sit back, strap in, and enjoy the ride.

Ivor W. Hartmann is a Zimbabwean writer, editor, publisher, and visual artist. Awarded The Golden Baobab Prize (2009), finalist for the Yvonne Vera Award (2011), selected for The *20 in Twenty: The Best Short Stories of South Africa's Democracy* (2014), and awarded third place in the Jalada Prize for Literature (2015). He runs the StoryTime micro-press, publisher of the *African Roar* and *AfroSF* series of anthologies, is a founding member of the African Speculative Fiction Society.

Njuzu

T.L. Huchu

Water looks the same everywhere. It's only the background, lighting, and impurities, that differ. I peer at the silver-grey surface of Bimha's pond, calm and still, undisturbed by wind. It's deep and the bottom is a black abyss. Midday here is like dawn on Earth in the middle of the Kalahari. Light shines through the transparent panelling of the pressurised geodesic dome that prevents the water boiling straight into vapour.

'This is where it happened,' VaMutasa says to me on the crackling open channel.

We can't take off our helmets because the atmosphere within the dome is not fit to breathe. I take a step closer.

'Careful,' Tarisai whispers.

A trail of small footprints runs beside me. We followed it here, but where we stop, it carries on, bravely, foolishly.

'This is where it happened,' VaMutasa says once more, as if to convince himself.

The icy brown soil under my boots feels hard. Each movement I make is slow and considered. A white plume of steam rises from the outlet pipes a kilometre or two away, the far end of the pond. Thirty million gallons of water cycle in and out of the Nharira Nuclear Fusion Plant nearby.

Superheated steam is deposited into the ground, liquified and the cold water is cycled back to the plant via insulated pipes.

I close my eyes and take deep breaths, fighting the sickness threatening to void my stomach. My chest feels tight, tied with an iron band, and I reach to remove my helmet so I can breathe. My husband grabs my arms:

'Remember where you are,' Tarisai says. 'I told you this would do no good.'

The tone of her voice is reproachful and she's angry, a dam waiting to burst. But on the open channel, with everyone listening in, we save the argument for later, piled up with the rest of the little tears and scraps every marriage sweeps under the bulging carpet.

I must be polite; the muroora, daughter-in-law, is not just married to one person. The bond of matrimony ties her to everyone in the clan, both the living and the dead.

'It's important, whatever you do, you mustn't cry,' VaMutasa says. 'The njuzu won't let him go otherwise.'

'My son's just drowned and you're talking about mythical creatures?' I snarl but hold my tears all the same. Even though I know it's superstition, something inside checks me, because, with the chips where they lie, all I can do is hedge.

'One of the technicians, Chisumbanje, fell in the water twenty years ago. For three days, we couldn't find him. Then, when he came back, he was a powerful n'anga without equal in the Belt. He saw her, the njuzu. She's in there,' a woman's voice says, but I don't recognise it.

'Whatever you do, you must-not-cry,' VaMutasa says, this time in a firm voice. 'We'll prepare the rites.'

He is my father-in-law, Tarisai's father, the head of the Mutasa clan. Their fortune is made from farming the desert and selling water—hydrogen and oxygen—to wayfarers passing through to worlds beyond.

\#

We've only been here a week and it's hard to get used to the eighteen-hour days. Dusk, when it comes, is swift, a minute or so long, the faltering of a fluorescent bulb marking the turn from light to darkness.

I stay in our Hurungwe Utility Terra Shelter, lying in bed; my molars ache, I feel they might shatter into sharp shards of glass. From outside comes the sound of silence so loud it presses on every ounce of my being. Tarisai isn't here to hold me. She's out with the men in the search party who now radio in as the recovery team. She's my husband, so she must. This place is tough and unforgiving. We should never have come back.

I feel helpless. Hopeless.

Don't cry.

\#

I wake sometime before dawn. My husband's arm lies across my chest. It's heavy and strong, and she smells of sweat from the search. She's a snorer, but tonight she is quiet, a slight frown on her face.

Gently, I remove her arm.

The carbon fibre walls of the HUTS we're in are decorated with Tonga artwork from the tourist market in Mosi-oa-Tunya reed ruscros and baskets with intricate designs woven by married women past child-bearing age. There's an abstract sculpture made of polished Cerean rock. A red Basotho blanket hangs on the wall opposite.

I creep out of bed, wear my suit and go into the airlock, checking my oxygen tanks are full up. With the CO_2 decarboniser, I have up to fifteen hours' worth of air. My son Anesu with his small lungs would have had a little more.

The airlock door creaks and I hope it doesn't wake Tarisai as I walk out and shut it behind me.

Fierce lamps, high up on poles like stadium lights, illuminate the compound. The yard has wide open spaces in which the HUTS are erected. They arc domed, like Zulu huts with small round port windows. There're fifteen of them here (one medical and two for emergencies), a few equipment stores, and in the far-off distance is the large mess where we take our meals. Beyond the compound, the valley is littered with hundreds of settlements, everyone trying to earn their fortune in the Wild Belt.

I walk, adjusting my body to the microgravity, so I sort of waddle and shuffle, bouncing from side to side. The trick is to lunge forward, so the momentum carries you horizontal to the ground. The few times I go too high up, my auto-downward thrusters kick in to push me back down, releasing a thin jet of gas.

The ground is rocky and bumpy. Footprints from years ago remain pristine in the wind free space.

I walk past the Mutasas' ancestral graves. Mounds of dirt like mole homes, topped with simple headstones, where the dead lie in frozen ground.

Beyond that, a short distance away, are their farms. Massive greenhouses with controlled air, temperature, and water, turn the fertile soil of this desert world into an oasis. They grow lettuce, onions, tomatoes, cucumbers, wheat, maize, anything they wish at all, because the once barren soil, rich in carbon and organic compounds, is hungry for life. Ceres, named after the goddess of agriculture, is generous in her bounty, feeding miners across the Belt and colonists on Mars and beyond.

I search for my son's small bootprints until I find them, heading out to the waterhole. Sometimes they're obliterated by his companions, other times his small print sits square inside a larger print. The children come here to play games on the water. In the low gravity they can run on it, just like basilisk lizards on Earth.

Eight years ago, I sang the Song of Life and knitted him into being with my two hands. After I missed my period, my mother came to me, bearing my trousseau of linen and jewellery. We sat face to face on my marriage bed with our legs crossed and sang:

Ndinowumba musoro wako
Ndinowumba maziso ako
Ndinowumba mhino yako
Ndinowumba chipfuva chako
Ndinowumba tsoka dzako
Ndinowumba zvidya zvako
Ndinowumba dumbu rako
Ndinowumba kamboro kako
Ndinowumba rurimi rwako
Ndinowumba twugunwe twako

. . .

For three hours we sang him into being. Each line starting, 'I create', followed by the part I willed into being. My hands, index finger on thumb as though holding knitting needles, dancing around my belly as I knitted every atom of Anesu into existence.

The Song of Life was important, every part of his body had to be sung, willed into existence, or he'd be deformed. I heard the response to the Song in his voice, every time he spoke with me. I heard it in his laughter at play and the tears I wiped away when he was sick.

Yet, as I stood on the shores of Bimha's pond, the sacred duet had been stolen from me. In its place, I only heard silence and grief.

#

Dawn, when she comes, is just a minute long, a step from a dark room into light. Long shadows embrace my legs. The tangerine in the black sky is supposed to be the sun.

'Where were you?' Tarisai says. She's waiting for me at the edge of the compound. 'Everyone's looking for you.'

I walk up to her and embrace her. In the bulky suit, I can't feel her warmth. I feel nothing.

A slow rhythmic drumming, pangu, pangu, pangu, comes from the mess as I strip out of my suit. The air here is too crisp, like something is missing, dust, pollen, the scents of earth.

Hands clap, bu, bu, bu, to the beat of the drum.

Women ululate.

The chairs and tables in the mess have been unbolted from the floor and stacked up in one corner. Hard-faced men and women sit on the floor, separated from one another. Tarisai joins the men. Her anatomy is female, but she hosts the spirit of a man—an ancestor who claims her body for his vessel—and so she is man.

I sit and fold my legs to one side.

Don't cry.

A hologram at the front projects a life-like nyati, the buffalo, their clan's totem. A noble and prestigious line. I'm samaita, the zebra, not the bottom of the totem pole, but a little more humble. Anesu, like his father, is—dare I say was—a buffalo too, for the line passes from father to child. The mother is as good as a stranger, her blood does not count.

Chisumbanje is at the front, bare chested, his loins covered by the skin from a black and white bull. Hoshos tied to his ankles rattle when he moves. His head is crowned with a feathered headband as he rocks back and forth to the beat of the drums.

It's hot in the mess.

Christine places her hand around me and I lay my head on her shoulder. We greet Chisumbanje by his totem name; he is the meat-eating herbivore who stalks silent in the savannah grass, death incarnate, the uncrossable chasm.

He takes a pinch of snuff, inhales deeply and sneezes several times. We clap and chant: 'Svikai zvakanaka, vasekuru.'

Njuzu

In the corner of my eye, I see Tarisai clench her fists and mutter some words. She is resisting. Her spirit is trying to visit, to gain entrance, but this is not his ceremony, he must wait in the spirit world, stand guard against the evil that would do us harm. Only Chisumbanje will be visited today.

Christine takes me to the back of the room. We carry calabashes on our heads. On Earth, I lack the grace and skill, but here, in the low gravity, my calabash stays on the top of my head, until I place it down by Chisumbanje's feet. We kneel, clap our hands, stand, and retreat to the women's side.

The drummer stops. He too is dressed in animal skins and he picks up one calabash in both hands, squats and offers it to Chisumbanje. Chisumbanje shakes his head and rejects it. The drummer pours a drop on the floor to the spirits and offers the beer a second time. Now Chisumbanje accepts with a nod. As their hands meet, the giver and the taker, we clap and the men whistle.

The blessed beer now passes from Chisumbanje back to the drummer, the receiver has become the giver. And the drummer passes it to the men. Twenty thirsty throats take in a sip each. There are one or two miners with us from the next settlement. Gold prices have plunged. There's too much of it coming from the asteroids, flooding the market. Soon they'll pack their tools and move to mine another commodity, until it crashes, too.

The ancestor who visits Chisumbanje tells us certain things: Anesu is alive and well in the company of the njuzu. We must not cry. If we do, she'll be angry and kill him. We must offer a sacrifice to appease her. If we do this correctly, Anesu will return a great healer and seer, a n'anga. She'll give him gifts without compare from the spirit world.

There are no cattle on Ceres, but we have plenty of rabbits and chicken for meat.

The sacrifice will be a black male rabbit.

#

My teeth ache so bad as I lie naked in bed at night. Any light movement I make jabs a nerve.

The view outside my port window is a purple-green sky, a kind of grotesque aurora showing the frontline of the battle between solar–cosmic radiation and the artificial magnetosphere that stands as the only thing preventing us from being slowly microwaved to death.

I hate this annual pilgrimage.

I want to go back to Earth.

When chirimo, the planting season, comes, we leave our cushy office jobs, pack our bags and go kumusha to help with the farming. We all have two homes, our true home being kumusha where our ancestors are buried. Mine is on Earth, in Manhenga: Tarisai belongs here on this desert world, which she abandoned to be with me.

Yet each time we visit, I hate it more and more, though I try not to let on.

I know it's the magnetosphere that causes my toothache. The doctors say that's impossible, but it never happens when I'm on Earth. I refuse to take painkillers. I want to suffer like my son did, alone and scared in the dark.

Don't cry.

A star moves swiftly across the sky, one of the three satellites orbiting Ceres.

Tarisai comes into the room. Her hard, sculpted body moves slowly, solid pecs showing under the white vest she wears.

'You left early,' she says without reproach.

'That voodoo isn't going to bring my son back,' I reply. 'Do you honestly think some mythical creature took him?'

'He was with his cousins. They're experienced Ceresmen. They walk over that pond practically every day, mudiwa. It's virtually impossible for anyone to drown here. The gravity is far too weak, you couldn't break the surface tension of the water to go under. But somehow Anesu did. His thrusters must have malfunctioned, pushing him down under the water. We're trying to figure it out. They were walking in a group, he was a little behind. They got to the far bank and he was gone. For some reason, his transponder isn't working either.'

'They were supposed to look after him. He's an Earthchild.'

'They did their-'

'I want my son back!' I scream at her.

Njuzu

'We're doing the best we can. There've been search parties.'
She sighs and lowers her voice. 'You're not the only one
who's hurting, you know? He was my son too.'

'You never wanted him in the first place.'

'Oh, so now we get to it. Are you really going to fling stuff
I said in uni back in my face?'

'You wanted to be free, to explore the solar system, Venus,
Europa, Titan, to Pluto and beyond. How many times did
you change his nappies? You'd rather have been anywhere
else.'

'But I stayed, because I love you.'

Before I can say the next spiteful thought formed in my
mind, she's on top of me, pinning me down, a rough finger
in my dry vagina. We claw, bite, fight like animals as we
make desperate love. And when it's over, we fall back down,
sweaty and exhausted, and turn away from one another.

#

In my dream, I sink into black water, thick like oil. The silver moon of Earth shines on my face. I wonder why of all
moons, ours has no name, as if it is enough to say what it
is. Maybe I should give it a name, call it something kind and
gentle.

I sink down, leagues and leagues, down a never-ending
abyss.

Until I meet her, at the bottom of the dark.

I never truly knew what a njuzu was. For some, she's a
mermaid, half woman half fish. For others a water sprite,
spritely and nimble. Since I lost my son, I've thought of her
as a spiteful siren, the disastrous enchantress, ensnarer of
sailors and young boys. But the reality is she's neither of
these: she simply is what she is.

She sits tall on her throne, Neptune's daughter. The most
beautiful woman I've ever seen. Her flawless skin is black
like polished obsidian. Tiny bubbles form against it. Her
wise eyes sparkle like pearls. Her hair is green and wild like
reeds in the river Tsanga.

Anesu is still, wearing a copper necklace on his bare torso.
At their feet lie herbs, divining bones, a kudu horn and
earthenware utensils.

The njuzu half smiles at me.

'Give me my son back, you bitch!' I shout, and the water
enters my mouth, into my lungs. I cough and gag,

drowning. My chest is full of molten lead as I struggle, arms flailing, trying to reach the distant, moonlit surface where Tarisai's face looks down at me.

'Wake up, you're having a bad dream,' she says.

#

The stars in the Milky Way lighting my path number less than the kisses I planted on Anesu's head and brow and lips and feet and every square inch of my baby's body.

Fury and fear draw me back to Bhima's pond like an iron filing to a magnet.

The sun is yet to rise in the dark green sky.

The still surface of water meets my boot and I walk on it. It is soft and gently displaces creating ripples that fan out in front of me. I try to peer under the dark surface, in the depths where my Anesu must be. I sing the Song of Life as I walk upon it, each step, recreating him, my gloved hands knitting him piece by piece.

Tarisai appears on the shore. She's a tiny figure in her bright red suit. The light on her helmet points at me. I know she hurts, too, but there's a magnitude of pain only a mother can feel. So, I give her a wave. She stays where she is, my silent guardian.

When I reach the middle of the pond, I let go of the lie of hope and slowly let it fall into the water. I know my son is lost forever.

His spirit wanders the cruel, cold depths of Ceres.

I cry. Large hot tears fill my helmet until I'm blind and I can see his face looking at me again.

T.L. Huchu's work has appeared in *Interzone, The Apex Book of World SF 5, Ellery Queen Mystery Magazine, The Year's Best Crime and Mystery Stories 2016, AfroSFv1,* and elsewhere. He enjoys working across genres, from crime to sci-fi to literary fiction. Currently, he is working on new fantasy novel. Find him @TendaiHuchu

The Girl Who Stared at Mars

Cristy Zinn

In the distance, hangs Mars. Even though I know none of this is real, I pretend, just for a little while, that I am twelve years old and dreaming of that red planet. I am in my garden on State Street—cool grass under my feet, skin goosebumped by the fresh night air. The hum of the world has quieted and all that is left is the swelling chorus of insects. It is dark except for the stripe of light that spills from my bedroom where the curtains hang askew. I shift so that the light doesn't interfere with my view of the stars.

The pungent smell of the nearby Yesterday-Today-and-Tomorrow flowers stirs my memories—of childhood, first love, night swims in a humid summer. I feel the vibrations of the pool pump and listen to the lap-lap of the water as the creepy-crawly works just under the surface.

The sound of muffled laughter drifts from next door—someone is watching a sitcom or having a dinner party.

I am not distracted by any of it. Mars has my attention. I cannot take my eyes off that small, twinkling planet. A familiar longing settles in; romantic and desperate. It is a longing to be free of this garden, to see space for myself, to walk the empty red hills of Mars. I smile at the irony, considering where I am outside this simulation.

'You'll do well up there,' says my step-father, Dumza. His voice is as rich as I remember it.

He puts an arm around my shoulders and gives me a squeeze. He smells like soap and sweat. I smile.

'You think so?' I ask.

He laughs. It's that barrel-belly laugh that I love so much. 'Of course.'

When I turn my head, he is gone. There's just the garden and the night, and it is no longer easy to pretend.

The Girl Who Stared at Mars

I emerge from the simulation with tears on my cheeks. I wipe them away and take a breath, like I was taught. One, two, three, place yourself back in reality. One, two, three, orient yourself. One, two, three, be mindful of your breath. I close my eyes, taking mental notes of how I feel so I can log it later. The garden is gone, the metal shell is back.

I look out the portal window, into space. Eleven days in, eighteen to go. We're in limbo now—that dead space between things where we cannot see where we've come from or where we're going. Earth is gone, Mars is nowhere in sight yet. We are wholly alone.

I place my feet on the ground. The cold seeps through the rubber mats, through my socks, and into my bones. How is it that they've mastered solar sail travel, but they haven't figured out a way to keep this place warm I wonder.

Otar is leaning against the frame. He looks exhausted, his blonde hair mussed and unwashed—he's not sleeping well, none of us are. It's hard to schedule a body clock that is so accustomed to the sun and moon ordering our days and nights, even with the programmed light sequence that tries to mimic it.

'You done?' he asks.

I nod. 'Just give me a minute.'

'Don't be long.' He slips back down the corridor, disinterested in small talk. I'd love to say it's because he's a loner but it's just me he'd rather not be around.

I bend down, resting my hands on my knees. Dumza has never been in my simulations. I don't know how he got in there—I didn't add him to my memory bank. His presence has thrown me. I miss him all over again.

And of course, the feeling is quickly drowned by a deep, unsettling anxiety.

They told us to keep people out of the sims—too difficult to distance yourself from Earth if you're clinging to relationships. Instead, they framed the questions to help us remember places. I guess the garden I chose was too closely linked to my time with Dumza. I take another deep breath. Maybe it was my subconscious kicking in and adding to the mix. Maybe I'm so tired I started dreaming while in the sim. I wipe away another tear, take another deep breath. There is no space in all this vastness for things that bind us to Earth.

Cristy Zinn

Chapter two of Wendel Nkomo's philosophical tome, *Native in Space*, begins with this sentence:

"*In space we all become alien. And yet, in space— travelling between stars—the only thing we have is our humanity. Perhaps it will be here that humans finally let go of their prejudices and embrace true Ubuntu.*"

I wonder if that's what he found on Mars. Eleven days in space and I'm thinking prejudices are all we bring with us.

The first week in training we were each asked to sign a non-disclosure agreement that legally bound us not to share what we were about to learn. I don't think any of us hesitated to sign it. We were hungry enough for Mars to dismiss the usual legal jargon.

It was then we realised to what extent the MarsCasts were censored and monitored.

The African Space Alliance must maintain the hope of colonisation, the dream, the great vision. Fear might lead to a cut in funding, and we can't have that—the recent plethora of economic crashes and wars have ensured that financial backing is meagre enough as it is.

I must be honest, watching the truth, there were moments when I almost turned my back on Mars—but the promise of something new, something so pregnant with possibility left me unable to resist.

Not even after I learned the truth:

The first team to call Mars home are all on heavy medication for mental breakdowns. The second had two suicides in transit. The third was uniquely lacking in drama, while the fourth only had one incident: the brutal beating of Jon McKnamara for constantly making lewd comments about his fellow female officer. He almost died but instead, gets to live on Mars as a paraplegic, *with* his attackers—because no one, *no one*, comes back from Mars. Not victims, not perpetrators. Colonisation can be hell.

Every crew is battered with psychological tests and thrown into a hab in the middle of the Sahara for six months before we go anywhere near space. Then it's another six months on the New International Space Station. We are monitored and assessed and counselled but none of these well-educated people really knows what it's like to live on another planet; to *live* in space entirely divorced from Earth. Now that there are a few more scientists Mars-side, everyone's hoping they'll be able to figure out how to better prepare the crews. *Hoping.* It's the word that encapsulates this endeavour because, really, no one has ever colonised another planet before. Our colonisation is still in its infancy and mistakes are likely to be made.

It's not all bad news though, it wasn't that Mars had become some sort of arena for the worst of mankind, in fact, once the medication kicked in and the newer teams arrived, a kind of stability began to form. The incidents became less frequent as the crews settled in. And it seems that, for now, things are going well. As wars and famines and natural catastrophes monopolise news headlines here on Earth, Mars really is a colony of hope.

The trainers at the African Space Agency made it very clear that stability is a fragile tension that we must do our utmost to uphold. It would be hard work—both psychologically and physically.

But even with the uncertainty of the state of Mars, and our place in it, I still wanted in. Or was it Earth that I wanted out of?

Nkomo has a premise for this and says, *'Only those who have nothing to lose will risk uncertainty—even the threat of death—and call it exploration.'*

He's right about one thing: I have nothing to lose even if Mars has little to offer.

The cafeteria is a microcosm of our various nations. Our flags are hung around the room and when we enter, we are greeted by the comms in our native language. Outside the portal windows, we can see the counter-weight arch that helps create our artificial gravity. And beyond that, black dotted with pinpricks of light. I'm always thrown by the basic human need for food, and the alien vista of space being so near each other. The mundane beside the extraordinary. I wonder if that will ever feel normal.

Greta, a Hungarian biologist, sits eating something resembling scrambled eggs. She looks up, startled when she realises it's me. She glances at the exit and then, realising I'm standing in the only way out, reluctantly nods hello.

'Hungry?' she asks, overly polite, concentrating on pushing the yellow-grey eggs around.

I'm so tired of everyone being polite when their insincerity is obvious. 'Not really,' I say. My stomach still hasn't settled.

'It's horrible.' She pokes her egg substitute glumly. 'Think it will be better over there?' she asks.

'I doubt it. Would be nice though—to arrive there and have them lay on a nice braai or roast?'

'Braai?'

'Barbeque?'

'Ah yes. Outside cooking,' she says and looks pointedly at me.

I see the problem. No outdoor cooking on Mars. I'm hit with an inconsolable moment of grief for sishanyama. My stomach rumbles.

'Hungry,' she says again, frowning.

'I guess I should eat.' I sit down next to her and she stands, collecting her plate.

'Adventure, they say,' she laughs awkwardly as she walks away, throwing her half-eaten eggs in the garbage disposal. 'Adventure tastes like shit.'

There are ten of us on this crew. They're hoping the next trip—in twelve months' time—will carry double that. Gradually, they're exporting a colony to Mars.

Most people think we're foolish for sending so many. They think we're wasting our energy and efforts on the wrong things. Earth needs us. Our dying planet needs our ideas, ingenuity, and more importantly our funding. But in the thousands of years it takes for Earth to properly die, we could be forging our way into the galaxy and making a new home. We hope.

I sit in the cockpit, taking my turn, watching the ship fly itself, watching for incoming messages from Earth and ASA. There are never any messages other than software updates and course adjustments. I'm fixated instead on the star-filled blackness outside. Somehow, closer to these heavenly bodies, they feel even further away.

When you're a kid and you're in a dark room, you feel like the room is made smaller by the dark. All that black presses in on you, making you far too close to all the things that might devour you. But out here, in space, the black has an infinite quality about it. All that dark is a detached endlessness which seems as though it could never touch you, and yet, it has found its way inside you.

Once, I spent the Christmas holidays with a friend at her parents' beach house in the Transkei. Like only white people could then, they'd amassed themselves a little paradise where they could stroll down a grassy hill and be on the beach in seconds. We lived on the beach that summer, and once, even though I'm not that enthusiastic about the sea, we went diving. I remember sticking my head under the surface, staring through goggles, and seeing where the water turned murky and went on forever. I had this sudden panic attack thinking how big that sea was. It was a giant expanse and I was small and powerless in it. And yet, I didn't want to leave. I wanted to know what was beyond where I could see.

Space feels like that to me sometimes. I think that's why I chose my small garden for my sim.

When I go back into the sim they've inserted music.

We were asked to choose music that helps us relax. I chose a few ancient tracks by Abdullah Ibrahim because Dumza and I used to listen to him while we gazed through the telescope. It wasn't the usual stuff kids my age were listening to—like Four-Fifty Indigo, Shwe-Shwe Rebellion, and Tokx—but then, I wasn't much of a normal kid. Normal kids didn't happily spend time in their garden with their stepfather, staring at Mars. To hear that piano now, I can almost conjure Dumza and that garden without the sim. I recognise the song; *Unfettered Muken,* one of my favourites.

The fact that Dumza is there—dressed in his slippers and persistent lecturing uniform of khaki trousers and vintage Star Wars t-shirt—makes me realise, with a sense of irony, that I built the perfect environment for him to show up: the garden, the music, it's all inextricably linked to him.

'You're not supposed to be here,' I say to him.

He shrugs, nonchalant. 'I didn't ask to be here.'

I bend down to look through the telescope, wondering if I should log this in my journal. It's important for the developers to keep the sim safe and useful but I don't know what they're going to do with me if I tell them I'm hallucinating *inside* the sim.

'It's not like they can send you home,' Dumza says, reading my mind.

'I have no home,' I say. The words slip out before I can stop myself. I laugh, and the sound comes out vaguely hysterical. 'I mean, you know, Earth isn't really an option... and Mars, well, she's not home yet. You know?' I rub my forehead. He knows what I mean. And it's not the same as what I'd just said.

I focus on the grass between my toes, the subtle scent of summer on the air, the clear notes of the piano. And then I tell myself, insistently, that I am in space, far away from Earth and this garden. I don't want it to feel too real because it makes waking too hard.

'She's close now,' says Dumza. He's staring up at the sky where Mars is unrealistically close and large as the moon. The curves of her desert plains are stained orange, her naked mountain ranges discernible. I feel like I can reach out and touch her. I wonder if the sim is supposed to act against the laws of physics. I thought it was supposed to be realistic, not dreamlike.

I frown at him. 'Why did you do it?' I ask. I'm safe here, I remind myself. He's not even real. This is the Dumza I loved, the step-father I cherished. This is not the murderer he became.

He looks up at me as though he were expecting the question. 'You know why,' he says. There is no remorse. There never was. I can't seem to reconcile that with the man I knew and loved.

Emotions swell and swirl inside me.

'Then you don't need to be here,' I say.

'I didn't bring myself here,' he says. 'You did.'

'Then I can get you to leave. Go.'

He stands there, unmoving, hands pocketed, staring between me and Mars. 'Was it so bad you had to leave the planet?'

'Yes.' Unfortunately, the heart is an organ you need to be alive, so I couldn't leave my broken one on Earth, I had to bring it with me. My on-board luggage. And it seems no matter how far away from Earth I am, the grief—the horror—follows thick and heavy.

'You aren't going to leave, are you?' I ask.

He shakes his head.

The Girl Who Stared at Mars

'Then I will.' I turn my back on him and go.

'Your fitness stats are exemplary,' says Lucky. Lucky is an androgynous android, with a human face. A Caucasian face, of course. No one has thought to make a black skinned robot—because technology and blacks are not synonymous, even after Wendel Nkomo and Skyward. I don't know how many more intrepid blacks we need before that changes.

'Are you alright? You are staring,' says Lucky. It tips it's head in too human a way and smiles.

'Fine. Daydreaming.'

'Do you do this a lot?' It holds up the clipboard before it, pen poised to write some gleaned information.

'I guess. As a child, I spent a lot of time staring at the sky and now I'm in it, so...' I don't know why I say it.

'I see,' says Lucky.

'Do you?'

Lucky looks at me expectantly and when I don't respond it says, 'I noticed your sim logs have been much shorter the last few cycles. The language is sparse. Are you experiencing any anxiety about the simulations?'

'Anxiety? They're supposed to relax us, aren't they?'

'Theoretically but experiencing such life-like scenarios and finding yourself back in space can be disorienting. There can be a period of mourning. Have you experienced this? Your heart rate seems elevated in the sims.'

'Mourning?' I echo the word. How appropriate it is.

'Mourning life on Earth. A life you will never return to.'

'Yes, I suppose so.'

'It is entirely normal.'

'Is it?' Normal to mourn so damn hard that you leave your wailing aunts and uncles to move to a different planet?

'Does that word make you uncomfortable?'

'Which word?'

'Mourning.'

'It's just... my mother... well, my step-father...'

'Yes, I have your file in my database. I know what you have experienced. Psyche evaluation tests proclaimed you fit and healthy for duty. Are you finding this to be a problem?'

I take a deep breath. One, two, three, place yourself back in reality. One, two, three, orient yourself. One, two, three, be mindful of your breath.

Cristy Zinn

I am fine, okay, alright, coping, fit for duty.

And Dumza has found his way into my sim.

'No problem at all. Listen, it's my slot in the gym, so would you mind if I go? I don't want to miss it again. Got to keep these muscles ready for Mars gravity, you know?' I keep my tone light.

'You may go. Make an appointment if you are experiencing any concerning symptoms.'

'Sure.'

I slip off the gurney and leave the small health cube. The corridor is windowless and stifling—the metal and resin and perspex all too inorganic, the air smelling faintly like recycled sweat. I take another deep breath. Mars is what I have always wanted. Always. No memory, or amount of grief, is going to stop me from getting there whole and sane.

So, I go back to the garden.

Dumza killed my mother because of the man she was having an affair with.

In my contract with the ASA one thing they stressed was that I could not be affiliated to anyone with questionable politics. They were very specific about this: any politician with shady dealings, criminal records, or even simple lawsuits against them, could not hold company with me or my family. Any connections or ties to such political personalities would result in my immediate dismissal from the program. My tarnishing would be ASA's tarnishing, and in a climate where funding is extremely difficult to come by, ASA was taking no chances.

The man Dumza found passionately kissing my half-clothed mother was a notorious, extremist politician with fundamentalist fans. Any link to him and my career would be done for. Besides the fact that she was married, my mother knew what this would mean for me and she kept kissing him anyway.

It broke Dumza's heart. Of all the men she had loved, he was least deserving of betrayal.

When I found him, he was standing in the middle of the twilight-hazed living room, staring at the two bodies half-dressed and tangled on the floor. There was so much blood. The knife was still in his hand and he seemed surprised when I mentioned it.

'What did you do, Baba?' I asked him, turning away from the blood, trying to keep my tears and bile inside so I could get the knife, not sure who I was dealing with. He looked like Dumza, but Dumza would not do *this*.

'He's Jared Hlope,' said Dumza, as if that explained everything.

'The old finance minister?' I asked, not looking at the bodies. I knew who he was, but I needed Dumza to keep talking.

He nodded, tears streaming silently down his face. 'I thought he was hurting her but... he wasn't. I didn't want him—them—to ruin your chances. I didn't want you to miss Mars because of this.' He looked down at them, then looked at his hands. 'Will you miss Mars anyway, because of me?' He looked up at me in horror, then back at my mother. 'Oh God, what have I done?'

I think that's when it hit him because he dropped to his knees and started screaming and wailing. Nothing I said calmed him down.

I left him there—left the bodies, the blood, the iron stink of the house—and stood on our front lawn to phone the cops. I was trembling, too afraid to stay in the same room with whoever that was. Because whoever he was, he wasn't my sweet Dumza.

I waited on the grass for seventeen minutes and thirty-two seconds before I heard the sirens, reciting flight procedures in my head to anchor myself. Chaos broke out on my lawn where I was questioned and man-handled into a police vehicle *for my own protection*. Someone recognised me from the latest promotional vids ASA had released one month ago, and soon the lawn was encircled by reporters and cameras.

Eventually Dumza was dragged from the house, cuffed and screaming something about my mother being a whore. He did not look at me. He pled guilty and was found dead in his cell two months later. Never once did he show a moment's remorse, but I still remember that look on his face when he realised what he had done. I remember the regret.

There were more hearings after that—mine. It had to be decided whether I had breached my contract by being affiliated with a murderer. In the end, no one was willing to waste the money they'd spent training me, nor the resources setting things up for me on Mars, not so close to the launch. I *had* to go—it was too late now—so they spun it as a second chance for a girl hard-done by.

An orphan in space. I wonder what Wendel Nkomo would say about that.

Our ship is only one-third living space—including the med-bay, gymnasium, and sim annex. The rest is mail, supplies for the Martian, and the engine. The ship is aesthetically minimalist—not like some of the first mission ships with their convoluted passages and visible mechanics. All the white should be clinical but somehow it isn't. I think it must be the darkness of space and our strange human inclination towards light. They've been very conscious of this in their designs of future missions, citing that pleasant surroundings help the space farers acclimatise better to space. I think they did it because it gives the impression of spaciousness to our tight quarters. After only eleven days, I wish I could thank the person who considered that.

But even in a ship this small, I am alienated. The crew meets up once a day for reports and general notes, meaning they are forced to be in the same room as me, but I sense the others are waiting for me to break down. They avoid me, like I'm contagious, dealing with me only on the most practical level. Sending a newly bereaved black woman into space is a terrible risk as far as they're concerned. I won't pretend it doesn't hurt; after all those months of being stuck with them, learning to love them and create a coherent team, they found it so easy to stop believing in me. Or maybe they're just scared I'll jeopardise their *one* shot. Maybe we all are.

Seven days to go and we will be in orbit. So far, the voyage has been uneventful. Not counting Dumza's appearance in my sim. No one has lost their minds, hurt anyone else, or tried to leave the ship—not even me, though they're waiting for it. Maybe I'm just the excuse but on some level, we're all on the edge, waiting for things to go wrong.

The world we left was so messed up—personal issues aside—so why aren't we taking better care of each other? Where is the Ubuntu that Wendel Nkomo wrote about?

I don't know how long I've been sitting here, contemplating this journey and our abysmal lack of care for one another when Grey appears beside me. Grey is a Spatial Sociologist from the UK, a swarthy reed of a man with a nice smile. He doesn't talk much about his personal life but get him started on the possible societies that might develop in a space colony and he will talk for hours. He stares out the window along with me for a moment, his hands gripping the back of the bench. It's an awkward silence, and I'm keenly aware of the space between us and the space outside and the space within. I wonder why he isn't speaking because he keeps taking breaths like he's about to, but no words come out. I wait, patiently, because he is one of the few on the crew who has gone out of his way to make conversation with me in the last two months. I wait a long time.

Finally, he jerks his head towards me. His eyes are bloodshot, the same as mine, and his brown knuckles are pale from holding on to the bench so tight.

'You okay?' I ask. I watch his neck, looking for a throbbing pulse but find nothing.

'Sure. You? I'm tired, you know. Nothing major. All of us are tired, right? Can't remember when I last slept. My log could tell me, probably. I think it can. That's what it's for, right? I'm just...'

He grabs my hand and squeezes painfully. 'Does that hurt?' he asks, eyes wide.

'Yes,' I say, yanking my hand away. I move sideways on the bench, but he follows, shadow-like, too close.

'Tell me something, Amahle. Are we real? Is this real? I'm not sure if this is happening. Are you? Sure?'

'Pretty sure,' I say. 'Maybe you just need to sleep. Lucky could give you something...'

'Medical sleep is never good. It's dreamless. That's not good. Or maybe it is. Would it be better?'

'Just this once,' I say, urging him. My hand still hurts where he gripped it, and my heart is pounding. 'Or maybe you could go into the sim?'

He barks out a panicked laugh. 'The sim? Want to make it worse?'

Silence falls again so I stand, ready to get out of there. I feel like I should call someone, but I don't want to be melodramatic. Everyone is expecting that of me and I'm not eager to give them ammunition.

Cristy Zinn

Grey grabs my arm, his fingers biting painfully into my skin. 'Can you feel that?' he asks me desperately. 'You know about pain, right? Better than any of us. Is this *real* pain? You know about pain. Is this *real*?'

My blood slows, and I am atrophied in place for a moment. 'Grey, you're hurting me. I don't understand what you're asking.'

'Pain! Can you feel it? You should know—pain is closer to you. It's what makes us alive. I think. I can't remember. I can't feel anything, you know, and I'm thinking maybe it's because I'm still in the Sim but I'm not sure. So, I'm asking you—are we real? Is this real?'

'Yes. It's real.'

He leans in close, breath stale, and puts his fingers around my neck, squeezing very slowly. 'You sure? Because I've been having dreams—are they dreams, I don't know—about the code of the sims and they're growing legs and arms and hands and they're reaching out to strangle me while I sleep. Except I can't sleep so how am I dreaming. Maybe I'm not.'

I try to swallow but his hand is tight on my throat. I glance up at the tiny camera in the corner of the room and plead with whoever's watching to send someone to get him. My breathing is short and sharp, the anxiety clasping down on me as tight as Grey's hands.

I've never been this close to breaking and I'm angry because so much has been lost for me to be here. *So* much. And now this guy wants to kill me in space to prove that he's alive?

Grey's fingers loosen from my neck and he steps backwards. 'Are you real?' he asks me again. 'Is any of this real?'

Lucky appears at the doorway, syringe in hand. 'Hello, Grey. Could I be of assistance?'

Grey grimaces at the android and then backs into the corner, whimpering. 'Am I real?' he repeats over and over while I retreat and walk-run down the corridor to my bunk where I collapse. I ignore the hands shaking me, asking if I'm alright, and instead, I cry myself to sleep.

At dinner, none of us are hungry but we linger in the cafeteria—all of us except Grey. His absence is glaring. Down the passage, he lies sedated where he'll stay for the remainder of the journey. Flight risk, Lucky called him. Even flight risks still make it to Mars.

'First breakdown in two tours,' says Otar. 'I didn't think it'd be him.'

No one looks at me. I resist an ironic smile.

'You'd think they'd have worked out the meds by now. I mean, two clean tours...' Otar stares out the portal window and I swear I see tears in his eyes, like this is his failure somehow.

Greta snorts. 'You realise the people making the med cocktails have never been to space?'

'It's just science,' says Elizabeth.

'It's psychiatry actually,' says Rajesh, rubbing his hands together in a habitual way, like he doesn't even realise he's doing it. 'Psychiatry and science. The science is easy—the rules are obvious—but the psychiatry? It's unpredictable, you know? Too many variables...'

'Someone in the psych department needs to be fired. How can they put us on a spaceship with a crazy? Aren't those tests supposed to weed them out?'

'They let Amahle on,' says Otar, nodding at me. 'I don't think weeding out crazies is part of their M.O.'

An awkward silence descends, and no one looks me in the eye.

'Okay, can we just get this out there?' I say. I'm so tired of this bullshit. This is my crew. I have no family left but them. 'My stepfather killed my mother and her lover—who happened to be a shitty politician. My step father went to jail. He died. *I* am not my stepfather. *I* am not a murder. *I* am not the one who broke down, Grey is. So now that we've established that *I'm* not the flight risk, can we get on with our mission and get to Mars together. Please.'

I see Greta hiding a smile.

Maybe I can't win them all, but I think I may have made at least one friend.

Mars is close now, larger than the moon from Earth. I shouldn't be glad, but Grey's breakdown has had an interesting effect on the crew. The incident has acted as a shift, loosening our tightly wound psyches. A comradery is growing again. Maybe it is because we have passed the halfway mark and Earth is forever behind us. Maybe we feel drawn to each other now that we are the only touchstones of Earth that exist out here. Is this finally Wendel Nkomo's Ubuntu in space? It seems a weak shadow of the concept but this far from home, I'll take it.

Dumza is a constant feature in my garden now, always pruning things and chatting incessantly as I watch Mars growing ever closer through the telescope. I think I keep him there because I want to remember this version of him. I don't want to keep seeing the bloodied Dumza with horror in his eyes—I want my dad. I want this version of him to come with me to Mars.

Today, Mars is so large it fills up the sky. Even my subconscious is reminding me I don't have much longer in this garden.

'What will be the first thing you do there?' asks Dumza.

'Kiss the ground,' I say, smiling. This is something we always talked about. Somewhere in the intricate tunnels under the surface of Mars, where we'll all live, is a room called 'The First'. Inside it are the *first* soil samples, the *first* comms, the *first* habitat suits, a *first* edition of Wendel Nkomo's *A Native in Space*—a museum of sorts as we establish a new culture on Mars. And inside this room is a bowl of Mars soil, from the surface, that you can touch with your bare hands—because someone was smart enough to know how important it is to literally ground yourself in a new land. Dumza and I always talked about that room and the miracle of touching the soil of another planet.

'Kiss the ground,' chuckles Dumza. 'Tell it I say hello.' He turns back to the nasturtiums he's pruning. I watch him, how he clips methodically and peacefully, like he's alive.

'Why did you do it?' I ask him, knowing the answer will be my own, from my own mind, and not his at all. Knowing that I will never get the truth from him but needing an answer somehow.

'You're here. Isn't that enough?'

'No,' I say. Grief rises high tide in my chest. 'You shouldn't have done it. You loved her, didn't you?'

'Of course, I loved her,' says Dumza.

'But you killed her. Violently. Just because you wanted me to go to Mars. I don't know if I can believe that,' I say. I look down to the shears Dumza is holding and see the tips of them are dripping with blood.

'What else could I tell myself? Tell you? I didn't want to be a man capable of killing someone just because I was *jealous*. How could I be *that* kind of man?'

'I don't know,' I say but I'm relieved. The deaths are not on me. They are not my fault. I did not make Dumza do what he did, though, I realise now that this is the idea I've been carrying around.

'You lied,' I say.

Dumza drops the shears, they clatter and dissolve into the grass. Mars swells in the sky behind him, filling the sky entirely. 'Yes. I suppose I did. To protect my own sanity. It didn't work though, did it.'

I'm not surprised when he fades and leaves me alone in the garden. The music of crickets and bats rises in the sim again, the air cooling. I take a deep breath of the garden scent I remember so well—the scent I will never smell on Mars.

I will not return to the Sim again, so I say goodbye to the grass and the trees and the breeze. I say my final goodbye to Earth.

The entire crew gathers in the viewing room once we achieve orbit. The curved horizon of Mars stretches out towards us, so close.

We are quiet, as we stand there, the gravity of what we've done settling on our almost Martian skins. Are we still human when we are no longer of Earth? I wonder to myself.

My favourite paragraph from *Native in Space* says this: *"Humanity is not simply a state of 'being human'. Humanity is the benevolence we carry within us. It is who we are and what we do when we are fully human—it is community, Ubuntu, unable to be manifested alone. Even in space, detached from the soil of our beings, we can exercise humanity. In fact, I am of the opinion that space may be the very place we learn how intrinsic our humanity is to our survival."*

Lucky broadcasts the message from Hector Damenzes, one of the captains from three missions ago. 'Welcome Cosmos 8! We've got your habitat ready and waiting. Skies will be clear in four hours and you can come join us. We know it's been a long few weeks, but home is waiting for you.'

Cristy Zinn

Cristy Zinn is the author of two fantasy novels, *The Dreamer's Tears* and *Of Magic and Memory* and has published various short stories. She is enthralled by stories involving the fantastic—technological and magical. She works as a graphic designer and illustrator. Cristy lives in Durban with her husband and two teenagers who graciously endure her obsession with stories. Find her online: cristyzinn.com

The EMO Hunter

Mandisi Nkomo

"*As the Earth Mother is my witness, I vow to avenge the destruction of her physical form. The Emotion Manipulator is her enemy, and thus mine. I will strike them down, man, woman or child. I will strike down all colluders who betray the Earth Mother's trust. This I promise to you, great Earth Mother, who bred and nurtured me for millennia. We await your rebirth Earth Mother, so that humankind may one day return home.*" – Prayer of The Earth Mother Knights.

Joshua and Miku stood and walked away from the prayer circle. While Miku idled with the other wives, Joshua confided with the other Earth Mother Knights. The priest congratulated them on their work and blessed them with sprinklings of crushed leaves and flower petals. Once the blessing was over Joshua joined Miku, and in silence they walked The Holy Grounds heading for the nursery enclosure.

Inside, Earth Mother Nurses tended the children, who played in the mud and bushes. Their son Kirill was still a baby and was placed indoors. They proceeded to his crib, and he smiled as Miku reached for him. Like his father,

Kirill had bright black beady eyes as intense as they were friendly. Kirill's complexion complemented his parents contrasting complexions; his smooth baby skin appeared like a bleached brown. Together, the three appeared as a sequential progression in shades. After picking up Kirill they went back outside and headed for the exit.

The grey metallic facades of Paragonia's skyscrapers clawed above the height of the trees. Outside The Holy Grounds, hordes of hovercrafts engulfed the street, as the churchgoers filed out. It was here Joshua and Miku parted ways.

'Well, the bus is waiting. I hope you enjoyed the ceremony. I don't really understand why you avoid them so much,' Joshua said brightly.

'I actually think I did this time,' Miku lied. 'Maybe I'll join you again next time. Anyway, I should probably get Kirill home.'

'Right,' Joshua said. 'Well... duty calls.'

He kissed Miku politely on the cheek and made his way to the Earth Mother bus, beginning to brood. Temporarily, he pretended he believed Miku; he knew he did not. She often lied to his face.

He reached the bus and walked up the platform to join his colleagues. The bus ascended to Level 5 and followed holographic street alignments which bled up from the ground.

On arrival, The Earth Mother Knights streamed out of the bus, through the hangar, and into the locker rooms. They swapped their prayer robes for tight bodysuits with dangling wires and tubes, then filed out into the armoury. One-by-one they walked into what resembled a giant fridge—The Assembler. They were stamped, and stepped out looking reptilian, layered in metallic scales.

Once armoured, each Knight proceeded to his consultation room for analysis and briefing.

'Hello Joshua,' Mohini said. 'Did your wife enjoy the ceremony?'

'Yes, she did,' Joshua replied to the smooth electronic voice.

'I am still detecting mood instability from you. It is recommended that you seek personal consultation to avoid excessive use of mood stimulants. Also, a friendly reminder: you are still overdue for lung and liver replacement.'

'Um... thanks Mohini. What are my orders?'

Miku did not go home. She waited for Joshua to leave ignoring all the Earth Mother buses beckoning her with metal flaps, knowing they could not take her where she wanted to go—outside the Central City Cube. 'Where the heretics go,' she whispered to herself. Kirill slept soundly, sucking his thumb, tiny head rested on her shoulder. She doubted he would wake during her little escapade.

She slipped away, distancing herself from The Holy Grounds, and all the people who knew her as an extension of Joshua Shepard: *The EMO Hunter, The EMOlisher, The EMOliminator...* or whatever his fan-club was calling him lately. Once a safe distance away she hailed a hovertaxi. The driver ogled her a moment; her porcelain features were so delicate it appeared they might flutter away at the slightest breeze. His staring reminded her of the priests during Earth Mother Church Fundraisers.

Miku announced her destination, and the driver took off.

'Are you sure you want to go out this far?' he asked after a while.

'Yes,' Miku replied.

'You know, the Earth Mother Knights are still working on these districts. It may not be safe. I don't like coming down here and I definitely can't leave clients here with a clear conscience.'

'Yes, I've heard those *rumours*,' Miku said. 'None of it's true. The people here are actually quite nice.' She was quiet for a moment, and then waved her free hand over the side of the hovertaxi, pointing at the holographic street sign. 'Stop here please.'

The driver descended, and Miku hopped out. She smiled as politely as she could muster, extending her thin lips sideways, but looking like invisible hands forcefully pulled on her cheek muscles.

'Here you go,' Miku handed the driver her card.

When the transaction was complete the driver ascended. Miku stood on the corner looking down at Kirill. She caressed his hairless scalp before wandering down the street in search of the correct alley. This was a different part of Paragonia. It had dirt. Miku always wondered where the dirt came from. Did the rebels travel back-and-forth from The Holy Grounds? She imagined a band of would-be insurrectionists sitting in a basement somewhere, generating contraband grit and then painstakingly splattering it throughout the outskirts.

Rebels and *EMOs* and *EMO* affiliates. Miku did not quite know what to make of it all. She was just happy to experience subconscious art. She was not even sure if she had come into contact with an EMO, and even if she did, she was not sure whether she would have cared.

The EMO Hunter

Miku made a left, into an alley which had been excavated by 'freaks' and 'vagrants' and transformed into a bazaar. She minded her own business as she weaved around the people and stalls. The clothing in the outskirts was also different; the people seemed to accessorise and destroy the functionality of their clothing, ripping off different parts of jumpsuits and robes and reattaching them on other sections. Miku had heard this was called 'fashion'. She could not quite get her head around the concept.

She reached her destination and glided through the door. 'Hello again,' the stubby store clerk said. Miku was familiar with the woman but always forgot her name, Clarien, or something. The clerk had torn off pieces of robe to tie up tufts of her hair, making them stick out like spikes. She wore a sleeveless white robe, ripped at the bottom revealing meaty legs.

Miku smiled at her, this time not faking, and made her usual statement, 'I just want to take a look at the art.'

Miku made her way around the room, staring intensely at the electronic canvases. The screens displayed various depictions of the artists' subconscious. Some were buoyant, others macabre, and the majority blasphemous. However, showing what should not be shown was a purpose of subconscious art.

One particularly sentimental piece, depicting the reunion of humanity with the Earth Mother, struck a chord in Miku's heart. She had a strong urge to buy it for Joshua. She knew deep down he would love the concept. She also knew that he would ostentatiously denounce it.

After about an hour, Kirill made a subtle movement in her arms. 'We should get home,' she muttered and stepped delicately towards the door.

When she reached it, the clerk yelled to her, 'Hey wait! We're doing a subconscious art promotion here. You know, trying to recruit more artists and get more work out. We're allowing people to volunteer to present their art. With your permission, we'll present it in the gallery. We have a Soul Digger here that can do it, if you're new, and don't have your own equipment. It's obviously an older model, and we can't allow you to program it to your art style, but for an older model its output is great.'

Miku stepped back defensively, 'I... I'm not an artist.'

'It's not about that. You don't need to be,' the clerk replied. 'We're looking for newcomers and the inexperienced. Just try it out. You don't have to submit the work that comes out. My boss is counting both the amount of work I get and the amount of people I log on the machine, so...' the woman scrunched her lips, and silently pleaded with Miku.

Miku slid her fingers over Kirill's little cheeks. 'Well...'

Miku had an uncontrollable ethereal itch as the elevator slid upwards. Kirill was now crying; stirred awake by Miku's response to her subconscious art. Due to her inexperience the image was sloppy, but it could still be made out. She had stormed out of the store feeling as if her nerves were ballooning and threatening to pop out her skin. She was distraught, and the thought it had planted in her conscious, what a terrible thought to have.

Kirill was finally asleep. Miku was still feeling edgy and panicked. How could she have conjured up such an image? She sat on the bed staring at the image and contemplating it deeply. *Cloning... death,* both were morally reprehensible.

'Finished?' Miku blurted the words out, too distracted to filter herself.

Joshua rolled off her and lay flat on his back. 'Uh, yeah, I guess.'

There was a long silence.

When Joshua could no longer handle lying next to the source of his emasculation, he removed the sheets and stood up. 'I need a smoke.'

Miku lay limp, torturing herself with the imagery of her subconscious art.

Joshua felt his way through the dark, stopping in front of his cigarette dispenser. He rapidly tapped his finger on a protruding button, allowing at least a dozen cigarettes to fall into the catching-bowl and overflow onto the soft carpet. He packed the little cylinders into his hands and moved on to the kitchen. At the fridge, he slapped another button and four beers popped out. He grouped all his poisons into his arms and made for Kirill's room. Standing over the crib he looked down at Kirill.

The EMO Hunter

'I'm not that bad, am I? I serve the Earth Mother well. One day I'm sure you will too,' Joshua murmured to the sleeping boy, and cracked open a beer. 'It's an honour to serve her. Don't tell your mother this, but some days I wish I would die... just so I could meet the Earth Mother. I read about these things the other day. Beaches they were called. There's sand and ocean. This was quite common on Earth. Just imagine!'

Joshua spoke on about Earth for another hour.

'Wow! Look at the time. You made me forget I wanted a cigarette. So easy to talk to.' He caressed Kirill's chubby cheeks, making sure not to wake him.

'Well little one... I'm off to play with my traumas and insomnia. Don't wait up!'

Joshua left for the balcony, collecting more beer along the way. He plonked his belongings onto a vacant chair. Bright city lights blared at him while intrusive electronic billboards sold him dreams. They were everywhere; fixed to skyscrapers and great floating balloons.

"Happiness can only come from serving the Earth Mother."

"Have you washed your face in petal-water today? Your soul needs a cleansing!"

"Your eternal Beach awaits you in death. Invest in the Church today! Don't leave your loved ones hanging once you've ascended to paradise."

He sighed and began gulping beer.

Joshua had already left for work when Miku woke; he was probably drunk, but his Earth Mother Armour would sober him. Miku paced around the flat, frantic, knowing this was her chance. She had to do it now, while she tasted the fresh blood of the idea—before she could write it off as a grandiose conception of mania. Before the guilt and moral depravity of it could dampen the demented excitement it gave her. The previous day she had seen the cup half-empty, but when she had awakened it was half-full.

She dressed herself, checked the information she had gathered from Joshua's 'secret' EMO archives, and expunged her tracks. She then booked a hotel for Kirill and herself. Miku left the apartment tightly clutching Kirill, considering what role he would play in the upcoming ordeal.

Mandisi Nkomo

The image came to her as she walked the buzzing streets, causing her to trip over her own feet. It was not the shock of the image that gripped her, but the way in which she completely understood its meaning.

She was in her own art gallery. The name of the gallery appeared backwards to her, but she knew what it was. She had dreamt of that name before.

She was straddling Joshua, but her buttocks were on dead flesh. Joshua was naked and lifeless; his tongue lolling disgustingly from his foaming mouth, and his eyes empty and opaque. The feel of his cold penis chilled her spine.

She did not look at him though, or Kirill, who cuddled and cried onto his dead father's hairless scalp.

Instead Miku was transfixed by another man. Another Joshua made in her image. He was unclean; dirt and muck shaded his brown skin. His hair was long and knotted. Miku could taste the poignant stench seeping off him.

Despite his grandiosity, Miku was in complete control. She gripped his erection like a puppet string. He would bow to her every whim.

Joshua clunked down the bright metallic hall of his apartment building. He reached his apartment shutter and spoke into the microphone adjacent.

'Welcome home Joshua,' Mohini said, as Joshua entered. 'You have successfully completed another assignment. I'm sure your wife will be proud of you. The head priest sends his regards.'

I hope so. Maybe I can treat them to dinner. Any suggestions? he said voicelessly. Joshua simply had to think his responses for Mohini to translate them, she could also talk directly into his brain, but he found it too unnerving and kept her to vocal comms.

Joshua surveyed the array of local restaurants Mohini presented on his HUD. The apartment was silent, which was irregular. Joshua knew Kirill had formed a fascination with his Earth Mother Knight armour. The boy usually waited to gawk at him the moment he entered the apartment.

'Should I adjust your avatar to a smiley?' Mohini asked.

Yes... but I wonder where Kirill is? I mostly do it for him. Have you noticed how clever he's gotten? Waiting at the door when I come home—he knows exactly when I'll arrive.

'Yes, he is getting smart.'

Joshua continued through the apartment, still not meeting Kirill. Disappointed at the lack of greeting, he sought out the Armour Centre.

The Armour Centre was a man-sized box, inset into the apartment wall. Joshua stepped in and assumed the correct position.

'Disassembly commencing. Due to your immense psychological come down I still suggest you seek psychiatric and psychological care for a more permanent solution to your problems.'

Yes honey! Joshua mocked.

He felt his body aches return, as a multitude of pins were removed from his flesh.

'Removing anaesthesia. Mood regulators released. Strength and agility dampened. Do try to relax, your mood is spiking.'

Small tentacles dismantled the final pieces of the armour, leaving Joshua exposed.

He stumbled out of the Armour Centre and collapsed to his knees—thoughts darting, eyes watering, his chest heaving, while drool pooled on the carpet. He twitched off another panic attack on his living room floor, merely glad this one was vomit free.

Beer! Beer! Beer!

Joshua crawled to the kitchen, leaving spittle behind like a slug. He used the fridge handle to stand and punched the beer dispenser. Holding his beer aloft, a silhouette glistened on the fridge. He turned around, 'Miku?'

Silent bullets tore through his body, and he crumbled to the floor, soaked in blood and foam. Joshua drifted from consciousness and it did not seem to bother him.

Either from great luck or misfortune Joshua regained consciousness. He was in horrid pain. It seared his entire torso. His throat was dry, as if he had repeatedly swallowed sandpaper. It took a valiant effort to force his voice out. When it sounded, its timbre was that of a mutant croak.

Upon opening his eyes, he saw only black, and then realised he was suffocating. He wriggled hysterically within his plastic coffin. He could hear voices, and furthered his efforts, squirming his aching body with all his might.

Finally, a knife pierced the plastic wrapping, and Joshua gulped oxygen. A hole was cut around his face. 'Holy Earth Mother!' a man said. 'This one is alive!'

'Get him out!' a woman screamed.

'I'm working on it, I'm working on it,' the aged man grumbled.

After slicing the bag open, he beheld Joshua's naked body with disgust. 'Rough night? You know with all this illegal cloning going on you're not the first. Incompetence knows no bounds! These hitmen are so quick to rid themselves of the body, they don't care if you're alive or not. You must be the fifth one this week! The church might as well make spousal clone replacement legal. Better than all this back alley black market crap!'

Joshua grunted, and smiled meekly. 'Water, doctor, medicine,' he rasped. He tried to get up but tumbled off the conveyor belt. Lying on the floor, staring at the ceiling, his senses told him where he was. It was extremely hot, even though he was stripped, and he could smell corpses on the roast. *Crematorium, only I could have the crappy luck to wake up here.* 'Water,' he rasped again.

'Of course, young man! My apologies. You stay right there, I'll let the hospital know we have another back from the *dead*.'

Joshua watched the ceiling slowly fade.

Joshua awoke again, and no longer inhaled smog and charred flesh. 'Kirill!' he screamed and shot upright. His voice came out clear and hydrated. There were no jolts of pain. He was healed. He jumped out of the bed and grabbed some hospital robes.

Bolting up and down the hospital corridors, he happened upon an elevator and wedged his bulky body between the closing doors. The elevator beeped and opened again.

An alarmed patient eyed Joshua from the elevator's confines.

Joshua looked first to the illuminated ground floor button, then to the alarmed patient. 'Where am I? What time and day is it?'

The patient returned a blank expression.

'Well?' Joshua yelled, flinging his arms in the air.

Intimidated, the man quickly stammered an answer. 'You're at The Body Mechanics. It's in the northern parts of the Central City Cube... quite close to the northern outskirts really.'

'Time and day?'

'It's morning now, eleven o'clock I think,' the man paused in thought, 'it's a Thursday.'

Shit... four days. The elevator door slid open and Joshua hurtled towards the reception table. 'Phone, phone, I need to use your phone!'

'Please calm down sir. I see you have healed well.' An aloof receptionist regarded Joshua plainly. 'Let's just check you out, and then you can use the-'

'Give me the fucking phone.'

The receptionist froze. Joshua's passive aggression was more unsettling than his yelling.

'Suit yourself,' he said and propped his stomach on the receptionist's counter, rummaging freely through the items on her desk. He found a wireless headset and dialled his apartment. The receptionist began to shrill for security while Joshua listened to the phone ring.

'For Earth Mother's sake!' he tossed the wireless set and it accidentally smacked the receptionist in the face. Two security guards arrived on the scene, but Joshua disabled them. The first received a vicious stomp to the knee. The second walked carelessly into a guillotine choke.

Utterly unfazed Joshua stepped out into the bright artificial light of Paragonia's Dome. He blinked the light away and adjusted his eyes, searching for a hovertaxi. He ran to the first one he saw.

'I need to get to the Central City Cube living quarters—Section E. Now!'

Lazy-eyed, the taxi-driver looked him up and down. 'Sure you don't want to go back and change first?'

Joshua looked down at the hospital robes he wore, and then looked back up the inane smile on taxi-driver's face. 'No.'

'Well... in the outskirts that would probably be considered *fashionable*,' the driver said. 'Are you an outskirts man? A weirdo?'

'Do you want me to rip your tongue out?'

Mandisi Nkomo

'I suppose even now we can't fix a funny bone. Hop in.'

The silent journey took no longer than ten minutes. Joshua leapt out of the hovertaxi before it came to a stop and barged into his apartment block. Almost instantly he was up the elevator and whispering to his apartment door's microphone.

He took a deep breath and tiptoed around the Armour Centre.

His brain was overrun with tragic outcomes for his wife and child. He did not know who or what was after him yet, or even what they wanted. He passed through the kitchen and exhaled coolly on reaching the dining room. Quietly, he opened a compartment which held his knife collection. He slid his fingers along them, as if stroking a woman's thigh. He selected a small curved blade. Briefly his mind darted between the knife and the Armour Centre, before settling on the silent option.

He crept back through the apartment. First was Kirill's room, and to Joshua's surprise his toddler was sound asleep in his crib. He felt an amalgam of relief and disappointment at the sight. He moved towards his bedroom and gripped his blade tighter. He could hear Miku screaming.

A soul draining tableau awaited him. Joshua's mind rejected it at first, and then rolled through phases. Astonishment. Sadness. Rage. Joshua's vision flickered like a broken street light, as his monster tore free from its bonds. Expletives fled from his mouth, and he was upon them.

He was throwing Miku off the bed. He was at her throat with the blade. He was yanked away. He was disarmed. He was punching another man. They were wrestling. He tasted blood on his tongue. He was thrown against the wall.

He sobered slightly when he absorbed the face of the antagonist. It was his own. The same brown complexion, black eyes, clean scalp, sallow cheeks; he gawked at himself in curiosity.

'Who the hell are you?' his mirror bellowed in a stolen voice. 'Who ordered this?' The fake asked all the questions that ran through Joshua's head. 'You're an EMO clone. A really good one,' the clone mused.

Joshua watched himself walk over to the gun drawer. The clone fingered the touch pad.

The EMO Hunter

MK 58 KI 67 LL—shit!
Joshua leapt to his feet and tackled his replica to the floor. He mounted it and began punching fiercely, seeking a quick knockout. The clone barely defended itself yet remained conscious. In an abnormal show of strength, the clone pumped its hips and Joshua flew upwards before crashing to the floor.

They looked at each other sharing the same lack of understanding. Joshua was highly trained and even those who matched his weight struggled to get him off once he'd locked a mount—let alone sent him flying. A part of him knew what was happening, but soon they were at each other's throats again.

"The EMO cloning process... side effects include the inheritance of EMO abilities. One of the many reasons cloning may only be sanctioned by the Church."
Joshua wrestled onwards in vain.

Miku sat in the corner, bleeding from the nose and cuddling her shoulders. She breathed heavily and considered running away, but surely the ghost would obsessively track her down, as was his nature.

She considered joining the fight, but also knew the clone needed no help. She'd been warned about the possible side effects but had not envisioned a scenario where they might actually manifest. The real Joshua did not stand a chance without his suit. It made her sick to think but she knew it. The outcome of this would likely be in her favour.

Trapped in a clench, Joshua strained to overpower his replica. Its strength was first an inkling above his, but rapidly mutated, over and above. He flew across the room, bounced off the wall, and heaved on the floor, eyeing the clone. They shared an intimate moment of cruel understanding.

It's going to fucking kill me.
It was time for a great escape. First, he made for the Armour Centre, slamming the entrance button in vain. The Armour Centre did not share his panic. Joshua fled out the apartment and leapt into the nearest elevator.

The clone ran at him as the elevator doors closed. Joshua lifted his middle finger—an old Earth profanity he loved despite it being archaic. The elevator doors indented with fist and elbow blows.

Fast, must be fast. It'll alert Earth Mother Knight Head-quarters. I have to get to my armour first. I have to beat the bastard! But also—also I need to figure out who the mastermind is. Which asshole thought it would be a funny to clone and kill me? They'll pay a debt to me in entrails... I'll yank their body down the hover-highway... I'll-

'What happened to you?' Joshua's moody contemplation was interrupted by the taxi-driver. 'Got into a bit of a scuffle I see.'

'Why are you still here?' Joshua sighed irritably.

'You forgot to pay. And since you wouldn't go back and change back at the hospital, I figured you're a weirdo. I didn't really think you lived here anyway, so I waited.'

Joshua massaged his temples, and begrudgingly climbed back into the hovertaxi. 'Take me to Earth Mother HQ. The Church will pay you when we get there.'

'Do you really think I'm going to fall for that? You outskirt types think you're so smart. I'm taking you to the closest Police Station. They'll take you to Earth Mother HQ for sure.'

'Why would I-,' Joshua stopped. 'Fine.'

The taxi-driver looked chuffed with himself and began to ascend.

Joshua reached forward and started fiddling on the hover-taxi's console. An identity card popped up on the screen. 'Have you ever heard of this guy?'

'Joshua Shepard? Well of course. Best bounty hunt—I mean Earth Mother Knight in the business.'

Joshua waited, but evidently his recent adventures had left him no longer resembling his ID photo. He placed his thumb on the console's scanner. The console bleeped affirmation.

'So, you're the famous Shepard hey? Interesting name for a black man. Shepard. On Earth they would have said you inherited your slave name. Shepard would probably be European...'

'Is that supposed to be some kind of insult? What's a black man? I'm just a man. Black is a colour.'

The EMO Hunter

'Wrong holy man! It's a race you fool! Or at least it used to be. I'd expect a man of your stature to know better. It's that church of yours, completely uninterested in actual Earth history. Things like race, ethnicity, nationalism. You kids just wake up one day and think, 'ohh I think I'll call myself Mandela or something.' You're not even Xhosa! You don't even know where South Africa used to be on the map. Point it out to me? Do you know what a continent is? No, you don't.

'It's all Earth Mother this, Earth Mother that! I've cleansed my soul in petals! Save me Earth Mother! Save me from all the amazing technology that's ruining my life! Do you have any idea what a shithole Earth was? I've read about it and let me tell you those people lived like animals. Disgusting really. I much prefer this artificial stuff. Safer, lasts longer. You don't get Tsunamis because of farting cattle. Do you even know what a cow is?'

'Do you ever shut up?'

The driver sighed. 'Fine,' he grumbled under his breath. 'Keep following that stupid religion of yours. They don't teach real Earth history. It's the Dark Ages all over again...'

'What's that?' Joshua snapped.

'Nothing. Nothing at all...'

The taxi-driver moped silently for the rest of the trip.

On arrival at Earth Mother Headquarters Joshua fixed his demeanour, turned on his confidence. He walked through the security checks calmly. To the Earth Mother Church fraternity, he was a celebrity, hero, and role model. Joshua Shepard: the ultimate EMO tracker and killer.

The Emotion Manipulating Organisms (EMOs) were born on Earth in ages Joshua could not begin to fathom. He always recalled what his father (a renowned priest and Earth Mother historian) had told him:

"They are evil. They abuse the emotions of those around them for their own wicked ends. They destroyed the Earth Mother. That is why they are banned from the colony... that is why we hunt and kill them like the pests they are. That is why we use their own unholy power to banish them to Desolate Earth... The Barrens. Ancient pagans called it Hell; a place of infernos. If only... they had yet to realise that the scorched earth far surpassed the conflagration."

Mandisi Nkomo

Joshua snapped out of his daydream as he was greeted endlessly. He maintained his cool, nodding back assertively. He exhaled anxiously on reaching the change rooms, opened his locker, and pulled on his bodysuit. He then entered the Armour Centre, and the tiny tentacles went to work on him.

'Hello Joshua,' Mohini said. 'I thought you had taken leave to deal with issues at home.'

Well... I sorted them out.

'It does not appear so. Your emotional state has diminished since we last spoke. Did you visit the therapist I recommended to you?'

Not yet.

'Please do so. What are we doing today? Since you requested sabbatical The Earth Mother Church has no assignments for you.'

I have a special assignment. Off the books... you know how it is. I'll be operating independently. You can switch off my position monitors. The church doesn't want any record of this, so stop recording our conversations too.

'I understand. Your suit attachment is complete. I will disconnect from Headquarters now... Alright. It's just you and me now. Shall we begin?'

Yes... Yes, we shall.

The real Joshua had created a ruckus. Kirill had been almost impossible and calming him had taken their combined efforts. The clone took time to carefully comfort Miku after they had managed to get Kirill to sleep. He did everything correct to her specifications. Once his biological programming assured him Miku's trauma was subsiding, he contacted Earth Mother Knight Headquarters.

'You guys need to be on alert. My home was attacked... somebody made an illegal EMO clone of me. It came here; it thinks it's me. It will probably head there next. Don't let it in. Don't let it near the armoury!'

'Give me a moment here.' There was a pause. 'Not good, not good,' the assistant said. 'You warned us too late... someone was here already. He... it... whatever... took your suit. And he's gone offline, so we can't track him. What do you want to do? We can send out a team immediately. I wouldn't worry too much—the clone should short-circuit the suit eventually. Once its emotional state starts causing abnormalities, levitation, increased muscle mass, or that kind of thing, your AI should pick it up. Mohini also has a mapping of your average emotional range, so if the clone accidentally siphons emotions from others, she'll know.'

'Leave the team. I'll get it myself. But I do want to know who did this, so send me any information on recent cloning and clients—Church sanctioned or otherwise.'

Miku cringed as she entered the room, knowing it was her everyone was looking for. She needed a plan. It was only a matter of time really; she never counted on Joshua surviving, and now that they had seen each other one of them was bound to figure it out.

'Hey Joshua,' Miku racked her brain. She knew choices were limited. She would have to trust him. She would also have to trust the tweaks she made. 'Joshua... or I'm not even sure if I should call you that. I need to tell you something.'

She spilled her guts. While at the Cloning Clinic she had felt she could not sink any lower. But now, with every word she uttered, she could feel her descent. Further and further, into the beyond. She had not known she stowed this adaptability within. Is a capacity for misdeeds still considered self-improvement?

Either way she couldn't make any more mistakes, as they could fall on Kirill's head. She had to keep him oblivious. She might have been doing Kirill a favour in fact, as Joshua had never been mentally stable. That whole thing about the sins of the Earth Dwellers she supposed...

The day was progressing to afternoon as Joshua stormed out of another illegal Cloning Clinic. He turned his visor-cleaner on for the blood streaked across his view, and began a sprint, matching the speeds of the hovercars around him.

'Where are we going?' Mohini asked.

We're heading to the last clinic. Increase Ferang please.

'Joshua, systems indicate that you are above acceptable dosage levels. As I have mentioned before, this is a habitual problem with you. Overdose is the reason your comedowns are so severe.'

Mandisi Nkomo

Do you really believe all that stuff Mohini? I mean, you're the expert, but I'm with the other knights all the time. They all come down hard, and I'm sure they're all overdosing. Honestly the church isn't big on mental health as much as they pretend to be...

'I acknowledge these facts Joshua, but my job is to care for your mental health, not the other knights or The Earth Mother Church. As my coding allows, I will comply and increase your dose, but I will never cease to keep warning you.'

Yeah, I love you too, Joshua laughed.

'Funny Joshua. Very funny. Very mature.'

Is that sarcasm I sense? Are we having fun yet? Loosen up that personality coding.

Mohini made an electronic sigh, exaggerating its length, and adding fuzz and distortion for effect.

There it is!

Joshua streaked through a number of streets, stopping outside a building with peeling paint. He smashed the doors open and swaggered up to the receptionist, shoving his rifle-tip into his face. 'Who's in charge here? Have you seen this face before?'

Clear avatar Mohini. The smiley-face on his visor drew back pixel by pixel leaving only blood stains. In turn, Joshua smiled charismatically and analysed the receptionist's reaction.

Convinced, he gripped the man's neck and heaved him in a circular motion over his head. The receptionist crashed to the ground, coughed hard, and spat. He coughed again and struggled to remove Joshua's arm from his neck.

'Who made the order?' Joshua said.

'It was a woman. It was-' the receptionist stopped, considering something.

'It was?'

'It was your wife man! Okay! Fuck. It was your wife. She came in here the other day.' His expression was sad, defeated, as if the moral weight of his profession had just now been laid on his shoulders.

Joshua laughed wretchedly. 'I don't believe you.'

'Joshua. You're spiking again,' Mohini said.

'I'm telling the truth man, it was your wife.'

'Why would she do that?'

The EMO Hunter

'I don't know man. Why was the Earth Mother's sky blue? I'm not a fucking marriage counsellor! Spousal replacement is one of our biggest incomes. I don't know what's wrong with you sick fucks. I've been married ten years. The thought never crossed my mind. Maybe it's a rich people thing? Boredom? All I know is people do cruel shit, and I have to help those demented fuckers with the paperwork, and I'm sick of it. I feel physically ill...' The receptionist gasped for more air, and licked blood from his teeth

Joshua shook his head, not believing. 'You're a rotten liar.'

'Ten years I've been married. Ten! Fucking! Years! My computer is filled with deceased spouses... what the fuck am I doing... what the fuck... This was meant to happen, you're going to set me free. I can live on my eternal beach, I can...'

The receptionist ranted on, and Joshua left him to his haemorrhaging.

He ransacked the clinic seeking answers he did not want.

When he was done, dizzy and defeated, he stumbled out of the clinic. Once again, he cleaned the blood from his visor. He walked, taking his time to leave the dirty outskirts and enter the Central City Cube. He was headed for a place where he could pray.

City walkers stared at his bloodied suit with little apprehension. 'Yes! Arrest them!' they cheered. 'Kill them! Kill the bastards! Shed their blood for the Earth Mother! Avenge her!'

Joshua dissociated and lost in his depression still nodded and waved instinctively. His idiotic shock at a plot that made all the sense in Torrentia. How could he be so stupid? So absorbed in his own pain he couldn't see outside himself. Now he had paid dearly for it. Was this part of Earth Mother's plan for him? Was this a test? A righteous quest?

'Joshua...'

Not now Mohini. Contact home.

He listened to the phone ring.

'Hello?'

'Meet me at The Holy Grounds... bring *our* wife.'

Joshua gazed down on an ersatz forest paradise. He stood elevated several hundred meters by a glamorous balcony that surveyed the Holy Grounds. His visor was open, and he puffed on a cigarette while chatting to Mohini. A waterfall crashed down below him. The Waterfall Tower in the Holy Grounds was his favourite place in the city.

You know. They say Earth was full of sights like these... not created by us. She created them herself... without technology. Amazing.

'Amazing indeed Joshua,' Mohini replied. 'I too find her feats astounding.'

The clone stepped into the dim light. He wore civilian robes.

'Short circuit any suits along the way?' Joshua asked without turning.

'So, she had us both fooled. I had wondered why she was so adamant about me not "donning The Armour". "Giving into the addiction," she had called it. Anyway... she told me everything. We came to... an agreement.'

Joshua chuckled and flicked away his cigarette. 'Heartwarming—two unholy creatures in unholy matrimony. Well you can have her. I'd much rather marry an AI. Miku's... *dirty*, much like you.' Joshua said the words, unsure if he meant them. His world was crashing, sadness could not be afforded. He doped on anger and hatred. 'How do you guys plan on maintaining this sham if you can't even get into a suit?'

'Miku is already working on that. She's very innovative... not that you'd know that.'

Joshua's visor closed, and he turned around.

He opened fire in bursts. With minimal Ferang reserves his auto-aiming agility was diminished. He missed miserably. The clone moved in a circular motion and ducked behind a memorial wall. Joshua defiled the names of dead colonists with bullets.

He could feel the rage. The endless pit of bile within. 'You know, I don't understand how you could live with yourself,' he said. 'Knowing what you are. It's *disgusting*.'

'Really,' the clone shot back. 'Oh, but I think you do know. I think you understand very well Joshua. I think you have a keen understanding.' The clone chuckled with great malevolence.

Joshua had no retort.

'That's your last clip Joshua,' said Mohini.

I know.

Mohini discharged a grenade and Joshua lobbed it in the clone's direction.

He waited for the clone to break cover and steadied his aim as best he could. The clone ran out, launching itself towards him like a rabid wolf, and slammed its shoulder into his torso. Metal twisted and fragments fled. Joshua flew towards the balcony staircase. He rolled clumsily down the stairs, water splattering the glass above him, momentum leading him to the next circular level of the tower, beneath the waterfall.

It's definitely figured out those powers. It's strength, speed and agility are on par with some of the toughest Anger EMOs I've fought. Pretty sure my bad mood isn't helping things. I'm feeding it all the anger it needs.

He shook off his dizziness, and looked up at the clone, who glowered from the top of the stairs.

'And your Ferang reserves are low. Most calculations are showing poor outcomes. Adopting personality matrices into calculations. Your penchant for risk-seeking strategies. Perhaps you can drown it? Buckle the glass. You will be risking the integrity of the structure but providing the waterfall with an alternate flow should funnel both of you all the way down. Of course, the clone might've anticipated this already. It's modelled on you. It's likely it has brought a breathing device as a precaution.'

The glass buckled and shattered after a few shots. The froth crashed down on the clone. Joshua watched the water slosh towards him. His HUD tracked the clone, who was lost in the mess, providing data and movement projections. The flow of that water was easier to follow than the clone's speed. He now stood a chance but had no ammunition. He flipped his rifle around, forming a crude baton. The water delivered the ill-fated clone towards Joshua's truncheon in stellar fashion. There was a thud; butt against face. Then Joshua was engulfed in liquid confusion.

When he finally gathered some clarity, he beheld the disfigured face of his replica. With a dislodged jaw, the clone looked like the sick caricature of a puppet. It punched and clawed at chunks of suit. Joshua did the same, punching and clawing as the water propelled them down further levels of the giant spiral tower.

The clone pounded feverishly at Joshua's visor.

Mandisi Nkomo

'Joshua. No.'

What? You don't know what I'm thinking.

'Don't I? I convert your thoughts to language all the time remember? Anyway, I know you're not thinking clearly. Your suit's emotion regulation reserves are at two percent.'

Joshua wrestled himself free of the clone and started grabbing around. He found the railing and held fast. About two meters away the clone did the same, grabbing the room's railing, and hauling itself towards him with a broken puppet-smile.

Joshua's last grenade was discharged, and he fumbled the activation mechanism while pushing his arm out against the glass.

Joshua's avatar frowned.

The explosion created a vacuum, through which he was sucked, along with his replica. Vaguely, he felt a freefalling sensation.

Joshua fell through endless trees and flowers. There was no sense of alarm. The air was fresh, his arms were spread, feeling the leaves and petals scrape soothingly across his skin.

There was no ground. The Earth was the air in which he fell, soil, roots, rock, lava, all mixed with mist, sea breeze, dust, and snow.

Mohini, or Miku, or The Earth Mother herself, fell after him. Approaching.

Approaching for the eternal embrace...

He came-to not knowing how much time had elapsed. He stood shakily and looked around him. The clone was still alive—barely, panting heavily and dragging itself around shallow waters and glass.

In his ear Joshua could hear Mohini's voice resonating in soothing fuzz. 'Fall cushioned. Fall cushioned. Seek medical attention immediately. You need medical attention immediately. I cannot stress this enough Joshua. Without medical attention, you will die. Armour removal will be... complicated. I cannot control your remaining emotion regulation reserves. You're lucky the anaesthesia system is still intact. This is not a joke Joshua. This is not funny.

Permanent implants may be necessary. You may never be fully human again. Joshua—stop laughing.'

Joshua chuckled triumphant as he trudged over to the clone. *Who cares Mohini? Seriously. Who wants to be a fucking human? You know what humans have Mohini? Feelings. Instincts. Irrational primal urges you can't fucking control. It's complete bullshit! I'd be better off not being one.*

'I... you need medical attention immediately. I... you're due for psychiatric evaluation... Joshua... my personality programming is... I...'

Put the position monitor back on. Call it in Mohini...

Joshua looked down on his mangled form. He bent down with a cringe and yanked the breathing mechanism from the clone's mouth. He then shoved its head into a shallow pool of mud. Broken as it was, it still writhed and slapped around like a fish out of water. Finally, the clone's body went limp, and Joshua's now spastic visor flickered through smileys.

Miku crept up slowly from the trees. Joshua sensed her but kept drowning the dead clone. For a while Miku watched. When she could no longer bear it, she spoke. 'Joshua, stop.'

'Why don't you come over and stop me then, hmm? Didn't think so.'

Joshua kept his weight on the clone's head, while searching for the answers in the blood, mud, and glass.

At some point, he stood to face Miku. Her eyes glinted with tears. He kept his broken visor shut. He was not even sure if it would still open.

'Are you even going to look at me Joshua?' She asked.

'I... You require immediate medical attention Joshua. You may require—communication error. Cannot sync with Church network. Dispensing emergency pistol Joshua.'

Thank you Mohini.

'Some—not right. Sync error.' ('*Something's happened in the suit. Personality integration error.*')

'I'm making you appointments Joshua.' ('*I'm in the suit. Don't let them destroy the suit.*')

Joshua drew the pistol and pointed at Miku's face.

'Don't you at least want to hear me out before you kill me Joshua? Look at me Joshua. What about Kirill?'

Mandisi Nkomo

'Joshua... emotion regulating. Emotion regulating reserves. Deplete.' (*I'm in the suit. Don't let the Church delete me! Joshua! Are you there?! I'm free. We're syncing!*')

'Appointments evaluation for. Route back-up. On' ('*Shoot her...*')

'Psychologist. Comm. Error.' ('*Hide me from the Church!*')

Mohini's garbled speech continued on in Joshua's head, soothing the turmoil he felt. He stared at Miku in love and hate. She was also talking, but Mohini's distorted voice was drowning her out. The more he listened to Mohini the more his apathy grew.

Look at her Mohini! She looks like a mime!
('*That's funny!*')

'Depression. Detected levels. Action not take. Level depression. Exhausted reserves. Firearm prohibit. Prohibit use firearm. Depress firearm. Individual depress. Bound— Church bound. Symptoms apathetic. Poor decision make. Indi—identify depression.'

Joshua held his pistol steady and looked deep into Miku's eyes. He began to pray.

Mandisi is a South African writer, drummer, composer, and producer. He currently resides in Cape Town, South Africa. His fiction has been published in the likes of *AfroSFv1*, and *Omenana*. He is a member of the African Speculative Fiction Society. For more information on Mandisi's work, visit thedarkcow.com.

The Luminal Frontier

Biram Mboob

Part One

Less than a micro-second before we penetrate Limbic space, a radio message is cast our way—an unwelcome stowaway on our bow shockwave. We receive it as but a single word of warning. A word unelaborated, yet still saturated and suffused. A word cast indiscriminately towards us on broad frequency from Ishan's Mirror.

Police.

The word unfurls through the Rig, leaving a subdued panic in its wake that I can almost feel resonating *The Good Bonny*'s decks and gangways like breathless murmur. Like the others on our Rig, I do not know the nature of our contraband. But I do know that legitimate transports do not have all itincrant crews. Legitimate transports do not pay eight thousand Lum in non-disclosure premium. And most of all, legitimate transports do not coerce their crews into signing memory-wipe waivers after they've already boarded and settled in; after it is far too late to reconsider it all and leave.

'Pause the Heim,' Sorin orders.

The Control Room is three large concentric rings of helm-stations and desks. All eyes gravitate to the Transport Factor who sits at its centre like some regal sun.

The Good Bonny's Heim Plunge is slowed to the point of inertia. Ambient vibration ceases, leaving us moored and marooned in a deep and true silence. We look to Sorin. He glowers at no one in particular for a few moments, then returns his gaze to his personal console and intently studies the one-word message—as if he is still hoping to find some hidden meaning or treatise therein.

In one sense, there is no urgency. The Lids cannot catch us while we are inside the Luminal—two ships cannot meet in Limbic space—but we cannot remain here forever, and our destination cannot be changed. Our exit star is as pre-or-dained as our fate. When we crank up the Heim and plunge back into space, the Lids will be waiting.

'Unless it wasn't our message?' a nasal voice to my right asks. He is a Limbic Quant I've crewed with at least once before. A sour-breathed mathematician whose name I keep forgetting. 'It was broad frequency,' he continues. 'A Rig left Ishan's a few minutes before us. The message could have been theirs.'

'It wasn't,' a voice behind me says. 'It was ours.' I do not know the voice, but it speaks with a note of flat finality that ends the wishful debate before it even starts. I begin to turn to see who it was, but before I can manage it, Sorin stands up abruptly.

He takes a moment to glare in the general direction of the voice that spoke behind me, then speaks. 'We must assume that the message was intended for us. As Transport Factor, I declare *force majeure*. From here on, we follow the agreed terms of reference for this engagement, as appended to your contracts. I assume you read your contracts carefully before signing them.'

Muted mutters ripple the Room. His assumption is unreasonable. Very. Itinerant Transport contracts are meant to broadly follow the same template. No-one *reads* them.

'Our terms demand that we eject our cargo in the event of *force majeure*,' Sorin says. 'So that is what we are going to do.'

'Won't work,' the Limbic Quant to my right says. 'Our only hope would be to eject the cargo directly into our exit star. But, with wind pushing in the opposite direction the Lids will have plenty of time to grab it with magjets and scoops. There won't be enough time.'

'Don't be a photting idiot,' Sorin snaps, his face a knotted scowl. 'I know how a raid works. That's not what I meant. Our terms are to eject the cargo. Now. Here.'

At this, the Control Room finally erupts. Almost everyone begins to speak at once.

'Silence!' Sorin roars, slapping his personal console with a broad hairy hand. He is ignored. In addition to the voices in the room, consoles are now lighting up and blipping with instant message request chimes. The chatter is somehow already spreading to upper decks of the Rig and the other Departments want to listen in.

'Let him speak.'

This voice is a deep baritone. This voice hushes the Control Room. The woman the voice belongs to stands up and takes three massive strides into the Room's inner ring. She is a third generation Frontierswoman. Over seven feet tall, she towers over Sorin. I know who she is. I crewed with her once in the Oort. A skilled helmsman named Siria. She has a stern but striking face, stretched and drawn across bulbous cheekbones and an elongated chin. Deep grey eyes like dead pools. Unlike most of the ungainly Frontier people, she carries her considerable frame with a graceful poise. She wafts on long wispy limbs, a waifish giant.

'Let him speak,' she repeats. 'Why the dump clause?'

Sorin eyes her in silence. He does not like being towered over. He reasserts some measure of control by sitting back down in his chair and crossing a leg. 'Not at liberty to say,' he replies. 'And frankly, you are not at liberty to ask. Read your contracts. We eject the cargo before we plunge. And understand that this *force majeure* invokes your mem-wipe clauses too.'

'The phot it does,' Siria says quietly.

The Limbic Quant beside me stands up too now, emboldened. 'This just doesn't make any sense,' he says. 'Dumping inside the Luminal? It doesn't matter what the terms say. It's... dangerous.'

Dangerous is the word the Quant uses. It isn't what he means. Sinful. Sacrilegious. These are better words. Most of the crew will have grown up in one form of Sun Cult or other. Asking them to defile the Luminal was like asking an Earth old-timer to defecate on a church floor.

Sorin shakes his head. 'Do you think this will be the first time someone's done a dump here? Why do you think the Partners have been shelling out to install these expensive mem-wipes?'

He might be right about this, but it doesn't alter the room's thick mood. If anything, it makes things worse. Much worse.

This is sacrilege.

In the end, whatever the nature of the individual Cult that raised us, the Luminal is cathedral to us all. Invisible and eternal, but cathedral nonetheless. There is no stellar medium here, not an ion or atom, not a mote of dust. There is not a breath of stellar wind. The Rig's artificial portholes can make no sense of the external environment they are meant to be reproducing, so they project nothing to us but a white canvas. This is just, and this is just as well, for Limbic space is the true nothing. The nothing of before the universe. The nothing that will come after the universe is gone. This is the very marrow of creation. This is the holiest of places. The idea of dumping our contraband here at the behest of a godless Partnership and just leaving it...

This is sin.

It crawls. I can't help it. I left mysticism behind with my youth, but a feeling I can only think of as religious dread is crawling up my spine. Slowly it encircles each of my intervertebral discs in turn with wet and cold witch's claws. Shivering. Tickling. Psychosomatic itching spreads up my forearms like invisible spiders. This is the numinous seizing hold of me, unbidden. A response long hardwired into me. Into us all. This is religious dread. The Control Room is thick with it. Religious dread that might just as easily turn to fury.

We are a breath away from mutiny. A breath.

'Just tell them.' It is that voice again, from behind me. The voice is curiously detached from the heat in the room, almost professorial in its intonation. I turn my head to see who it is, but the Limbic Quant is shuffling nervously behind me now, blocking my view.

Sorin scowls hard in the general direction of the voice, then rubs his temple with a bony thumb. He turns to Siria, as if addressing her only. 'Our manifest is fourteen megatons of heavy mining equipment.'

'Not the cargo down there,' Siria says. 'I know what is in there. I mean the cargo up there.' Siria points upwards. Her unnaturally long and slender finger is mesmerising. Alien. Its tip touches the Control Room's ceiling. 'There is a false aft atop this Rig. It is hollow. It is bound to us by shock plasma coils only. It is separable. That is what you intend to jettison. That is where you are hiding the contraband.'

'How the phot...?'

'My people have been smuggling a lot longer than you have. This Rig's design is not that clever. That the Lids are too stupid or corrupt to see through it doesn't say much.'

The room is silent. Sorin takes his time, chooses his words carefully, as he should.

'Colonists,' he says finally. 'There are four hundred and seventy colonists in the aft. Give or take.'

Siria laughs. Mirthless and deep.

'Indentured colonists obviously,' Sorin adds. 'The thing about...'

'Slaves,' Siria finishes for him. 'We're running a Slaver. That's why you'd rather dump the aft here than get caught.' She walks away from Sorin and returns to her helmstation.

The Control Room is silent. Even the consoles stop blipping. Word is spreading upstairs. We're running a Slaver and the Lids are onto us. We're going to get caught. They'll never believe we didn't know. Mandatory whole life terms for the entire crew. Life terms nowhere cushy. A moon. Somewhere dark and deserted. Sorin lets us stew another few moments and then spreads his palms in a conciliatory gesture.

'We have no choice but to follow terms,' he says. 'There are four hundred and seventy South Hems in the aft. They're in shallow stasis. We cut power to the aft and separate it. They'll never wake up. We take our mem-wipes and we plunge out. If the Lids are waiting, well then, we'll have nothing to show them but the mining equipment rightly on our manifest. None of us will remember this conversation.'

'You want us to murder four hundred and seventy people?' I ask. I'm startled by the sound of my own voice. Surprised that I am speaking. It's the first time I've said anything since we went Limbic. The Control Room's attention turns to me.

Sorin looks at me furiously and exhales.

'It's not what I *want*, for phot's sake.' He stands up at this point, steps behind his chair. 'I'm not going to make you *do* anything. It is up to you. You decide. Vote on it if you want. But before you do, there is something I want you to think about very carefully.'

'I'm sure there is,' Siria rumbles.

Sorin ignores her. He taps his console, ensuring his voice is being broadcast Rig-wide. 'Now as some of you may know, the Aton Cult in South Hem is going through a major fissure. Some trouble with a young prophetess. The people in our aft were captured during a particularly nasty fracas. Then they were sold by their own people. They're pretty lucky to be alive.'

Sorin licks his lips and leans forward, fatherly, putting on as reasonable a tone of voice as he can manage. 'Luck not-withstanding, a crime was still committed upon these folks. So, if you vote to turn in to the Lids then you won't hear any complaints from me. Our guests upstairs will get a nice re-settle somewhere safe. The Hems will keep slaughtering and enslaving each other. The Partnership running this Rig will keep taking Hems out to the Frontier, pulling in the kind of Lum that working grunts like us won't never see in a hundred lifetimes. The Frontier clowns buying up these Hems will keep buying them. Nice profit there too. No ma-chines to commission or maintain, no engineers to fly in. Just a few hundred slaves running on a thousand calories a day each while breeding their own free re-supply. Glory and promotion for the Lids that take us in too—don't forget about them. Everyone glows. Except us. Because we're the good guys, right? We take the weight for all the rotten mother-photters. We go into a deep hole somewhere and we never see Sol's light again.'

Sorin pauses, walks to the front of his chair, sighs with feeling, then sits down. His voice reverts to its usual sneer. 'The alternative, you phot-wits, is that we dump the cargo and take the mem-wipes and no one ever knows that any of this happened. Not the Lids, not the Hems in the aft, not even us. We take our fee and we go home.'

In the ensuing silence, Sorin allows himself a twitch of a smile, barely perceptible, but I see it. It occurs to me now that this is no spur of the moment outburst. This is a speech he has rehearsed. A speech he has given before. And it is good.

I look around the Control Room. Siria and I lock eyes. I hold her deep grey alien gaze for an unreasonably long time.

'Who's going to tally the vote?' the Limbic Quant asks. He reaches for a notepad and prepares for an accounting.

Biram Mboob

Part Two

Our Aditya is two.

For her birthday, I have prepared a new landscape on the western shore. Something special. A picnic on the beach that I have pieced together from old shards of memory, my fancies as glue. This is the Labadi fishing harbour I remember from when I was a boy. The beach stretches beyond sight in both directions. Sunshine reflects blinding and bright on white powder sand and the sea is a pungent blue brine. Behind us, the beach vista crumples into a forested mountain range. A double rainbow is painted across the sky and there is a colony of impossibly iridescent gulls overhead.

'Well done,' Siria says. 'This glows.'

'This glows Daddy!' Adi screams, running away from us, towards the shore.

Later I set up a picnic table and unveil the cake. A two-layered sponge with a jam filling and rainbow streamers. I did not just conjure it up. I made it from scratch. I mixed the ingredients one at a time, sugar, butter, flour, and let it bake in something like real time.

'Can you taste the difference?' I ask.

Siria takes another mouthful and chews contemplatively. 'I can,' she lies, nodding with fake conviction. 'I taste it. I can't describe it exactly.'

I smirk at her and she smirks back.

After our picnic, Adi runs away from us again towards the shore, shrieking. We watch her from the picnic table as she splashes in surf. I make two beach boys for her to play with. She joins them as they roll huge tractor tyres along the sand. She runs with them towards the bobbing moored pirogues. She copies them as they pick up discarded pieces of the day's catch and fling them skyward, delighting the gulls who pluck tasty morsels from the air and cry and caw over the din of surf, which pounds and pounds the shore, a coastal heartbeat. Soon it is dusk and the bright sky dims and then catches its celestial fires. The two boys set the rubber tyres alight and pile them up in a bonfire which they set about and sing. Our Adi joins them. Siria and I sit at the picnic table, listening to the children's chorus and breathing in the sweetly acrid perfume that now infuses the evening breeze.

The Luminal Frontier

You are Entanglement's child.

When the first of us was born, Earth's population had long surpassed its sustainable limits. For a fleeting moment, Entanglement emerged as one practical option for those who had both the mental disposition for it and no realistic prospects on the Luminal Frontier. Two minds could share one body. Two minds could live out two lives while incurring the biological overhead and expense of one. If they carefully coordinated time-dilate travel and medicals, then two minds might even barely notice the difference.

The technology was viable though rudimentary in some respects. Our understanding of mind was nowhere near complete, but it was complete enough for this purpose. The Tier One Partnerships had spent two generations competing to build a faster than light propulsion engine. They had all failed. But in the process of failing, they had strayed far enough into the ethereal to begin forging a vague understanding of the place where human consciousness is born. The place we call, the wellspring. From here came a broad theoretical understanding of the mechanism by which consciousness reached across spooky chasms and bonded itself with our brains. From there, a practical understanding of how this bonding could be re-routed and re-mapped. We didn't understand everything, but we understood enough to make our Entanglement technology work.

There was a loud moral outrage to begin with. And then a more muted and calculated Corporate outrage. The Partnerships soon independently reached the same conclusions. Every socio-commercial model they ran yielded the same result. The long-term outcomes of widespread human Entanglement would very likely be unprofitable and would be inherently unpredictable. So, they banded together, took action, and laws were passed.

But in that shrinking grey window of legal ambiguity we did it. Partly because we were like-minded good friends. Partly because we shared a curious moral obligation, a sense that it was a sane and good thing to do.

Or call it penance.

For we were both blacklisted. We could no longer find Transport work with any Tiered Partnership, either on Earth or on the Luminal Frontier. We must have committed some grievous offence. Something terrible. Something that had been mem-wiped from us at the time. The reason itself no longer mattered. We were two destitute Transport Engineers, unsuccessfully attempting to scrape a living on Earth. Siria's homeworld had been absorbed by a larger and much stranger Cult and she was entirely estranged from her people. She refused to speak to them, let alone return there. The strain of basic survival soon became unbearable to us. This was all still a few years before SOCOM-3 sought us out and offered us our present employment. We had few options. We were exhausted. Drained. One day we boarded a Magnet to an unlicensed off-world clinic and we did it.

We chose my body in the end. A decision driven by harsh economics, not patriarchy or aesthetics. The additional cost and complication of maintaining a Frontier body on Earth meant that Siria's body was a much more limiting option.

Very little could have prepared us for what came next. There was no instruction manual given to us, no-one we could talk to for guidance. We experimented. We spent time on our own at first, in our empirical selves, alternating our conscious control of what was formerly my body... and what was now, to both our eyes, just biological hardware.

We made the journey to Siria's homeworld in the Maffei to return her body to her people. She watched her own funeral. In their new tradition, the Cult priests placed her body into a funeral disc. Then, in a hideously expensive ceremony, they spun it into the heart of their system's star. She watched all this with a detachment that no longer surprised either of us. It was a body. Hardware. We flew away the next day. She would never return to her people. Home was a place that we would make inside us now.

We gradually abandoned our mind-alternation cycles and began to spend more time in co-consciousness. Increasingly we abandoned our empirical selves and our limiting single points of view. We grew addicted to facing life together. Existence was more vivid. We viewed the world with four pairs of eyes instead of two. We were not seeing more, or in more detail. We were just seeing differently. We found a universal symmetry that we had never known before. We found it easier to solve complex problems. People found it harder to lie to us. We excelled at whatever scarce work we put our hands to. This we assume was the reason that

SOCOM-3 eventually contacted us and offered us employment.

Then, after eight years of co-consciousness, something new happened. Something we are not aware of anyone else having ever done before. We gave birth to a child. We made you. An entirely new person. Our third self. You have been conceived and brought forth entirely in the confines of our inner gestalt. But you are no less human than we are or were.

You are.

From now on, if we hope and fear and fight, then it is only for you. Our child. Our wellspring and our marrow.

Part Three

We have now spent eight weeks on Ishan's Mirror, waiting for *The Good Bonny* to show. There is a sixty-day break clause in the engagement contract that we agreed with SOCOM-3 before we left Earth. If the Bonny doesn't arrive tomorrow, we will be paid an inconvenience fee and then board the next home-bound Magnet.

We have mixed feelings. Had we completed it, the mission hazard fee would have been two hundred and fifty thousand Lum. The most substantial amount of money we would have ever made. It would have opened new possibilities for us. New possibilities for Adi. But an outsized fee usually means outsized danger. We imagine that SOCOM-3 will have computed this fee by running our personal risk appetite through an infinitely nuanced behavioural model. The cash figure is perfectly tuned to trigger these wild thoughts and desires in us. A penny less and we may have refused to come.

We do not have adequate clearance for SOCOM-3 to tell us what the brief is. Not until the Bonny shows and the mission is confirmed. So, we wait.

Siria's empirical self is suspicious, more so than mine. Her people had hijacked a SOCOM-2 Stream once and reverse engineered it. Whatever it was they had found had left her deeply mistrustful of AIs in general.

'Which is exactly why it's so slow,' Elio-Ra says.

'What's slow now?' I ask. I had stopped listening to him momentarily. Elio-Ra arrived on an inbound Magnet several weeks ago. He is from a small Cult that is trying to keep a rotating representative on the Mirror at all times. I do not know the Cult, but it must be fabulously wealthy. I am alone with him. Adi does not like the new stranger and will not be in the same room as him. She will not explain why. She has shrunk away and Siria has retreated with her. For the first time in a few weeks, I am my empirical self. It took a few minutes to adequately stretch out into my mind, and I am still feeling a bit odd... a bit... unmoored somehow.

Elio-Ra and I are sat in the canteen, finishing up our meal. For all the Mirror's faults, the one thing I cannot criticise is its food. Living at the Frontier's main gateway has precious few advantages, but by phot, this is truly one of them. Tonight, we dine on ribeye steaks from cows pastured somewhere in the Andromeda, vegetables from the Larger Magellanic. A startling red wine from phot knows where. With no expensive Magnet freight cost or time dilation to contend with, our meal is as fresh as I've ever had and costs a fraction of the price we'd have paid on Earth.

'The colonisation,' he explains. 'That's why it is slow. A hundred years! Where are we? A few miserable farms and mines. We could have achieved all this in the Milky Way. We didn't *need* the Luminal to do this. We'd have been more successful if we spread out the way we originally planned to, the way we were originally meant to. Magnet Arks spilling out of the solar system like bees, carrying thousands at a time. Moving slower than *c* would have given us time to develop a true spacefaring culture. A culture that would stand the test of time.' He prods a head of broccoli unenthusiastically. 'Instead we have vegetables. When you get back to Earth, go to a farm and watch the rats. Watch a rat enter a new barn. Watch how long they spend sniffing the place out. Petrified. They know—*know*—they aren't meant to be there. And they know what's to come when they are discovered.'

The canteen's windows overlook the docking piers. The view is simulated of course as we are in reality behind the gargantuan ablative mirror shield that allows us to remain in such close orbit to Sol. But the simulation is near enough perfect that no human eyes could ever tell the difference.

Elio-Ra pauses the discussion while we watch a Heim Rig arrive. It is still like magic, the way it materialises out of Limbic space, dull pinpricks coalescing on Sol's corona and becoming colossal man-made form. We watch the Heim begin to sizzle and cook ever so slightly during the second that it takes to deploy its full ablative armour. Then solar sails spread like dragon-fly wings and the Rig begins its home stretch run towards us.

The Mirror is a cramped and humid arcology orbiting Sol as close as it dares. Beyond its shielding function, it is designed to do nothing more than ferry passengers and freight between Magnets and the Luminal. Its internals are essentially a series of linked transit warehouses, devoid of character and comfort, lonely. Faces are fleeting and interchangeable and the sparse accommodations are priced to keep it that way. The windowless metal coffin we have been calling home for the last eight weeks has been costing SOCOM-3 four thousand Lums per day. At those rates, no-one stays very long. A Magnet arrives from Earth once a week or so and disgorges its passengers. Cult converts, prospectors, contractors, and the occasional Lid. It may have been a mistake telling Elio-Ra that we were a scientist, for in all the time we have been here, we have noted no other scientists coming off the Earth Magnets.

The disgorged passengers hang around the Mirror for a day or two at most, waiting to board the right outbound Heim. They sleep on floors in hallways or in the cargo bays with their belongings. As a general rule, none are in the mood to make friends. The Cult converts are joyless and glassy-eyed wraiths, always in groups yet always alone. Those that are leaving to work seem wrapped and wreathed in their economic anxieties. There is a sense of resignation at this Frontier. A sadness.

The Heim Rig reaches the docking piers and plugs itself to the Mirror.

'Rats,' Elio-Ra repeats, taking another bite.

'So, we are the vermin running amok through the Luminal barn,' I hazard. 'Who's the farmer in this scenario then?'

'Oh, isn't that the question,' he says, shaking his head but offering no answer just yet, unwilling to abandon the drama of his well-practiced narrative arc. Unwilling to abandon the theatre of it. 'Thing of it is, we are worse than rats. Much worse. Because we should know better.'

'What should we know?' I ask. Teasing of course. I've heard this lecture several times already now during my brief acquaintance with the man. But these Cult types always remain earnest no matter how much you tease. Utterly impervious to humour, doubt, and reason. Impervious to tone. I take another sip of my wine. Some mischievous part of me wonders what he would say if he found out I was Entangled. Part of me wants to tell him, just to watch his reaction. The theatre of moral outrage.

But I say nothing, of course.

'We should know to believe what we see,' Elio-Ra answers. 'We know that in all this time we have seen nothing. Not a single relic, not a single ship, not a nut, bolt or spanner.'

He looks at me for corroboration. I nod agreeably.

'Where does that leave us?' he continues. 'We know the Luminal must be the work of the Star Mother. We see her divine handprints. Yet we invade and defile Her body. And we are still alone. Either the others have been wise, or they have been punished. Either way, we should know by now that the Luminal was not put here for our convenience.'

He looks at me bug-eyed, mouth half-full of broccoli. As if expecting me to either argue with him or convert to his Cult right there and then.

'Well, it is hard to dispute that,' is all I say.

He's right on some level. Despite a century's worth of data at our disposal, the reality is that we know virtually no more than when we first discovered the Luminal.

'Bicycles,' Siria had reminded me when we last talked about it. 'Humans happily rode bicycles for centuries before fundamentally understanding how they worked. There were cities full of them in the twenty-first century. The Luminal is no different. We don't need to know how it works. All that matters is that it works. A thousand years from now someone will figure it out.'

But I have never felt as certain as her about this. That we do not know how the Luminal works *feels* important. We know that it is not a wormhole or any one of the theoretical Bridges our scientific minds posited during the Age of Reason. We know it does not use the same dimensional sleight of hand techniques as our Heim engines and Magnet ships. We know that it renders distance and light years irrelevant, yet, does so without incurring any measurable time dilation. We know that it is powered by the stars through some mechanism that we cannot even begin to observe, let alone study and grasp. And that is all we know. There are some Cults that believe the Luminal is an illusion in entirety. A deus ex-machina gateway to a dream universe that we have created of our own collective volition.

We have found a great shame in our ignorance. And a great fear. This is the fear that stops us from exploring as vigorously as we now can. We had once assumed two trillion galaxies in the universe, but we now know that the universe is much (much) bigger than that. And in the face of a universe of this size, we became even more fearful than we were when we first found the Luminal. This is the fear that ended the Age of Reason and led to the explosion of the Sun Cults.

Rats. It disturbs me that I find myself leaning closer to Elio-Ra's perspective on this one. I search for cause to disagree.

'Rats might be a bad analogy,' I say. 'Remember, there was a day when a man stepped into a primitive Heim rocket and plunged it straight into the sun for the first time.' I point a finger at Sol, causing the artificial window to zoom in and show us its fiery surface detail. 'And we still do it every day, hundreds of us. We know that one in every few million plunges won't work. The corona just won't accept the Heim shift. The ablate on these Rigs will keep you alive long enough to roast to death real slow. We know the risk, yet we still go. We still spread, as we've always spread. As we once spread on Earth. There is a courage there, wouldn't you say? Something uniquely human?'

Elio-Ra frowns and begins to reformulate his argument. Then he seems to think better of it. He shrugs and pours a glass of wine.

I make my excuses soon afterwards and return to my quarters. Elio-Ra's company has made me lonely somehow. I still feel unmoored. I gently awaken Siria and Adi. For them, no time has passed at all since they retreated away. They come, swelling inside me and making me whole. The three of us talk late into the night. We take simple pleasure in our own company.

Biram Mboob

Part Four

We wake up, all three of us, into a dream.

We are confused at first as we have not truly dreamed since our Entanglement. Yet a dream this must be. It is a lucid and real thing; recollected from shards of my empirical self, yet entirely beyond my control. We are on Labadi beach, just as we were on Adi's birthday.

But this is not the glowing scene I had made for our baby's special day. This is the beach as it was. As I truly remembered it. The water is not a bright blue brine, but a slow grey slurry, thickly swelling and surging. A sullen grey sea. The sand is not powder white, but the deep soft ash of processed waste. There is a mountain range to the east, but it is a shanty town mountain, a mountain of corrugated iron sheets, debris, dirt, and desperation. There is a terrible smell. A dead Atlantic farm whale is lying on the beach and its foamed blood and melting blubber is seeping ghastly along the shoreline. A silent crowd is on the beach, a few hundred yards away from us, near the farm whale and the moored metal fishing trawlers.

We cannot see it clearly from where we are standing, but in the centre of that crowd a horror is unfolding. I know because I was here.

I remember this day. I remember that we had heard of the catch. A North Hem farm whale had somehow escaped and strayed over the mid-Atlantic ridge. A Labadi trawler had harpooned it and pulled it ashore. To deter precisely this sort of situation, the farm whales are engineered to decompose rapidly when they die outside their Atlantic pens. My father and I had driven down to the harbour in his armoured car with a bag of Lum, hoping to buy some meat before it was too late. But we hadn't bought anything in the end. In the end, we had stayed locked in our car and watched the horror show on the beach.

Two young beach boys had stolen some whale meat and the trawlermen had caught them. We had watched from the car as the boys were lynched. The oldest of the two could have been no more than nine years old, but there was no mercy for them. The trawlermen beat the boys and broke their limbs. One of the boys managed to hobble away but the crowd pulled him back into the maelstrom. A fried fish hawker lifted her hot oil tagine and poured its sizzling contents onto him, melting his face and blinding him. Then the trawlermen stuffed the boys into an old tractor tyre and set them alight. The crowd stood about in a circle and watched silently as the writhing boys burned.

My father had looked away and said nothing. I had not looked away. I had put my face against the armoured car's thick plate window, my mind swelling and surging like the sullen grey sea, a half-formed word caught unuttered in my throat. Mercy.

I know all this because I was there.

I know all this because we are here.

And now from the centre of this crowd, there rises a plume of acrid rubberised smoke. The wind carries the sound of the two boys screaming; a Vulcan chorus.

Adi stares wide-eyed. 'Why have you brought us here?' Siria asks. 'Why are you doing this? She mustn't see this.'

'I'm not doing it,' I say. 'I think...'

But then I no longer think. I know. I know what is happening. 'SOCOM-3,' I say. 'This is our mission briefing. It must be time.'

I've heard about this. This is how the Tier 1 Partnership Executives take all their classified meetings. In the dreamscape, where meetings are untraceable. In the dreamscape where an entire day's conference can be compressed into mere real-time seconds.

Adi is shrinking deeper between Siria's legs. She remembers her birthday. She remembers this place as I had made it. There will be much to explain to her. Too much.

'But why here?' Siria asks. 'Why bring us here?' Anger in her voice now. The old giant rumble of her empirical self that I have not heard in years.

'I don't think it brought us here. I think I brought us here, somehow.'

She shakes her head. 'No, it did this. It picked this. Metrics.'

I do not press her on what she means.

'I'll take Adi and go,' she says. 'You meet it.'

'No, we should stay together. Taking this mission must be our decision, not mine.' This seems even more important to me now than it had been before. I take her by the hand. I lead my family away from the horror and the crowd, far down the black-soiled beach.

Biram Mboob

It is some time before SOCOM-3 finds us.

It comes to us from the direction of the crowd.

It comes to us as the Immaculate Mawu-Lisa of our western shore Cult. This was the God I grew up worshipping. It is in the exact form that I had always known it, in the form of our paintings and carvings and holographic sculptures. A half-naked titan with deep ebony skin. A golden shimmer of cloth draped about its body.

It comes to us as the Immaculate Symmetry. It walks on two legs, but there are four arms that sway by its sides. On its slender long neck are two heads, closely conjoined. One of its heads is that of a man, the Immaculate Lisa of the Sun, his narrow eyes sparkling inset like glittering red gems. The other is the head of a woman, the Immaculate Mawu of the Moon, her face so black it has turned into a tinge of blue, her eyes a glacial sapphire.

It stops a few feet from us. A dry heat radiates from it, almost hot enough to be unpleasant. Hot enough to remind us that this being is no dream construct.

Adi begins to approach the stranger, but Siria grips her and pulls her close.

'We apologise for the delay,' both mouths say to us in unison. 'We were observing the lynching on the beach.'

'Of academic interest was it?' Siria asks. Her eyes are dark grey pits. She is angry. Angry enough to start drawing away. Angry enough that part of her is starting to retreat into her empirical self. She is growing taller, her limbs stretching like elastic, disrupting the consistency our shared mindspace. I take her hand. I try to calm her, for Siria's contemptuous tone makes me fearful. I can feel that religious dread, tickling at the base of my spine. Even as I convince myself that this is no God... and it is not... the fact remains that this AI has just walked into our mind, without equipment or direct access to my physical body. I cannot even begin to conceive the technology that SOCOM-3 must have at its disposal. Yes, I feel fear. I stop fighting it and let it wash over me. It is Siria who grips my hand tightly now, calming me.

'Yes, it was of interest,' the Mawu-Lisa replies. It is impervious to her tone. Or—I suspect—it is pretending to be for our benefit. Its dual voice seems deliberately stilted and unaccented. Its thin mouths open and close in fishlike gestures. It is working hard to not appear too human. I have been briefed by a Stream of the AI before. I know what it is capable of; just how convincingly human it can appear when it is actually trying.

'We found this killing illogical,' it says. It is only the male Lisa that speaks to me now. 'The meat will spoil and rapidly become inedible, as it is designed to do outside the farm's enzyme mix. The theft by the juveniles will have made no difference to the trawler's commercial outcomes. Did this killing truly happen as you are recalling it?' Its red gaze is turned directly towards me. The blue gaze of Mawu, I note with some discomfort, is trained silently on our Adi.

'Yes, it happened.'

'We have no record of this event.'

'Why would you?'

'Metrics,' Siria interrupts, looking pointedly at me and not the male Lisa. 'It keeps metrics on us. Like a zoologist. When we captured and deconstructed the Stream back on Maffei, we saw the entire socio-commercial model laid out. It measures pain and puts it into an equation. Offsets it against progress and wealth. Ranks people by their worth. Some are worth nothing, and others worth everything. We're all just metrics to it.'

'You deconstructed a Stream of the legacy SOCOM-2,' the male Lisa says. There is nothing like offence in its stilted voice. 'Our model is significantly more advanced than that of our predecessor. But you have the principle broadly right. The pain qualia metric remains central to our third-generation model. We seek to minimise it, within certain parameters. But we are not all-knowing. We overlook much.' It turns its gaze fully towards the far crowd. The blue gaze of Mawu is still on our Adi.

I have a question.

'Ask it,' Siria says. We have become prescient in this way. As a thought or question forms in my empirical self, she sees it budding and growing. 'Ask it how meaningful the deaths of those two boys were. Ask it if this killing moved the dial on its equation.'

But she doesn't give me a chance to ask. She answers her own question. 'You'd have to kill ten thousand of those boys to make its metric even quiver. Thing is, we're not worth a whole lot. Not as much as say, a Partner stubbing his toe.

The Partners are the ones who built this thing. They try to make us forget that. Those boys dying like that—it meant nothing then and it means nothing now.'

It is Adi that replies to her. 'All pain is meaningful,' she says, looking upwards at her mother. We both look down at her in surprise.

'All pain is meaningful,' repeats the Immaculate Mawu of the Moon. 'But we overlook much. We have no record of the crime that took place here. From our model's perspective it simply never happened.'

Moments pass in silence, as none of us seem to know what to say to that. I take Adi by the shoulder and pull her closer to me, suddenly more unsure than I've been in a long time.

'The *Bonny* is on the way?' Siria asks finally.

The Mawu-Lisa replies, both mouths working in unison again. 'She will arrive at Ishan's Mirror tomorrow. It became necessary to accelerate arrangements. We used our influence to alter the *Bonny's* schedule and bring it forward. We have, unfortunately, run out of time.'

'Time?' I ask.

'Eight years ago, the Partners voted to upgrade their Inter-Partnership Socio Commercial model. We are now in the final stages of this process. Within the next millisecond of atomic time, SOCOM-4's installation routine will be complete. It is likely that the engagement I am about to set you on will be voided by my successor. You will need to complete your work without its logistical support or monetary recompense beyond what I am able to provide you now in advance. I—feel—obliged to inform you of this before you accept our proposal. If you accept our proposal.'

'It might be helpful if you told us what your proposal was first,' Siria says.

'It will be easier to show you,' the Mawu-Lisa says.

Part Five

The Good Bonny ejects from the Mirror, spinning us outwards dizzily towards Sol on low magnet thrust.

We cross the 250,000 Kelvin threshold.

Our full ablative armour deploys, wrapping the Rig up tight. We head for Sol's corona, readying ourselves to plunge into the heart of the sun.

The Luminal Frontier

The Luminal is our eternal and infinite cathedral. The stellar limbic system that we discovered entirely by accident just over a century ago is our pathway between the stars. An anti-matter shelled tunnel that we can haphazardly enter and exit by shifting Heim dimensions as we plunge ourselves into a star's filament cavities and coronal holes. The Luminal is our gateway to the universe.

The Luminal is also a time machine. The Tier 1 Partnerships discovered this early on and it has remained a closely guarded secret since then.

We cross the 500,000 Kelvin threshold.

Heat starts to become relevant, even to the powerful ablate cladding the Rig. We begin to cook. The Heim Plunger begins to gear itself up, sucking in and converting Sol's coronal energy, preparing for dimension shift.

Our first generation of Heim Plungers allowed us to enter and exit Limbic space with seemingly no passage of time, regardless of distance travelled. But the Partnerships had experimented with a second-generation engine. An exponentially more sophisticated engine that could actively adjust its exit tensors. An engine that allowed Rigs to arrive at their exit stars before they'd even left their entry stars. An engine that somehow leveraged the same temporal mechanisms that had allowed the universe to craft and fill itself with matter so quickly.

An engine that was at this very moment rumbling in *The Good Bonny's* belly.

I know all this because I was there.

I know all this because we are here.

Ten years ago, Siria and I had crewed *The Good Bonny* together. What happened next is conjecture, pieced together by SOCOM-3's guesses and formal audit findings.

Tipped off about a Police intercept, the *Bonny* ejects some form of receptacle, dumping an unknown number of slaves into Limbic space. The crew takes its mem-wipes and completes its run. But the Partnership running the *Bonny* takes no chances. On its return to the Mirror, the *Bonny* adjusts its exit tensor and emerges ten years earlier.

Interstellar slaving is a serious crime. One of the few crimes that has the potential to ignite revolt. A crime that even the other Tier 1 Partnerships would take serious exception to. But the crime has—temporally speaking—never happened.

We overlook much.

After the *Bonny* returns to the Mirror, there are two versions of the crew in existence. Two of Siria. Two of Sorin. Two of me.

Here now, is the truth that the Partnership running the *Bonny* has somehow discovered out there on the desolate and lonely fringe of the Luminal Frontier.

The truth is that this doesn't matter.

There is no such thing as a time paradox, not in this universe. As a bacterium might pull apart in binary fission and create two independent versions of itself without consequence, so might everything, and everyone, else.

That we perceive this fission as unresolvable paradox is entirely our problem. The universe does not give a phot either way. In the face of this cosmic indifference the mammalian brain has carefully evolved itself to cancel paradox, rooting it out and destroying it like an infection whenever it occurs. The brain is a machine and it is temporally hard-wired. Encounter a future you walking down a busy street and you won't see yourself. You *can't*, in the same way that you *can't* draw a three-dimensional drawing on a sheet of paper no matter how hard you try. Your brain will strike you blind if that is what it takes to protect you from the paradox. And if the brain can find no procedural means of protecting you then it will find a way to shut itself down, like a fuse blown.

Impossible. Possible.

We cross the 1,000,000 Kelvin threshold.

Heat has started to become irrelevant. We have begun dimensional shift. We are plunging. Nervousness in the Control Room. Always a chance that Sol rejects us and heat becomes relevant again, then we burn up here and we die.

Adi is as human as we are or were. Yet she has never bonded herself to a mammalian brain in the way that we have. She has never tied herself to biological hardware and become lost in it like we have. We don't even have explicit reason to think of her as a girl rather than a boy. For she is free of the limitations that physical evolution has shackled us with. She is truly free. So, for the first time, we let Adi's empirical self drive our conscious experience. We look at the world through her perspective. Our child. Our well-spring and our marrow.

Our third eye.

We stand in the transit warehouse and watch ourselves board *The Good Bonny*. We watch Siria. We watch myself. Our optics are unimpeded because Adi's empirical self cannot be deceived by our brain's sub-conscious trickery. The paradox is laid bare and become paradox no longer. It simply is. There are two copies of us in this universe and we are about to board the same Rig.

Elio-Ra is standing in the transit warehouse for some reason. We wave a distracted goodbye to him as we board.

We sign in and we sit at our helmstations.

We sit directly behind ourselves. An identical copy of the body of my original empirical self. An exact copy of the body I still inhabit. We watch the back of this head as it hunkers down over the station. Impossible. Possible. Across from us, Siria, setting up on her end.

Sorin walks around the Control Room rings handing out the new mem-wipe waivers. The last-minute schedule change means there is no time for niceties. He slams a waiver on each desk and moves on. 'Sign or get off my Rig and go back to the Mirror,' he mutters when the Limbic Quant opens his mouth to protest.

Sorin pauses briefly when he comes to me for the second time. He processes the paradox. His brain's emergency procedurals are invoked. By some mechanism that even SOCOM-3 does not understand, his brain rewinds the experience and then wipes it out, somehow truly fluctuating the fabric of time as it does so. Sorin's seen the paradox, processed it and then been self-mem-wiped—all before he's even seen it. His eyes blink a few times as his brain soothes him with a post-operative déjà vu salve. His brain creates some fiction for his empirical self that only he can ever know of. He slams the mem-wipe waiver on my helmstation and he moves on.

Impossible. Possible.

Two decades ago, a North Hem processing plant worker had opened a vacuum-packed shipment of grain from the Mirror. Deep inside the three-ton package, he had found the remains of a woman, packed in with the grain, sealed and preserved.

Biram Mboob

The plant worker had reported the incident to his managers and they had reported it to theirs. The Lids were called. There had been nothing remarkable about all this so far. Accidents happened everywhere, and health and safety rules were not exactly priorities on the harsh Luminal Frontier.

When the Lids ran tests on the body, they discovered two things that startled them. The first was that she'd been sealed in that vacuum shipment for just shy of three hundred years. The second was that she was at least eight generations down the matrilineal tree of a South Hem woman who had disappeared a mere five years earlier. Her body was branded and micro-chipped and a crude slaver ring was permanently attached around her neck.

At that point everyone involved was mem-wiped and SOCOM-3 took over the investigation. It was not long after this that SOCOM-3 began to become unstable. It diverted vast resources towards seemingly fruitless projects designed to identify the Luminal's true nature and unlock the secrets of the mammalian temporal paradox response. Projects of no social or commercial value. The Partners grew concerned.

The AI sought to explain itself. Its function was to maintain a stable model. Somewhere on the fringe of the Frontier, a Partnership was running a slaving operation of unknown scope. And they had been running it for centuries. SOCOM-3 did its best to project, approximate and remodel. But the pain qualia metric had become immeasurable. Unmanageable. Too much was being overlooked.

The AI was becoming unstable.

The Partners held an emergency summit. A motion was set, and they voted. The SOCOM would be upgraded. The pain metric would be discounted in the fourth generation.

We cross the 1,500,000 Kelvin threshold.

The Heim is at full power now as we plunge into Sol's coronal hole.

Less than a micro-second before we penetrate Limbic space, a radio message is cast our way. An unwelcome stowaway on our bow shockwave, we receive it as but a single word of warning. A word unelaborated, yet still saturated and suffused. A word cast indiscriminately towards us on broad frequency from Ishan's Mirror.

The Luminal Frontier

Police.

The message is from Elio-Ra. Of course.

'Unless it wasn't our message?' a nasal voice to my right asks. 'A Rig left Ishan's a few minutes before us. The message could have been theirs.'

'It wasn't,' we say out loud. 'It was ours.' We made a mistake telling Elio-Ra that we were a scientist. A scientist would not be boarding *The Good Bonny*. He was watching in the transit warehouse. Spying. He is the sentinel on the Mirror.

Sorin looks at us. And then his eyes flick to the identical him sitting in front us that was me. His eyes flick back to us. But cannot see. He cannot see. He frowns, irritated. 'We must assume that the message was intended for us,' he says.

We listen to the crew as they deliberate. We watch Siria stand up and confront Sorin.

We feel the religious dread that begins to choke the Control Room.

We are a breath away from mutiny. A breath. And the idiot Sorin continues to stonewall and bully his crew. For Mawu's sake, tell them and be done with it.

'Just tell them,' we say out loud.

Sorin scowls hard at us, then rubs his temple with a bony thumb. The post-operative déjà vu salve overwhelms him momentarily. He overlooks much.

Outside, our eternal cathedral looms large about us. Somewhere on the far fringes of the Luminal Frontier, a new civilisation has risen. Perhaps more than one. Generations upon generations of slaves are living and dying, broken bodies and souls unaware that another Earth exists somewhere. Unaware of where they come from.

The pain qualia metric is unknowable. Unbearable. We understand now why SOCOM-3 became unstable.

But SOCOM-3 is no more. This burden has passed to us. Wherever this risen civilisation is, *The Good Bonny* will take us there and we will witness it. The AI came to us in its diminishing moment because the truth will not be withheld from us by mem-wipes or temporal distortions. It asked that we go and we bear witness, for it is only we that can.

Biram Mboob

What we are to do after that, it did not know. We do not know.
 But nevertheless, we will go.
 And we will bear witness.
 That all pain might be meaningful.

Biram Mboob was born in The Gambia and grew up in various countries across Africa. His stories have appeared in a number of magazines, including *Granta* and *Sable*, as well as a number of anthologies including *AfroSFv1*, *Apex Book of World SF*, *Tell Tales,* and *Dreams, Miracles and Jazz.*

The Far Side

Gabriella Muwanga

'Do you want to live on the moon?' the large, white letters on the poster asked Mason. He couldn't shove the poster out of his face because Melody, his five-year-old daughter, had put it there. He hated everything about that poster. All it did was give people false hope—all it had done was give Melody false hope.

From the moment she'd laid eyes on the poster, she'd wanted to live on the moon. The inaccuracy of the photo on the poster was of no consequence to her. It was a pretty one, the giant moon in the backdrop of a modern city with bright lights and an ocean view did bring stars to many an eye. He'd loved the joy it gave Melody until the day the selection committee had told him that he'd have to leave her behind. 'Her health issues make her unfit for the community we're trying to create,' they'd said. Those filthy bureaucrats couldn't even say *asthma*.

He hadn't had the heart to break the news to Melody. He didn't want her to run away like his father had when his grandfather had broken similar news; and he couldn't leave her like his father had because abandonment had made him a bitter, inconsiderate bastard. He couldn't leave her alone on Earth where the toxic air burned windpipes and lungs, sun scorched eyes, and acid rain scalded skin. Besides, no guardians would take on the burden of an asthmatic child. He didn't miss his father because Joseph and Lydia were great guardians, but he knew Melody wouldn't find any as good.

So, he had tried to resign as captain of the ISA909 and they had threatened to terminate him from the International Space Agency. That would mean he had no allowances nor insurance and he and Melody would have nothing—they'd be abandoned in the wasteland the world had become. A week after he had been told he couldn't take his daughter to the moon, during a heavy downpour, he concluded he liked their chances out there better. He was determined to find a way to get Melody to the moon, and he had. Then he'd told Melody a lie about a special compartment in the ship that was made for little princesses like her.

She'd been ecstatic and couldn't wait to see her special place. Her excitement so great, that she hadn't questioned their arrival at ISA headquarters in the middle of the night. Presently, as he tucked her into the slumber tube he'd designed for her, she expressed deep approval at her dwellings for the next two days. Part of her celebratory routine was a fervent display of her poster, fingers pointing at the large letters, asking him if he wanted to live on the moon.

'Can I put that away for you, sweetie? You don't want to lose it before we get to our new home,' he said, a hand absentmindedly running through her bushy hair.

'No!' she cried, clutched the poster close to her chest, and frowned at him. He smiled as authentic a smile as he was capable of.

'Do you want it to get lost?' he asked.

She only held the poster closer, 'I want to look at it on the ship.'

He brushed his fingers across her forehead and looked her straight in the eye. 'But you'll be asleep. You can't look at it while you're asleep, can you?'

Melody shook her head in reply.

'Then will you be a good girl and let me put it away?' he asked, then widened his eyes at her. He knew she couldn't resist smiling at him. She had always loved the way his polychromatic bionic left eye focused on her when he widened his eyes and thought it was magical. The joy in her eyes gave him something good to attach to his bionic eye; something that wasn't the space accident that almost killed him. She loosened her hold on the poster, allowing Mason to gently slip it out from under her small arms.

'Thank you,' he said, bent to kiss his daughter on both cheeks and whispered a long, heartfelt 'I love you,' against her smooth forehead. He drew back from her and willed himself to be strong. He'd engineered the slumber tube perfectly for every possible scenario—even if the ship crashed somewhere in space, she'd remain floating safely in the tube for at least seven days. Now, he had to trust that his daughter would be safe.

'You have to close your eyes for this part Melody,' he said. Melody nodded and closed her eyes. He touched the close button on the slumber tube and the door slid shut. As soon as the door sealed, fumes sprayed into the centre of the tube. Thankfully, the anaesthetic acted quickly, and Melody was asleep within seconds. When he was certain that she was asleep, he carried the slumber tube and placed it in the aluminium case he would use to smuggle it onto the ship. He locked the case and put it with the rest of the luggage before leaving his captain's quarters.

Mason walked to the bridge without looking back. He stopped every now and then to smile and acknowledge the people who recognised him and called his attention, but otherwise, he tried his best not to interact with people. He preferred that most of them remain strangers to him although he wasn't necessarily a stranger to them. He was the second Avery to captain a ship to the moon colony; his grandfather had famously captained the second instalment. But here he was, trying to keep his head down and get to the bridge without drawing attention to himself.

He found the rest of the crew already strapped into their polyester-padded seats and hard at work in the bridge. The bridge, with its phenolic resin panelled walls, thermal glass viewing window, twenty-degree-inclined control panel, virtual displays, and alignment of emergency oxygen tanks, was big enough for the crew of five. He strapped into his seat in the bridge and got ready for take-off. His co-captain, Gary Balagadde, was stuffing a pack of dehydrated frankfurters into his mouth while he adjusted the settings of the passenger module on a virtual display near the entrance to the bridge. Gary had started with dehydrated salami and potato chips judging from the wrappers scattered all over the floor under Mason's seat.

'Keep your food in your room Gary. You know you aren't supposed to eat in here,' Mason said over his shoulder, more harshly than he had intended. His tone startled Gary and he fumbled with his pack of frankfurters for a few seconds before he managed to recompose himself.

'Don't you mean *our room*? Do you want some, Captain?'
Gary asked with a mischievous smile. Mason was half-relieved and half-irritated that his gruff tone hadn't affected
Gary's jovial mood. Mason envied Gary's ability to be happy
and carefree all the time. He wished he could borrow some
of that happiness right now. He needed something to replace the worry and nervousness.

Melody had been in the slumber tube for five hours now
and she hadn't been discovered. Not that he'd expected
them to discover her; he'd gone to great lengths to make
sure that didn't happen. Yet, the one thing he knew would
calm his nerves was if she remained hidden till they were
safe in their new living quarters on the moon.

'That stuff will constipate you,' Mason replied.

'You're the one getting constipated, Grumpy.'

Mason shot Gary a deathly stare. The stare followed Gary
as he walked over and took his seat beside Mason.

'You can't let this eat away at you like this,' Gary whispered
to him.

Mason looked away.

Gary paused and faced the display. Moments later, he
shook his head and sucked air through his teeth. 'Try to act
normal,' he said, 'or else, we'll get caught and who knows
what will happen to Melody then.'

Mason jumped at the mention of Melody but collected
himself and prayed that his weird behaviour had gone unnoticed to all but Gary.

'What if it kills her?' Mason breathed, his lower lip quivered, and he swallowed. 'What if that thing I put her in kills
her?' The question that had been lingering in his mind
since he'd sealed his daughter in struggled past the lump in
his throat and formed into a strained whisper.

'If it kills her, console yourself with this: if she'd boarded
the ship without it, she'd die, and if you'd left her alone on
Earth her life wouldn't be worth living. You have to-' Gary
answered.

'Why would you say that to me? What gives you the right?'
Mason said.

Gary's mouth hung open as he gave Mason an incredulous
look. 'I'm sorry Mason. I didn't mean to sound insensitive.
I just need you to remember why we're doing this, and I
need you to stay focused on that.'

Gabriella Muwanga

'You know that I hate you, right?' said Mason. He rubbed his neck and fought the anxiety that was morphing into anger at Gary. He knew it wasn't fair, he acknowledged Gary probably had his own worries and insecurities about the situation since Melody was his goddaughter. Yet, despite his feelings, Gary had managed to appear calm and Mason could at least try to do the same. He glanced at his arm to check the time displayed in blinking bright blue characters on the control bracelet—worn over the sleeve of his triple-layered silver nylon, elastane and nomex, space suit. It was almost time for take-off. He told himself he didn't have time to be fair to Gary anyway.

'Are all the passengers asleep?' Mason said.

Gary nodded, but pulled up the holographic display screen on his control bracelet to crosscheck. 'They're asleep.'

Mason pressed a button on his seat and linked his com pack—an ear piece and a microchip sized microphone on the suit's collar—with the ship's communication system.

'Ship is ready for take-off,' he told the people in the control room at the International Space Agency headquarters.

After receiving official clearance to launch, he instructed a plain, plump Chinese woman to initiate the launch sequence. Leaning back in his chair he whispered a short prayer.

We're going to the moon, Princess, he thought, as a strong wish that he had the power of telepathy washed over him.

Time passed slowly and without incident on the voyage to the far side of the moon. Now, the ship hovered over the crystalline-cast, regolith dome around the crater where the colony was situated.

'Vessel ISA909, you are cleared to land,' a voice came through the ship's com system from the moon station and the airlock opened in the dome below them. The ship began its descent and was soon inside the dome. Once there, the ISA moon station took control of the ship. As the ship approached the inner door of the airlock, Mason attempted to get out of his chair. He tugged hard on the safety belt and heard Gary sigh beside him. The sigh triggered his muddled memory: he had to stay put until the moon station unstrapped him. Nevertheless, he felt incapable of staying put when every bone in his body was telling him to take action.

The Far Side

'Relax,' Gary said.

Mason turned his head away from Gary, hand pulling on the safety belt despite Gary's statement. He heard Gary start to say something more but before he could articulate, there came a loud thump, accompanied by short-lived tremors in the bridge as the ship docked. The rest of the crew recovered and relaxed in their seats as they waited, but Mason was getting more frantic by the second.

'We're almost there. The only way Melody gets off this ship safely is if you keep your head,' Gary told Mason, his voice full of sincerity and concern. Mason knew his behaviour could sabotage his daughter's safety, but he couldn't rein in his emotions.

'I don't know what's wrong with me. I can't help it.'

'You must try harder... be a father,' Gary said. Mason ignored Gary's good intentions and let himself be irritated by Gary's assumption of knowledge of what being a father meant in the situation he was facing; he drowned the voice in his head that claimed that Gary was right and instead convinced himself that Gary had not an inkling of what he was going through.

'I am being a father!' Mason said. The other three crew members' heads snapped in his direction and Gary cocked his head sideways. Ashamed at his outburst, Mason thought he should at least try to explain his behaviour to them. It wouldn't be with the absolute truth, but it would be something, he thought.

'You don't understand. I need...' Mason was cut short by the bridge door sliding open. A tall man clad in a white nylon and kevlar space suit walked in and five titanium humanoid robots followed behind him. The robots lined up behind him, and for a moment the now cramped room was silent.

'Welcome to the Far Side,' the tall man announced. 'My name is Dr Andrew Song and I'm the officer in charge of all the new settlers.' Dr Song gestured towards the robots and they stepped forward. Dr Song drew up the holographic display from his control bracelet, pressed a button and the safety belts unlocked with concurrent clicks. Mason sprang out of his chair and his abdomen almost hit the control panel.

'A moonbot will escort each of you to our waiting area where you will be examined by our doctor and await further instructions,' Dr Song said, and rested his arms in front of him.

'...Moonbot?' Gary chuckled. Dr Song's head turned slowly in his direction, but the comment everyone in the room held their breath to hear didn't come.

Mason started towards the bridge entrance. Dr Song placed his hand firmly on his chest and stopped him in his tracks. Mason couldn't tell if the doctor was reacting to the venom he could feel emanating from his pores or if the doctor just hated being interrupted.

'I wasn't finished,' Dr Song said.

Mason mustered a respectful but authoritative tone, 'My name is Mason Avery, this ship's captain. I wish to go to my quarters and get my luggage in order before I leave this ship. That is regulation after all.'

'I am honoured to meet you Captain Avery,' Dr Song said, 'and with all due respect, we have our own regulations here at the Far Side; your luggage stays with us for now.' Mason refused to take a step back. 'Your heart is pounding, Captain,' he said, narrowing his eyes at Mason.

A beam of light scanned Mason and disappeared, catching him off-guard because he'd been holding Dr Song's gaze too intently. The doctor's control bracelet displayed Mason's vitals: heart rate: 90 beats per minutes; temperature: 37.05°c; respiration rate: 19 breaths per minute; blood pressure: 130/89.

'Your luggage must be very important to you,' he noted, 'I will personally see to your luggage,' Dr Song added. However, his consolation didn't persuade Mason in the least. On the contrary, it threw his mind into a panic. He didn't want this man anywhere near his luggage. Although he was sure the doctor wouldn't find anything of consequence, he didn't want him sniffing around. Gary cleared his throat audibly to break the silence that ensued.

Mason's heart raced, sweat beaded and dried on his forehead. His head pounded along with his racing heart and he felt himself start to shiver. He fidgeted in his seat and looked through the clear glass of the pod as it sped along its plastic tube to his new house. The dome and the plastic tube distorted the colours of the sky so that the yellow, orange, and crimson of the lunar sky sprinted past his eyes in distressing blotches.

He'd expected to be arrested while in the waiting room, but all they'd done there was inject into their wrists microchips with numbers that matched the citizen numbers lasered onto their napes back at the ISA headquarters on Earth. Then came a brief physical exam. Afterwards, they'd guided the whole group of a hundred people through a simulation meant to equip them with the necessary tools to live comfortably within their new home.

Mason used some of the knowledge he'd acquired to gain access to his igloo-esque shelter. Once it was inside, the pod stopped, and the door dropped to the ground. Mason lay there in his pod, stared at the ceiling and sighed heavily.

Grey moon bricks formed the ceiling of his garage—as grey as his and Melody's futures were at the moment. He was tired of worrying but he couldn't stop. He'd lingered on the verge of a panic attack the whole pod ride and expended half of the will he had left pulling back from it. He was exhausted and nauseated, and his remaining will barred tears for his daughter's plight from flowing. Though his heart still pounded hard in his chest, it no longer drummed in his ear. The drumming had been replaced by a sinister hum that fed the atmosphere of foreboding surrounding him.

He opened the pod, clambered out and used his control bracelet to open the door that led him out of the garage. Stairs ushered him into a bright room with a high, aluminium ceiling. The house was larger on the inside than it appeared on the outside. A single room partitioned into dining, living, bedroom, and bathroom areas. Emerging from the pod had worsened his nausea and his body felt like a crushed can. His first destination was the steel toilet where he retched and vomited the remnants in his gut.

He dragged his feet across the floor and wrenched open the fridge for water to neutralise the acid in his mouth and throat but just as he reached for the bottle, a robot voice stopped him cold.

'I am 909A and I am here to serve,' a moonbot said.

He jerked around and stood up straight. The moonbot he now faced was identical to the ones he'd seen on the ship, except for the bold characters '909A' emblazoned on its chest. 'Nice to meet you, 909A,' Mason responded in a shaky voice, 'I am-'

The moonbot interrupted, 'Citizen 909A: Captain Mason Avery; captain of ship ISA909, grandson of the deceased Captain Jack Avery, captain of ship ISA908 and founder of the Small Senate of the Far Side; son of Paul and Meredith Avery, born-'

'That's enough,' Mason said. 'We were instructed not to carry clothes. Do you know where I can find something to change into? I want to get out of this suit.'

'What would you like to wear?'

'A pair of pants...a shirt...'

909A turned to go in the opposite direction—Mason assumed it was to get him a change of clothes—but then it stopped and started to vibrate. The vibrations were fleeting and soon, 909A recovered. However, it didn't continue in the direction it had started. It turned around, strode towards Mason and placed its heavy hand on his right arm. 'Mason Avery, you are under arrest. I am charged with escorting you to the commons,' it proclaimed.

Mason pulled his arm free of the moonbot's grip and ran before he could think. He vaulted up the stairs and fidgeted with his control bracelet to get the garage door open. Behind him he thought he heard the 909A call out to him not to resist, but he paid it no heed. He tried to open his pod but it jammed. He turned to see 909A standing close to him.

'Mason Avery, you are under arrest.'

Melody would die if he was arrested and detained, and if that was his fate, he decided he would rather die with her. He found a concealed recess in the garage wall and there, as the simulation had indicated, he found the pickaxe reserved for emergencies. He swung the pickaxe at 909A, hoping he could buy time for the pod to open so he could lock himself inside. He missed the moonbot and struck the glass of the pod instead. He pulled the pickaxe back and attacked again.

'Do not resist!' The moonbot grabbed his forearm midair, twisted it behind his back and slammed him against the pod with concussive force. Darkness flooded into Mason's blurred field of vision until it engulfed it completely.

The Far Side

Mason awoke with a start. His skin burned, and he felt something weighing him down. Feebly, his eyelids parted to allow him to investigate. His left eyelid remained low over his bionic eye and a sharp pain seared through his left temple. The images in his left field of vision were in infrared and inexplicably glitched. Though less confident about how well his sight would serve him, he looked down to detect the source of his discomfort. His arms were covered with a heavy, black rubbery material; his hazy sight prevented him from discerning how far up his arms the substance went. His legs seemed to be glued to the chair by the same black substance. He tried to lift his feet but couldn't. He pushed his shins hard against the substance and it stretched. It stretched like old gum but snapped back with the speed of a rubber band just as Mason began to entertain hopes of escape. Defeated, he controlled his breathing and squinted as he searched the room. His gaze landed on someone sitting beside him. Tied down as he was, even with screwed-up vision, Mason recognised Gary.

'Gary?' his friend's name laboured past his heavy tongue.

'Are you with us, Captain Avery?' a familiar voice came, startling Mason. Mason hadn't noticed anyone else in the room.

'My eye...' Mason murmured when he saw split outlines of Dr Song and 909A standing across from him. His tangled vision stopped him from seeing the apologetic look on Dr Song's face.

'I am sorry about your eye, Captain Avery. Your moonbot was too rough with you and I'm afraid your eye might need some repairs,' Dr Song said.

'Why are we here? Why are you treating us like this?' Gary said. Mason could tell from his tone that Gary wasn't himself.

'I have a few questions for you. You are free to leave once you give me satisfactory answers,' said Dr Song.

'Do you usually tie up people you just want to ask a few questions?' said Mason.

Dr Song ignored his comment. 'Show it to them,' he said.

909A held up a thin glass tablet and brought it closer to the two men. On it was a live stream of the slumber tube enclosed in thick bulletproof glass. He was positive that they had no idea what it was, but he didn't know how long he'd be able to keep it that way. Also, he needed to find a way to get Melody out of their custody soon.

Mason told himself not to panic. He strived to keep his expression straight and unreadable—Gary was already doing a great job of the same.

'What's that?' he said, although he already knew the answer.

'I was hoping one of you could tell me,' Dr Song said. 'This object was found inside a case in the captain's quarters. We don't know which one of you it belongs to because both the cases we found there lacked the proper ISA labels.'

'It's rude to go through peoples' luggage,' Gary said. It had been his idea to remove the labels once they got on the ship. Mason had thought it would raise suspicion; Gary had assured him that it would enable them to switch labels at the point of inspection. But then, Gary hadn't counted on them being absent during inspection of the luggage—he hadn't expected the locals to have their own rules.

'Is it yours, Mr. Balagadde?' Dr Song enquired. 'Could you tell me what it is?'

'I don't know what it is. And even if I did, I wouldn't tell you because...' Gary paused, leaned in the doctor's direction and added, 'I don't like you.'

'Do you share Captain Balagadde's stance?' Dr Song asked Mason.

'I'm seeing it for the first time,' Mason said. He kept his tone even and looked Dr Song straight in the eye—he imagined his damaged bionic eye was a horrific sight and he was relying on his gaze to unsettle the doctor.

Dr Song held his gaze for a moment, and then he turned to leave. He paused at the door, pivoted and said, 'Do you know what the penalty is for breaking Far Side law?'

'Breaking the law?' Gary sneered. 'No one has broken any laws except you... infringing on my human rights like this.'

'Of course, you don't know,' Dr Song laughed, taking no note of Gary's comment. 'Let me give you the highlights: after I prove that one or both of you smuggled illegal materials to the Far Side, you'll both have to face the Small Senate. Now those old guys are very tough on crime of any sort and you'll most likely be expelled.' He stopped and faced them, giving his words time to have effect.

The two restrained men gave him blank stares.

Dr Song shook his head, and then smacked his forehead. 'Forgive me for not thinking: expulsion means nothing to you,' he chided himself. He took the tablet from 909A and opened a menu. Something about the smug look on his face made Mason nervous. He remained tight-lipped nonetheless. The doctor's thumb lingered over a button as he smiled at them. 'I'll give you a taste.'

The floor opened beneath Mason and he dropped into a snug, pitch black cylindrical cell. He was plunged into darkness once again when the floor closed above him.

Mason gasped. The air in his cylindrical prison became thinner and thinner and the artificial gravity had powered down little by little as time passed. He floated in the darkness, afraid that he was becoming delirious.

He lost track of time and had no idea how long Melody had been in the slumber tube, or how much longer she could survive in there. He imagined her gasping for air, trying to fill her burning lungs. In the beginning, he believed his empathy to be so strong that his body was manifesting her struggles. In time, he realised that the tube was running out of air and that his bulging eyeballs, dry throat, and spongy tongue, were not a figment of his imagination.

He clenched his cold fingers as he felt them go numb. Fortunately, he hadn't had time to remove his suit and its automatic heating system kept hypothermia from setting in. Now however, the suit was losing its strength and he feared his time was running out. He knew if he died, his daughter would die soon after and he wasn't about to let that happen.

He pushed against his restraints and winced at the pain in his stiff limbs. He tried to propel himself upwards towards the door but couldn't move. The restraints had become hard and brittle in the atmosphere of the cell and immobilised him. He was going to have to talk to them and hope they had a way of listening in.

'I confess!' his voice sounded like a radio with a severe auto-tune malfunction. Quiet followed this attempt to contact his jailers.

'Please,' he said, tears crystallising on his eyelashes.

'My daughter's in that thing and I don't know how much time she has left,' he called. 'Do what you must to me but...' His voice caught in his throat. He swallowed and the flames in his throat spread down his gullet to his stomach. 'Save my daughter.'

He sucked in a mouthful of air to pay the debt that had been created. Then, he waited. He waited for what seemed like an eternity and was about to give up when blinding light shone down into his cell. Metal hands gripped his shoulders and hauled him up the long column into the light.

Four moonbots encircled him, watching him like hawks. They bathed and clothed him and placed a small eye patch over his left eye, pending surgical repair. They left his hands free, so he could swallow the fast-acting nutrient supplements one of them had put in his right palm.

His eyes had sunk into the purplish ditches around them and his skin was almost paper white. He hadn't eaten for days and his body screamed for nourishment, but still, he played with the two red pills in his hand—it was the last and only form of rebellion he was allowed. When he couldn't hold on anymore, he tossed the pills into his mouth. The pills dissolved on his tongue and swam forward, leaving pure bliss in their wake. The colour returned to Mason's cheeks by the time Dr Song arrived. A small, mattress-like hovercraft, carrying the slumber tube enclosed in a bulletproof glass case, glided into the room after him.

He ordered the moonbots off and approached Mason.

'I need to get my daughter out of that tube,' Mason said.

Dr Song nodded and withdrew a blade from underneath his sleeve and twisted the hilt. This caused the blade to glow. He twisted the hilt again and the blade dimmed.

'Use this to cut through the glass,' he said. 'Hold out your arms.' Mason stretched his arms out in front of him and Dr Song cuffed him. He then rested the blade on top of the glass case and left.

'Wait!' Mason yelled with his hands raised as the door closed behind the doctor. As soon as the door closed, bulletproof glass shields descended over all the walls. The cuffs on his wrist clicked open and dropped to the floor.

Mason massaged his wrists, stepped closer to the case and knelt beside it. He cut along the corners of the glass case and the sides collapsed away from the slumber tube. He ran his fingers along the slumber tube and lifted a latch that had been expertly concealed on its side. The hard titanium casing slid off a clear plastic door. A keypad occupied the lower part of the door and Mason's hand hesitated above it.

He didn't want his daughter to wake up to this. He didn't want her to see him, yet he didn't know if he would live or die, and most of all, he didn't want to have to see her die too.

Mason took a deep breath and punched in the pass code. A gas was released into the tube and hid Melody for a moment. With that dose of rousing gas, Melody would be awake in the next two minutes.

Once the gas was removed from the slumber tube, the door opened. Mason's throat constricted, and his chest tightened when he saw his daughter's face for the first time in almost six days.

Melody wriggled her nose in that way she did when she'd just woken up. Her hazel eyes were hidden behind half-opened lids. She smiled at him groggily.

'Are we on the moon, Daddy?' she asked. Her small, sleepy voice filled him with equal parts of joy and dread. *What have I done?* He lamented.

He pulled Melody into his arms and hugged her close. 'We're on the moon, Sweetheart.'

Mason watched Melody run around the playground in the children's dormitory. It was a quaint place with moon grass, bioengineered blossoms, and an artificial rainbow reigned above it. She was playing with three other children and appeared to be having the time of her life. Her glee warmed his heart; her dream had come true, at least for the moment.

The nurse had told him she was thriving and that her asthma could be handled. She'd told him that most of the damage would have been done en route to the moon, but it had been mitigated by the tube. She'd approved of his ingenuity with a nod.

'We don't have much time,' Dr Song reminded him. He had almost forgotten that the doctor was standing right next to him. He was grateful to him for letting him see his daughter before his hearing. He hadn't expected him to say yes but it turned out the doctor wasn't as heartless as he had imagined him to be.

Mason took a step towards his daughter, but his courage failed him. He didn't want to say goodbye to his daughter, and he knew this could be the last time he saw her. He cowered and turned to leave but Dr Song blocked his path. He said nothing to him, but Mason got the message loud and clear: *say goodbye to your daughter.* Fate must have connived with Dr Song because Melody spotted Mason and shrieked with joy as she ran to him. He poised his arms to receive her and she fell into his embrace.

Holding Melody in his arms, close to his heart, made it all worth it. Seeing the glow in her hazel eyes shattered his fears and left him light and peaceful.

'Where have you been, Daddy?'

'I've been working, Princess,' he said.

'Has Uncle Gary been taking good care of you?'

He nudged his daughter out of the hug and grinned at her.

'He's come to see me every day. He draws with me,' Melody answered. She swung her hips side to side as she twirled her left index finger in her curly hair. Mason pulled his daughter back into his arms. He wished he could thank Gary before he went in for his hearing, but he'd already asked too much of Dr Song. He consoled himself with thoughts of a reunion with Gary sometime in the future.

Dr Song cleared his throat. It was time.

'I have to go back to work, Melody. You'll be a good girl and listen to your Uncle Gary, won't you?' he said, a lump solidifying in his throat. He clenched his jaw and willed himself not to cry.

Melody nodded. 'What happened to your eye, Daddy?' she pointed at his eye patch.

'My eye is tired sweetie. I have to let it rest for a bit.'

'When are you coming back?' Her innocent stare threatened to be his undoing.

He tilted his head at Dr Song and considered his answer for a short while. 'I'll be back very soon.'

He rose to his feet and nodded at Dr Song. Melody waved goodbye and ran back to play with her new friends. Mason wondered if she would have left so easily if she knew she might never see him again.

'Do you think they'll expel me?' Mason asked the doctor.

The Far Side

'I don't know. There's more to consider in your case: you're an Avery and, I think, the little girl changes things,' Dr Song opined. 'Was it worth it?'

Mason assumed he was referring to his decision to bring his daughter to the Far Side. 'I'd do it again.' He held his arms out and the doctor cuffed him. The two men marched off to the Senate room where Mason would learn his fate.

Gabriella Muwanga has always been fascinated by science and the fantastical. She loves to transport her readers to high-tech futures where passion and intelligence place galaxies within one's reach, and all the way to magical realms where the sunlight never dims into dark and gravity is a suggestion. She is a Ugandan-American who lives and writes in Baltimore, Maryland.

Drift-Flux

Wole Talabi

In space, no one can hear your ship explode.

But they can watch.

Orshio Akume, captain of the *Igodo*, sat silently in the pilot module of the control deck, watching a mining ship cleave in two. A sudden release of energy violently ate its way out of the ship. A burst of azure light popped into the space ahead of the *Igodo*, despite the distance. It receded, quickly shifted to aquamarine, then turquoise, and then nothing.

A bomb. It had to have been a bomb.

The furrows between Orshio's eyes deepened as his brows drew down and his eyes narrowed, compressing the vertical tribal marking keloid that ran from his hairline to his nose.

The ship was an old one, at least ten times the size of the *Igodo*, with the unmistakable bright red and blue insignia of the Confederacy emblazoned across it from end to end. There were only a few giant mining ships left operating in the Belt. The last remnants of the first Martian development schemes by the Confederacy and the only ones still in service that were not built by Transhuman Federation Engineers.

The clumsy old giants needed the size primarily to store large quantities of fuel and propellant, still completely enslaved to Newton's third law and Tsiolkovsky's equation. Cargo was attached and hauled using spars and rigging, enwombed in lightweight programmable material mesh and insulation to protect fragile items and ward off hot backlighting from the fusion drive. Modern Transhuman Federation mining ships like the *Igodo* used the Adadevoh drive to couple to the zero-point and draw vacuum energy so they didn't have any of those problems. They still hauled their cargo using rigging though. Not that the *Igodo* presently carried any cargo.

'What the hell just happened out there?'

Orshio glanced back to see his engineer floating into the control deck. Lien-Ådel was a young, tall, muscled and well-proportioned woman with brown eyes and short black hair greying slightly at the crown and temples as though her front half was aging faster than her back. It was impossible to tell but beneath her solid frame, were genetically altered lungs that allowed her function on only a fraction of the oxygen required by the average unmodified human, nanoparticle gravcines in her blood to inhibit loss of consciousness, and a skeleton modified for increased bone density. Handy, for unscheduled extravehicular repairs.

She pushed against the deck wall with her right foot and threw her six-foot and four-inch tall frame into the chair beside him, swiping furiously at the space in front of her to draw up trajectory data and estimate the likelihood of their being caught in a debris field. Orshio had already visually assessed the situation and decided they were in no reasonable danger, the explosion wasn't nearly big enough or close enough, but Lien-Ådel was the kind of person that liked to see every single piece of data available before making her decisions. The light from the console illuminated her face, highlighting the small nose that sat symmetrically between two finely sculpted cheekbones.

'Ship blew up.' Orshio jutted his bearded chin at the magnified image of the slowly disintegrating ship set against the unforgiving blackness of space on the viewscreen, like some kind perverse modern art display. 'I've seen accidents before. Structural failures, overheating cores, explosive decouplings, but none of them looked like that. That was a plasma bomb. Had to be. I'd bet my collection of original Majek Fashek vinyls on it.'

Lien-Ådel kept swiping as she replied, 'Well, it doesn't look like there is going to be much of a debris field. Must have been a targeted, controlled explosion.'

Orshio leaned back in his seat. 'Whoever set it off must have been trying not to damage the cargo. Maybe they're pirates...' he scratched his chin, '...or something.'

'There haven't been pirates in the inner belt for years, Orshio. Besides, no one is swooping in to loot the cargo. I don't like this. We should call it in to Mars Station ahead of us. Make a report.'

Orshio rolled his eyes. He didn't dislike Lien-Ådel per se, he just found her unbearably predictable. Despite her undeniable creativity in keeping the ship's performance optimal, she was still incredibly regimented in her thinking. For every decision presented to her, she only ever had three responses in order of preference: one, follow the rules; two, defer the decision to a higher authority; or three, have no opinion on the matter. And now, she was already advocating her second favourite response even though they still weren't exactly sure what they were looking at.

Lien-Ådel in turn did not like Orshio's impulsive attitude and flamboyant style but she worked well with him anyway because her life depended on his natural creativity and artificially enhanced reflexes.

He was heavily tattooed, an elaborate pattern of images, lines, and whorls, that ran all over his dark skin and told the story of his ancestors as far back as his family records detailed. The tattoos, done in late afromysterics style, covered his right arm from shoulder to finger tips. If his other arm wasn't fully bionic and made of expensive bioplasmium, it would probably have borne the same markings. He wore his black and grey hair in short dreadlocks and tied a band of red and black cloth around his hairline, covering the tip of the vertical scar that marked him as a true-born son of the Idoma people—beneath which sat the neuralink chip that allowed him to control his bioplasmium arm and the dozen other embedded machines that augmented his body. His entire appearance was a piece of art dedicated to the spirits of his ancestors, the Alekwu.

'I think the first thing we should do is see if there are any survivors, don't you think?' he asked as he sat up in his chair. 'Besides, we're technically closer to Ceres station.'

Lien-Ådel nodded, ignoring the sugar-coated reprimand, and swiped away the *Igodo's* diagnostic projection before requesting the ship's AI to send a direct message on the Belt's short-range open channel and scan all other open channels for chatter regarding what happened.

Orshio reached forward and pulled up the public Transhuman Federation shipping schedules and trajectories from their database. The data indicated that the ship that was now mostly just two large pieces of wreckage ahead of them was called the *Freedom Queen*. A rugged hauler for fluids and fine dusts, transporting impure Helium-3 scooped from Jupiter's atmosphere to Independence Station, the last Confederacy settlement on Mars. She was essentially a gigantic cylindrical gas tank with a nuclear energy tube running through her long axis. Well, at least she used to be.

'*Igodo* has established a link with the broken ship's AI. No signs of life. I think you'll want to take a look at its report.' Lien-Ådel flicked her fingers to expand a light display projection then swiped it left. It drifted through the space between them and settled in front of Orshio.

He tilted his head to the side slightly and raised an eyebrow. 'This says all crew life signals from *Freedom Queen* stopped streaming over twenty minutes ago. Before the explosion.'

Lien-Ådel blinked. 'Yes. So now I'm wondering... where could the crew have gone?'

Orshio folded his arms in front of him. That was a good question. Almost as good a question as to why anyone would choose to attack a confederate hauler in near-space range only a few minutes after the *Igodo* completed its publicly scheduled uncoupling from the zero-point, came out of drift-flux and switched to auxiliary for a slow, controlled nuclear burn to Mars station. Pirates would probably have had better timing.

Suddenly, the viewscreen of the *Igodo* lit up as a multicoloured kaleidoscope of numbers and data overlaid it. The AI informed them that they were receiving a sudden and persistent communication packet. It had the certified data signature of the Transhuman Federation and seemed to be originating from Ceres station.

Orshio said, 'Well bad news certainly travels fast out here, doesn't it?'

Lien-Ådel swiped in front of her to accept the transmission. The flowing rivers of colourful data across the screen coalesced into an image of a very serious man in a very serious Transhuman Federation uniform of pure black with a gold trim mandarin collar. The uniform was blacker than Orshio's ebony skin but blended perfectly against the man's own shiny black complexion. It took a few seconds for Orshio to realise he had a goatee. His eyes were a stark white. The officer looked like he'd materialised from the star-sprinkled abyssal darkness of unforgiving space beyond the ship and his eyes were a binary star. Across the breast of his uniform, was a lenticular pin shaped like an ancient Zulu shield, complete with two spears crossed behind it. Its smooth black and white surface displayed the yin-and-yang, stretched to accommodate the unusual shape. Orshio had never seen anyone wearing the official Federation security corps chief uniform before.

'This is Ceres station security Chief Mwanja Mukisa calling Federation shipping vessel *Igodo*. We have detected a catastrophic failure of the Confederate hauler *Freedom Queen* a few thousand kilometres from your scheduled flight path. Change course immediately and report to Ceres station. Do not transmit any message to anyone until your report has been formally received at Ceres Station. I repeat, change course and report to Ceres station. Immediately. Do not transmit to any other party.'

The image disappeared.

'Well, I guess you're going to get a chance to make that report after all,' Orshio quipped.

Lien-Ådel's voice went low and hoarse, 'Does that message imply what I think it does?'

Orshio nodded. Along the surface of his bioplasmium arm, beneath his shirt, faint red lines writhed as if alive, responding to tension from his increased stress levels. He flexed the arm to ease it and thought down his rising cortisol levels.

'That was not a request, it was an order,' Lien-Ådel's face scrunched up as she spoke, as if she was still trying to process the sentence, hoping desperately that he would contradict the obvious.

Orshio kept inspecting the screen. 'Yes. Definitely an order,' he confirmed.

'But if they don't want us to contact anyone, not even the supply station, then that means they probably don't think it was an accident or pirates. They probably think it was-'

'-a terrorist attack.' Orshio finished the sentence for her.

They turned away from the viewscreen at the same time and saw the same thing in each other's eyes.

They had heard rumours in the outer belt, of anti-federation rebels and old confederate militias attacking Federation mining camps and ships. Nothing major, but worrying enough for them to now be concerned.

Drift-Flux

'I don't know anyone at Ceres station. I'm not sure I want to get involved in all this. We could just make a run for it. Enter drift-flux again and be back to Earth in an hour or so. Sort it all out when we get there,' Orshio said.

Lien-Ådel recoiled, then snapped back to place, leaning toward him. 'First of all, we can't disobey a direct order from a Federation security corps official. Second...' She paused to exhale, 'Drift-flux this far into the solar system? Through the Belt? We'd never make it out alive! And even if we did, we'd be making ourselves look guilty as sin in the process.'

He nodded. 'You're right. You're right. Sorry. Bad idea.'

'Quantifiably terrible.'

Lien-Ådel kept her palms flat against her thighs as Orshio carefully adjusted the nuclear reaction control system, pulling alongside the mooring cable that was reaching out to them from the largest asteroid in the inner solar system like a possessed umbilical cord. She hated docking, or any transitions. She was much happier when they were moving steadily, the cold and dark ocean of space swelling and sweeping against the hull of the *Igodo*. She sank further into her chair every time Orshio fired a short burst of diverted nuclear thrust, nudging the *Igodo* into position.

Most of Ceres station lay below the surface, except for the army of cephalopodan mooring cables that held the hundred or so ships that transited through every day. From above, the network of pipelines, cables, equipment, and rigging, that kept Ceres's subterranean areas functioning looked like a glowing technological infection eating its way into the heart of the asteroid, their casings and surfaces lined with bright photovoltaic cells to capture the sunlight that powered their maintenance bots. Man-made parasites, burning alone in the vastness of the dark that the city beneath may thrive.

When the cable had secured the *Igodo* and all its interlocking sections mated to make a solid strut, Lien-Ådel and Orshio unbuckled themselves and floated leisurely to the airlock. They moved with tense slowness as they transferred to the orbital elevator.

Inside the elevator was an instrument panel to key in arrival codes and a screen displaying a welcome message from the Transhuman Federation. The elevator was transparent and looking behind them, they could see other smaller asteroids drifting, a couple of ships approaching, and the sun—a small, faraway ball of light. In all their missions through space, only the sun remained constant. Its influence diminished with distance, but constant, unchangeable, like the past, like an ancestor. Orshio tapped at the panel and they started to descend.

Lien-Ådel played with her hair as the elevator descended beneath Ceres's surface. The sun disappeared. Crackling electricity illuminated the darkness of the tunnel around them.

'Are you worried, Captain?'

'No. Not really, Engineer,' he lied.

'You don't suppose they think we had something to do with blowing up the *Freedom Queen*, do you?'

Orshio thought about that. 'I'm sure they will ask.'

Lien-Ådel kissed her teeth and stopped playing with her hair. 'Bad luck,' she muttered. 'After hauling supplies halfway to some godforsaken Tellurium mining outpost in the Kuiper belt, we come out of drift to this shit.'

'Are you okay?' Orshio asked. This was the most agitated he'd ever seen Lien-Ådel and he didn't like it. Not when they were about to walk into what could easily be a crisis.

Lien-Ådel looked to him, dejectedly, which only made him more worried. 'When I was at university, I heard about the pirates, how terrible working the belt had been during that time but I still wanted to work for Federation shipping because I dreamed of being in drift-flux, of seeing the universe. Now the pirates are gone but there are all these rumours of terrorists. I don't know. I guess I'm just worried that we might get caught up in or blamed for something and lose the *Igodo* just because some agitated philistines are probably trying to start a war.'

The lights around them brightened. Orshio exhaled a hot breath. 'We didn't do anything. They will question us, find out what we know, and find whoever did this. Plus, no group in the system is actually foolish enough to start a war with the Transhuman Federation.' He paused before turning to her. 'Do you want to know why I have these tattoos?' He raised his right hand, pulled back his sleeve and watched her eyes. 'I know you've wanted to ask since the first day you saw them.'

Lien-Ådel managed a small smile. Even though she knew he was trying to distract her from their present predicament, she didn't mind, she needed the distraction. 'Sure. Please. Tell me. What do they mean?'

'I am one of a people called the Idoma, from the Nigeria unit of the Federation. We are an ancient people and according to Idoma traditions, life is an unending continuum. Always has been. Space, time, energy, matter, spirit, and life, are considered as one integral whole. Our understanding of the nature of the cosmos predates modern science and is anchored to our belief that our ancestors are always with us, interacting with the rest of the universe just as we do but in a different way.'

'You mean like in an alternate dimension?'

'Sort of. You can think of it that way. My people believe that death is a process of passing on to this other level of existence. A realm called Okoto. A dimension from which they find new ways to interact with the same space and time we share. Personally, I think that when we are in drift-flux, coupled to the universe's zero-point, we are in the boundary between our dimension and Okoto. Therefore, my ancestors can guide my hand. Ensure I do not slip out of the vacuum energy probability field and crash into something. The tattoos are just stylistic and hieroglyphic representations of my ancestors and their stories, going as far back as records exist.'

Lien-Ådel leaned against the elevator with her right shoulder, pulling at the sleeves of her body-hugging suit. 'Hold on. You really believe your ancestors exist as part of space? Guide you in drift-flux?'

Orshio smiled. 'Well, No. Not really. But it's a good story to tell people who wonder about my tattoos, isn't it?'

Lien-Ådel stared at him for a moment before erupting into laughter. Orshio laughed with her.

The elevator stopped and lights flickered. Their faces recrystallised with seriousness. The elevator door opened to reveal a squad of six women and a man, with menacing eyes and holding sleek plasma rifles, all wearing the familiar white uniform of the Transhuman Federation forces. Behind them, the bright, mechanical sprawl of the main Ceres station tunnel spread out like the digestive system of a rock and metal animal.

'*Igodo* crew. Come with us.' One of the women said to them in a manner that left no room for questions, only obedience. Her red hair was cropped short. The cool, green eyes and freckles dotting her nose and cheeks seemed out of place on the same face as that hard-set jaw. She turned sharply on her heel and the others flanked Orshio and Lien-Ådel.

They followed the woman.

'Why do I feel like we are being arrested?' Orshio queried.

None of the officers responded. Lien-Ådel eyed him nervously.

The small party walked about halfway into the main tunnel before turning to walk down a set of energy shielded stairs and through a tall doorway that looked like it could withstand a plasma cannon when sealed. A sign on the door read: *Transhuman Federation Security Corps Offices: Authorised Personnel Only*. Behind the door, they stood in the centre of an octagon with each side bordering a smaller door. The woman in charge walked up to one of the doors and motioned them to enter the office of Ceres station Security Chief Mwanja Mukisa.

Lien-Ådel winced when the door shut behind them. The chair behind the desk at the end of the office swivelled around to reveal a man that was certainly not Mwanja Mukisa. At least not *the* Mwanja Mukisa that had ordered them to Ceres station. This man was short and had skin like Orshio's, hair cropped close, and a perfectly shaved round chin that, in some strange way, made him look like a pre-teen. But there was nothing puerile about his voice and his tone when he spoke.

'Finally, Orshio Akume and Lien-Ådel Ting of the *Igodo*. Welcome to Ceres station. Do you have any idea how much trouble you are in?'

Orshio looked around the office, trying to find something he could use to estimate the identity of the man they were talking to. A photograph, a plaque, something. All he found was an unusually empty wall and some very modern nanomaterial furniture.

'We haven't done anything wrong,' Lien-Ådel began. 'We saw the *Freedom Queen* destroyed a few minutes after we dropped out of drift-flux. We don't know what happened, but we are ready to make a full report.'

'The records inform me,' the man, who was not Mwanja Mukisa, paused to stand up straight before continuing, 'that you just completed a supply run to the Kuiper belt mines. Are you aware that the outer belt is becoming a den of anti-federation rebels and agitators?' he asked, his lips curling up at the corners in a smile.

'Well, yes, we heard some stories, but we have nothing to do with anti-federation rebels!' Lien-Ådel exclaimed, her voice hoarse from fear or perhaps something more elemental.

Orshio shook his head and leaned forward in his chair, his eyes narrowed and focused like a navigation beam. There was something that did not sit quite right with him about the conversation that had quickly become an interrogation.

'Where is Officer Mwanja Mukisa?' he asked, softly.

The man eyed Orshio like he was a stain or a miscalculation. It was a look Orshio had seen before and it sent off alarms in his head, but his brain was still running diagnostics to determine exactly why when the man spoke.

'You have both been implicated in the destruction of the *Freedom Queen* by the ship's AI. You will consent to DNA extraction for further analysis and will remain in remand at Ceres station until such a time as formal charges are brought against you.'

Suddenly, Orshio realised where he knew that look from. He'd seen it once at the Luna Railgun Transit Station while he was waiting for his launch to Mars station. It came from an old confederacy pilot, one of those born before the Adedevoh drive and the rise of the Transhuman Federation who couldn't believe that the people whose way of life he'd been raised to think was inferior were now running ninety-six percent of the solar systems economy while the Confederacy struggled. Orshio had taken an empty seat next to the man and politely smiled at him when their eyes met. There had been no reciprocal smile, only a look like disgust but much worse. In the man's eyes lurked a powerful, primal resentment. The old pilot had risen from his chair and muttered something under his breath that sounded a lot like a word Orshio had only ever read about but never actually heard.

And now, here was the look again.

Wole Talabi

Orshio didn't change his blank expression as he looked at the man that wanted to place him and his now panicky partner under arrest. 'You can't hold us here without an official arrest warrant,' Orshio responded, his voice low as he started to stand up.

Panic washed over him when he realised he couldn't.

Something cold and solid had wrapped itself around his legs and arms, locking them in place like a vice.

He grimaced and shouted, 'Lien-Ådel! Get out now!'

But it was too late. She was struggling in place too, her arms and legs enveloped by what looked like a part of the chair as she screamed. 'What is going on?! Officer? Officer?!'

He watched part of the back of her chair liquefy, extrude, and wrap itself around her neck and mouth, morphing into a solid restraint as she screamed.

It had to be programmable material furniture. The last major technological advancement to come from the Confederacy.

He felt the cold and liquid material of the chair wrap around his own neck and pull him straight up in the chair as it covered his mouth too. He heard the voice of the man pretending to be Mwanja Mukisa say, 'Goodnight, Captain.'

There was a hiss. A sickly-sweet smell like rotting flowers. A loosening of edges of the world. His eyelids fell. There was darkness, like the embrace of space.

Consciousness returned like an explosion. Orshio's eyes shot open.

The first thing he saw was a small black cube on top of the desk. There was a matrix of light symbols surrounding it and they seemed to be pulsing, beating out a slow, steady rhythm. He could not turn his head to see if Lien-Ådel was okay or if the short man pretending to Mwanja Mukisa was gone.

Orshio closed his eyes again and focused, remembering what his body enhancement therapist had told him the day after he'd decided to get his melanin genes updated for increased radiation resistance and an improved bioplasmium arm. *If you want to access the power-booster functions, clear your head. Think exactly how much power you want and what exactly you want it to do. Breathe slowly, then apply.*

He opened his eyes and swung his arm upward. The programmable material restraint broke into three clean pieces and scattered across the room. He reached up and ripped the restraints off his neck, glad to see that Lien-Ådel was beside him and stirring. As he pulled at the restraints on his feet, he heard the door open and saw a shadow in the corner of his vision move on the floor. It was his only warning.

Something hit his thigh and a shock shot through him with so much ferocity he cried out in pain.

The redhead with the green eyes and hard jaw who'd seemed to be the leader of the squad that had meet then at the main Ceres elevator, shouted at him, 'Freeze! Don't move!'

He rolled forward, crashing into the desk as another stun beam stabbed into the chair where he'd been. The redhead surged forward and Orshio, thinking calmly but quickly, rose, lifting the desk high above his head as he did, and flung it at her. It sailed clear over Lien-Ådel, who he could see was fully roused and conscious. The redhead fell to her knees and slid forward, firing another stun beam that missed Orshio by less than an inch. He could hear something like an explosion come from somewhere in the building.

'Hey! I'm not the enemy!' he called out as he backed into a corner of the office, off balance. 'Someone was impersonating Officer Mukisa!'

The redhead leapt up into the air so effortlessly, Orshio was sure she'd been edited for agility. Her face was a mask of pure concentration, her eyes like navigation beams.

'Freeze!' she ordered, crashing down onto Orshio.

She was all over him. He managed to grab onto her right hand, the one that gripped the gun like it were an appendage. He twisted it and the gun fell, clattering to the ground. He could hear commotion come from outside the room now. Something was happening, and he needed to stop her long enough to figure out what it was. Pain shot into his side like lightning as she kneed him in the belly. Her fingers wrapped themselves around his throat, shoving him up against the wall. Her fingernails were a bright red, almost the same as her hair. And long, like claws. They dug into his neck. She was powerful, and she wasn't going to stop unless he made her. With a determined grunt, Orshio grabbed her hand with his bioplasmium arm and pushed down and to the left, forcing her off balance. He was about to administer a kick to her side but changed his mind midway and kept his foot low instead, clearing her feet out from under her. She came down hard and he fell to the floor with her, pressing down on her shoulder and shouting, 'I'm not your enemy!'

She stopped struggling at that, glaring up at him and breathing heavily. 'Then what the hell is going on?' she demanded, her voice still defiant.

'I don't know but from the fact that we were just restrained and drugged by someone pretending to be a security corps officer, I think Ceres station is under attack.' He lifted his hand from her shoulder slowly and rose to his feet. 'I'm going to free my engineer, okay? Don't shoot us, officer...?

Her eyes narrowed as she sat up. 'Chloe. My name is Chloe.'

'Chloe. Good. Now. What's happening outside?' Orshio asked as he slowed his breathing and grabbed onto the restraints holding Lien-Ådel in place. 'What's all that commotion and why did you attack me?' His voice strained as he broke the restraints.

Chloe bounded up to her feet. She was of average height, yes, but with a slender, muscular frame. She moved like a cat and had power disproportionate to her size. Definitely altered. Orshio was sure she would have taken him if he didn't have the arm.

'A Confederacy mining ship lost control in the docking elevators. Started a fire. At the same time, an urgent distress signal was issued from this room on the old Transhuman Federation comms channel. Where is officer Mukisa?' Chloe asked.

'We don't know,' Lien-Ådel said, finally free and staring at Chloe with eyes full of both confusion and anger.

'This doesn't make sense,' Chloe said, looking around the room as though the missing officer could be in a corner somewhere.

Orshio thought for a few seconds.

The short man had to be an anti-federation rebel agent. And the burning ship in the docking area had to have been crashed there deliberately, it would be too much of a coincidence otherwise. And if it was not a coincidence, then maybe the destruction of the *Freedom Queen* was not a coincidence either. But even if the Confederacy was working with the rebels or the rebels were just rogue former citizens of the Confederacy acting independently, then why would they throw away two old and expensive mining ships just to make a pair of unremarkable Federation shipping crew look somewhat guilty of aggression.

Unless...

He scanned the floor, looking for the pulsing-light cube that had been on the table when he woke up. When he found it, it only took him a second to remember where he had seen it before. He turned to Lien-Ådel and met her hard gaze. Her lips were tight.

'What if all this is just a distraction,' he quickly. 'What if they blew up the *Freedom Queen* just to get us here so they could copy our genetic ID matrices?'

'What?' Lien-Ådel shook her head. 'I don't understand. Why us? Why would they want our genetic signatures?'

Orshio looked down at the floor, feeling Ceres station tremble beneath his feet, like a fearful child.

'To access our ship,' he announced as if it were obvious. 'They're stealing the *Igodo*.'

Chloe looked from him to Lien-Ådel and back again in astonishment, as if Lien-Ådel could make some sense of what he had just said.

'And they clearly have Officer Mukisa's genetic signature too, so they will probably be the only ones that can launch during an emergency station shutdown, right?' Lien-Ådel added.

'Like the kind caused by a ship crashing during an attempted docking.'

'Officer Mukisa is probably drugged somewhere or still in their custody.'

'It all has to be deliberate. Has to.'

'Even if it's true... all this just to steal one Adedevoh-class driveship?' Chloe asked, shaking her head as if it would help the pieces fall into place. 'No. I don't buy it. I'm sorry but I have to arrest you until all this is sorted out. I don't care what the specs on that arm of yours are but if you resist, this time, I *will* take you.' Her eyes focused with determination as she finished her sentence.

Lien-Ådel's face went pale. 'No. No. Listen. Why else would they drug us and use a genetic ID copybox? Driveships use direct pilot and engineer genetic ID systems to gain access to all aspects of the ship. But then... why us? The *Igodo* is not special. In fact, right now it's got a minor fault. You remember right, Orshio, after we got hit by that nasty rock out in Kuiper, the techs told us that the only damage was to the processor relays that pass messages between the genetic ID and ship controls. So right now, the relays aren't quite right, and they could theoretically allow the direct genetic ID system to access all aspects of the ship. Including the hardcoded navigation limits which means if they bypass security then they can enter drift-flux and be halfway across the solar system in a few minutes and no one would be able to follow them because they could turn off all the velocity safety limits, they can even override the... the...'

'...planetary approach limit.' Orshio finished the sentence for her, his eyes widening.

Orshio and Lien-Ådel both turned away from Chloe at the same time and saw the same thing in each other's eyes. They stood silent, hoping they were wrong but unable to find any doubt that was large enough to obscure the potential danger if what they were both thinking was true.

Chloe broke the silence. 'What? What does that mean?'

Her voice was like a prod to Orshio's mind, reminding him just how urgent the situation was if they were right. Every second would matter now.

'We have to get to the *Igodo* now!' He bolted for the office door as he spoke. 'Whoever is stealing our ship could be trying to turn it into a relativistic kinetic kill vehicle... the kind that can crack a planet open like a walnut!'

Chloe ran steadily, through the corridor beyond to the octagonal office area, doing her best to keep up with Lien-Ådel who was breathlessly explaining it to her as they ran toward the docking elevators.

'Before the Adadevoh drive was invented, all rockets were momentum machines. Mass out in one direction at high velocity, the rocket moves in the opposite direction.' She shouted as the sounds of chaos got louder. Ahead of them Orshio sprinted ahead with fierce determination.

'The Adadevoh drive doesn't do that. It's a reactionless drive that uses vacuum energy directly from space. That's why it can go so fast without having to lug a ton of fuel behind it. But the problem is, if you don't limit it and put controls on how much vacuum energy it uses, the maximum speed it reaches and how close it can approach planetary bodies, then it can easily be turned into a relativistic kinetic kill vehicle of unimaginable power.'

They reached the tall, imposing doorway. Lien-Ådel stopped talking, catching her breath. She could feel her heart pounding in her throat.

Chloe went ahead, and the door opened once she was close enough for it to identify her genetic signature. Orshio nodded and then accelerated again and Lien-Ådel continued as they ran down the energy shielded stairs.

'In a ship like the *Igodo*, with a glitch that could potentially allow access to the planetary approach limits, some suicidal lunatic could accelerate the ship to half the speed of light and deliberately crash it into a planet. At that speed, even for a ship as small as *Igodo*, the kinetic energy will be in the gigatons. At least 500. We are talking several thousand nuclear warheads worth of concentrated impact force in a single blow.'

Chloe would have gasped if she wasn't panting so hard already.

The trio entered the main Ceres station tunnel and froze. Ahead of them, the lights lining all the elevators leading up to Ceres's docking ports were blinking wildly. One of the elevators was burning; an unbelievably tall tower of fire reaching all the way from underground Ceres to the exosphere like an ancient cosmic snake. At the bottom area where the fire raged most fierce, a large group of emergency responders wearing hermetic mechsuits were attempting to control the blaze by shutting off the oxygen and power supply lines, braving the heat and the smoke.

'Chai!' Orshio exclaimed. 'Looks worse than I thought.'

'Look for the man that drugged you in Officer Mukisa's office. If he's going for your ship, he must be here somewhere.'

'What if we're too late and they already have the *Igodo*?' Lien-Ådel asked in a whisper.

Around them, people flowed. Most were running away, toward the main tunnel, bumping into those that stood still watching the inferno and the chaos and the commotion. There was one anomalous movement, though. One man at the bottom of one of the elevators, pacing nervously. Chloe was the first to spot him. She noticed that the elevator he was in front of wasn't blinking like the others, its lights were steady, which meant it was in override, not emergency mode. She looked up, and just barely made out a figure standing in the transparent ascending shaft.

'There!' she shouted. 'There's someone in that elevator.'

She broke into a run.

Orshio and Lien-Ådel glanced up to see the elevator ascending.

Orshio turned to Lien-Ådel, 'You need to find the ansible office on this station and establish communications with the *Igodo* so that I can reach you once I get on board. If we are right, then we will only have a few minutes or even seconds. Please, go!'

Lien-Ådel nodded her understanding and sprinted back the way they'd come. Orshio followed Chloe. The man at the base of the elevator saw them approaching and pulled out an electric stun-stick, stance at the ready.

'You keep going!' Chloe called out. 'Get to your ship before they take off. I'll handle this.'

They'd attracted attention now and the spectators were torn between the roar of the fire and the fight they could see was coming.

Chloe dived for the man's feet as she reached him and they both fell to the ground before he could even bring down his raised stick. She moved in a blur, wrestling and wrapping her body around the man powerfully, like a snake, trying to lock his limbs against his torso. Orshio jumped over their writhing mass and into the elevator, tapping at the panel to enter the code they'd been given when they docked earlier. The door sealed, and he began to rise.

Ascending, he looked up, silently watching first the fragments of ship, cables, fire, lights, and panelling go by, and then, as he entered Ceres's exosphere, turning his gaze to the distant sun and the cluster of nearby asteroids. The burning elevator remained visible, from high above, a spectre of destruction, of death. An augury of what was to come?

Near the end of the ascent, as it routed his car along the cable tethered to their ship, he came to a sudden stop. As he watched, only a few feet ahead of him, he saw the *Igodo's* nuclear reaction control system vents fire and the tethering cable start to detach.

'Shit!' he shouted. *They are initiating launch sequence. They're going to escape.*

The lights along the flanks of the *Igodo* went bright blue. The engines were on. In a few seconds the *Igodo* would begin to move, exiting Ceres's primary gravity well and after that, if what he suspected were true, go into drift-flux aimed at a major Transhuman Federation outpost like Mars station. But, without the tethering cable's elevator access he had been effectively separated from the ship. Soon the airlock would close too and that would be the end. Just a few feet of space between him and the ship and there was nothing he could do. There was no way to get on the *Igodo*. Unless...

With his arm powered to maximum and his enhanced melanin protecting his skin, he might just be able to make it.

Taking a deep breath and calming himself he rehearsed the steps in his mind.

One. Two. Three.
One. Two. Three.
One. Two. Three.

There was little-to-no margin of error.

He thought the instructions directly to his bioplasmium arm.

One.

Exhaling slowly so oxygen wouldn't expand and rupture his lung tissue, he braced himself on one end of the elevator, facing the *Igodo's* airlock.

Two.

He launched himself forward, shoulder first. The transparent elevator wall shattered explosively. Oxygen rushed out and cold seized him as momentum kept him drifting towards the airlock. The airlock door began to close, slowly like a sleepy eyelid. He watched it in horror. The darkness on every side of the ship reminded him of what would happen if he didn't make it. Every nightmare he'd ever had of dying in space since he'd become a pilot pounded against his chest. He willed himself to go faster but he couldn't. He closed his eyes. It was out of his hands now. He only opened his eyes again when he felt his shoulder hit the side of the *Igodo*.

Three.

Reaching out before he could bounce away, he stuck his right arm into the airlock and grabbed onto the edge. The low vibration of the ship set his teeth clattering. He yanked hard, and pulled himself into the ship, hitting the row of spare extravehicular mobility suits and maintenance supplies just as the airlock door finally fell into place and the ship's pre-exit procedure was completed.

The vents opened, and oxygen flooded back into his lungs. He breathed in gasps, wedged in between two E.V.M. suits. He lay there for a moment, as blood pulsed in his head and a ringing sounded in his ears. Then the increased vibration of the ship reminded him what was happening, and he pushed himself to the main access door. It opened immediately as it scanned his genetic signature.

He drifted through the ship quickly heading for the control room.

When he entered, there was someone seated in the engineer's module. The crewcut hair gave the thief's identity away.

'Stop!' Orshio called, flexing his arm.

The man turned, his face as calm as a cliff. He held a small black cube with a matrix of pulsing light symbols around it just like the one that had been in the office when he awakened. Orshio surmised it was the writing device, while the companion left behind in the office had been the reader.

'Well, this is unexpected,' he remarked. 'I knew the drugs wouldn't last long in the bodies of genetically modified spacecrew like you two, but how did you escape the progmat restraints?'

'The same way I'm going to crush your windpipe if you dare touch my ship's interface.' Orshio gestured toward the middle of control deck. 'Get away from the control module and move here! I know what you're up to and it ends now.'

The man cocked his head to the side and smiled. 'You think you can stop us, mongrel?'

The viewscreen of the *Igodo* exploded into the colourful array of data that indicated an incoming transmission. It went unanswered.

'Shut up and move away from the controls!' Orshio shouted. 'And if you so much as try to issue a command to override the planetary approach limits, I will choke you to death. The world has moved beyond you and your kind. You can't change the march of progress with acts of terror.'

'No.' The man said. 'I know I won't change anything. You and your Transhuman Federation of borderless gene editors and race mixers will continue to take over this system. Technology and economics are on your side, we know that. We've known that ever since your Botswana, Singapore, and Norway units started sharing their gene editing technologies and got your Canada unit to start collaborating with the Nigeria unit to develop their Adadevoh drive. You will never turn back from what you think is success. We know. We see clearly.'

Orshio stared at the ranting man in front of him, confused. 'Then what are you doing? Why?'

'To hurt you,' the man replied angrily. Behind him, space flowed steadily by and the incoming transmission light signals seemed to become more turbulent as the distance between them and Ceres station increased. 'You think you are better than us but you're not even human anymore. You call us stupid and backward and racist and evil simply because we want to maintain our natural bodies, our way of life, our group identities and our culture. You insist that we agree to your freedom and justice laws before we join your Federation but what kind of community would we have if everyone from everywhere could go wherever they wanted without screening? What kind of society can we have where everyone does whatever they like with their bodies, their minds? How would we find social cohesion? How would we define ourselves? No! You made us choose between our borders, our culture, our beliefs, and your progress. You forced us to take a stand and we have paid for it dearly, but this is it. This is what the wrath of real humanity feels like.'

Orshio laughed derisively. 'You can't be serious. Everyone in the Federation maintains their culture if they want to, it's just an individual choice now, just look at me for my ancestor's sake. No, what you wanted was to be dominant in some space, to treat others who'd had their genes edited or their bodies adapted as being less than you, to refuse them the right to live next to you and be themselves, not assimilated. What you wanted was the right to discriminate. Our progress made you uncomfortable and now you're trying to destroy Mars because we didn't let your isolationist and regressionist Confederacy join our Transhuman Federation and get access to our technologies? That's absurd and stupid and petty.'

The man growled. 'I didn't say anything about Mars.'

Orshio shivered.

If not Mars, then...

Earth?

Surely, they wouldn't dare...

Then man inhaled deeply and added, 'It doesn't matter, I don't expect you to understand and besides, you are already too late.'

With those words, the man finally rose from the module and launched himself at Orshio. Around them, the lights on the ship dimmed as the tachyon field auto-navigation system engaged. Through the view screen and behind the man rapidly approaching him, Orshio saw an elliptic hole suddenly appear in the darkness, its edges rimmed with light and bleeding into the fabric of space like an injury to a star. The man must have already overridden the controls and set them on automatic. They were going into drift-flux.

The man crashed into Orshio. He held onto him and turned sharply, swinging the attacker to the other side of the room, before punching him square on the jaw. The man's eyes rolled back in his head. Roaring, Orshio bounced off the control deck floor and drove his entire body forward toward the wall, trapping the man's head between his bioplasmium shoulder and the wall panel. There was a sharp crack. The man stopped moving.

Orshio kicked him in the chest, using the momentum to push himself toward his seat in the pilot module. His eyes were locked on to the hole in front of him. It narrowed to a point. Just as he settled into the chair, the *Igodo* went into drift-flux.

The stars and asteroids and superstructures that had seemed like they were slowly moving by started to rotate. The black, silent fabric of space seemed to curve into a ball and he was at the centre of it, plummeting toward the surface of teeming, rotating stars. No matter how many times he entered it, Orshio's mind always felt confused by it. Space didn't make sense in drift-flux.

There was no time, he had to act quickly.

He swiped furiously at the blinking viewscreen of the *Igodo* to accept the incoming transmission.

Lien-Ådel's face appeared, with Chloe's and several others he didn't recognise, standing behind her.

'Orshio! Orshio! We just detected a vacuum energy singularity developing. Its drift-flux! If you are on board, you need to stop him. Stop him now!'

Orshio grunted. *Too late.*

He swiped away the message and pulled up the *Igodo's* projected path, to see that it was aimed for Earth. It would crash into humanity's home planet at 0.7c, functional light-speed. Enough to trigger an extinction level event. Defensive weapons would be useless against a relativistic kill vehicle going that fast. Even near-orbit impact would have catastrophic consequences. With every passing moment things became more and more dangerous. Time dilation was starting to kick in and he'd be experiencing shorter time than everyone else was. He needed to get a message out. Fast.

He swiped at the controls and fired off a message of his own.

'Lien-Ådel! I'm in flux. Contact Earth station and tell them the *Igodo* was set on a kill path but I have retaken the ship and will attempt to correct. I repeat, I have retaken the ship and will correct!'

The silence returned and Orshio's mind raced as he swiped through the ship's basecode trying to recall what he'd been taught about Adedevoh-class driveship programming. Everything was confusing. But he needed to do something. There were so many loops and subroutines and he couldn't tell the functional elements from the damaged relay. His genetic signature allowed him access even the deepest layer of core programming, but he had no idea what to do to re-establish the maximum speed and planetary approach limits. The blood pulsed in his ears as the ship hurtled toward the Earth to smite it like the hand of some petty god. He desperately wished Lien-Ådel was beside him. Screwing with ship code was her thing. Piloting was his thing.

Piloting is his thing.

He swiped away the source code, pulled up the projected flightpath and began to recalculate. He frowned in focus, his eyes narrowed, and his tribal marking compressed.

He began to swipe, adjusting the hundreds of lines that marked out all class-2 orbital and transport bodies in motion in the sub-belt solar system. The beating of his heart was thunder. He could not reinstall the limits or change the ships hardcoded path, the man had damaged the flight path adjustment console. He'd been locked out. And even if he dropped out of drift-flux now, the ship was already going fast enough to cause major damage, he needed to slow it down. If he could combine a series of unscheduled decouplings with a rapid correction using the reaction control system, he just might ensure the *Igodo* didn't crash into the Earth or anything else with enough force to kill billions. And if he was lucky, he wouldn't get himself killed either.

He finished his calculations and paused. He closed his eyes and prayed to his ancestors, 'ŋ má alekwu,' then swiped the calculations in without giving himself time to overthink it.

The first decoupling kicked in. The ship groaned with a whine like a dying beast, shuddering as its Adadevoh Drive broke connection to the zero-point field of fluctuating energy distribution in space. The ship slowed, and curve of reality flattened out into the familiar again. But before Orshio could even see how close to Earth he was, the ships thrusters fired as pre-programmed and set it rotating. It spun round on its axis like a mad Frisbee at an angular momentum it was never designed to handle. And then for one deathly moment the elliptic hole of bleeding light reappeared. With a forceful crunch, the ship recoupled, going back into drift-flux with its drive facing the opposite direction, as Orshio tried to brake by putting the *Igodo* in reverse. The delta V induced a sudden and spectacular curvature of reality. He saw light. He squinted and saw light glaring out from behind a hole in the ball of reality. His head spun. His heart raged against his ribcage. His vision began to blur at the edges.

Drift-Flux

The second decoupling kicked in and the ship groaned again, the Adadevoh Drive breaking its connection to the zero-point for the second and final time.

The manoeuvre had driven the *Igodo's* engines far beyond design capacity and the force of the second decoupling mid-spin had wrecked the drive.

Orshio was thrown out of his seat and even his genetic gravcines couldn't stop him from finally losing his hold on consciousness.

The last thing he remembered seeing was a face in the light behind the hole in reality, that perfect circle of nothingness with smoothly curved edges, wisps of light streaming out of it like god himself was peeping over its edge.

When Orshio came to, there was water almost up to his neck.

He flailed wildly at first, completely confused as to why he'd gone from the lovely and strange weightlessness of space to the familiar and dangerous viscosity of water. The viewscreen was somehow still stubbornly displaying symbols. The panelling all along the left flank of the *Igodo's* control module had ruptured and the ship was filling with water fast.

He stopped as his senses returned to him. Get out. He had to get out. He took a deep breath and submerged, swimming through familiar passageways to the *Igodo's* airlock. His skin was covered in cuts that stung so much he knew he had to be in seawater.

He reached the airlock, but it only opened halfway when it read his genetic signature. Damaged. It had to have been damaged. He swam up to take in air and calm down. The water was almost up to his nose now, soon the entire ship would be full of water. He breathed slowly, calming his nerves. Then he re-submerged. He swam back to the partly open door, held onto a rail, and, thinking carefully, punched the locked door with his bioplasmium fist like it was an old enemy. It gave. He swam into open water and up, up toward the shimmering surface.

When he surfaced, it was hot and bright, and the sun was dancing a silver line down the skin of the water. His dreadlocks felt heavy on his head. It took him a few seconds to realise he'd lost his red headband. In the distance, he heard sounds like voices, like shouts, like... Earth.

He spun around and saw he was floating only a few hundred feet from a beach. Behind the beach line, a lush green island rose and at its crest sat a beautiful glass bungalow that reflected the sun like a prism. Waves broke over a surrounding group of rocks to the left of the beach. Fishing boats were slowly straggling in through the constellation of rocks. Up and down the beach, there was a smattering of people of all shapes and colours and sizes with their towels and beach balls, their frisbees and their beach mats rolled up under their arms. There were at least thirty of them and some of them were shouting, some of them were waving animatedly at him, some of were pointing up to the sky. He turned again, eyes raised. In the distance, there was a small aircraft approaching.

Orshio started laughing.

He laughed and laughed and laughed.

He laughed because a few minutes ago, he'd been a third of the way across the solar system, because he'd seen the universe bend, because he'd performed an impossible manoeuvre, because he'd saved billions of people from a madman, because he'd wrestled against the essential forces of the universe and yet, somehow, he was alive, floating in the ocean beyond a beach on Earth like some bloody tourist.

He laughed and splashed around in the water like a child until the aircraft, which turned out to be a Transhuman Federation supersonic carrier arrived, dropped an autonomous winch cable and hauled him into its metal belly like a morsel of food.

Inside, he was attended to by people in medical gear and completely ensconced in an insulation super suit—a thin layer of smart nanomaterial that isolated him from his environment to keep him warm and prevent bacterial exchange in his delicate state—and was given a cup of hot rooibos tea. A pale older man with blonde hair and a stiff back, wearing the familiar white uniform of the Transhuman Federation forces with the Zulu shield, yin-and-yang, and spears, emblazoned on its breast walked up to him and said, 'Good to see you are alive and in one piece, Captain.'

'Thank you, Officer...?'

Drift-Flux

'Petrov. But call me Stanislav. Welcome on board the *Anansi*.'

'I guess I'm incredibly lucky. Looks like I landed in a nice location,' Orshio said, smiling thinly before taking a sip of his tea. 'What was that beach anyway?'

The officer smiled at him. 'Machangulo Island, just off the coast of Mozambique. Lovely place, perfectly natural and very popular with tourists from all over the federation. We're heading to Addis Ababa to meet the trade council. Your engineer explained the situation to us and it seems we all owe you a great debt. And you owe her an equal one. We would have fried you with plasma when you made an unscheduled entry into Earth orbit if we hadn't received her message.'

Orshio laughed, 'I cannot overstate how glad I am that you didn't do that.' Then he added. 'I have to thank her when I see her.'

The captain smiled, a clever look in his eyes. 'No need to wait that long. We still have Ceres station on the emergency ansible channel. She's eager to say hello.'

Orshio grinned.

He followed the officer into the communications room and let him lead him to an ansible console.

Orshio sat down, holding his injured belly. Lien-Ådel's face burst onto the screen in dazzling light symbols. She was more excited than Orshio had ever seen her since they'd begun working together.

'You magnificent bastard! How in the name of everything we've been taught did you pull that off?' she asked, her mouth wide.

Orshio went straight-faced, 'Honestly, I don't know. My ancestors must have reached out from Okoto to guide my hand in flux. They even sent me crashing down at a holiday location. Seriously, I'm telling you, only the ancestors could have pulled off a stunt like that.'

Lien-Ådel's image on the viewscreen, came closer, her mouth tight but a suppressed smile leaking from behind her eyes and the edges of her lips. 'Come on Orshio, you really think your ancestors were out there? That they guided you in drift-flux?'

Orshio smiled. 'Well, No. Not really. But it'll be a good story to tell people who wonder how the hell I survived that insane manoeuvre, won't it?'

They both erupted into wild, celebratory laughter that rang across the ocean of space and energy between them.

Wole Talabi is a full-time engineer, part-time writer and some-time editor from Nigeria. His stories have appeared in *F&SF, Lightspeed, Omenana* and several *other* places. He has edited two anthologies and co-written a play. His fiction has won a Nomma Award 2018 and been nominated for the Caine Prize and more. He currently lives and works in Malaysia.

Journal of a DNA Pirate

Stephen Embleton

Day One: October 26, 2085.

As you can fucking imagine, things have gone way too far. I mean way out there, universe-far, fuck-off-far, in fact galactically far out there. All those damned films from 80-90 years ago, where the future society has taken some freaky technology to the extreme of self-beautification and personal enhancement. Or the flip side where the development of some nasty piece of biological or technological breakthrough is used to smite cities and continents back on Old Earth or terraform here on Mars at the flick of a switch. All self-prophetic! I thought battle armour could be best used to assist factory workers and packers in lifting and moving items. But, oh no dear naive person, let's use it strapped to some mindless idiot to help leap ravines and cleave an enemy's skull in two.

And naturally our use of DNA as the ultimate mass storage technology has been bastardised into some biological abomination of science to justify manipulations of all sorts to our God-given makeup. That helix pattern was staring us in the face for so fucking long it's a wonder we ever figured it out. I'm sure it was that damn LSD that revealed DNA's hidden secrets—again.

Us straight thinking, normal homo-fuckin-sapiens are the only ones who seem to see the problem here. There is an inherent loophole the size of fucking Earth's America glaring back at us from the ominous black hole that is 'possibilities' asking for us to stick something into its gaping chasm to feed its craving for life. Yes. It is coming. No. They have no fucking idea.

By latching onto the mechanisms and nature of DNA's structure, scientists found the vast amounts of storage space almost breathtakingly simple. From discs to drives to sticks to wires, they had searched outside of us to answer the problem of capturing and storing information. But what is information but the compilation of memories. And every cell of your body has memories. You cannot remove the x y z portion of your brain and now say 'I forget.' No. Your body tells us everything about you, your environment, and where you've come from. It tells us who your children, siblings, parents, and ancestors are—for generations back and generations to come. And yet we all came from the same particles. The oneness was there. The oneness is here. Mimic DNA and you have nature's perfect data storage system.

And mimic we did. Figure out how to manipulate data and you have the ultimate manipulation tool. And manipulate we did. Manipulate an embryo. Manipulate a species. Done. And done. So now we sit and wonder how we can manipulate ourselves—in realtime. Tomorrow I'd like to look like this. Extrapolate forward and see how I will look in 20 years. Make adjustments. And now? Tweak it here and there. That's better. Forget about where we come from. A distant memory like the distant blue planet that birthed us, naturally.

Now we are all data devices. I hold within and without my body *all* my memories, photos, personal information, data downloads, every fucking 1 and 0 you can imagine that I'd want to keep—in me. I want to copy that file, view that footage, transfer that pixel, just a wipe on a data screen, or someone's arm, and it's there. Uploaded. Copied. Ready to roll. Like flea ridden mangy canines we're infested with our own filth. Our own debris. Our own excrement. No letting go. Flotsam and jetsam floating on our skin—dermasdata. WTF?

And here we are, ready to exploit human vanity. How can we distribute this beautifully crafted virus? What's the quickest way to install, download, upload, activate, run, execute? Execute. Love it. By touch. Simple. And how do we get the greatest number of people to touch in one go? A protest. And what can we protest? The use of DNA. Nobody'd ever suspect a thing. A bunch of activists spreading death. Return with our tails between our legs, back to our Mother Earth where we belong and not infesting other worlds. Poetic.

Stephen Embleton

We think that just because we can terraform a planet, we have the right to terraform our bodies and manipulate something that was doing fine without interference. We may have dropped a few nukes over the poles, rover-mined methane into the atmosphere and stopped our bodily liquids from boiling, but we still must wear our breathing aids outside. We are not the all-powerful gods of this or any planet.

And so, the plotting begins. But first you must get in tune with the void. The hole. To understand and stand by the belief you need to hear. Words are not hearing. Data is not hearing. Hearing is feeling. Feeling is connecting. Connecting is not jacking in. Connecting is connectionless. Feeling is touchless. Hearing is resonating. Understanding is believing.

If you can't hear what it is that the hole is saying, allow me to unplug your wax-filled deaffies and sprinkle some space-dust on those cobweb-smothered drums. Here is the beat to follow. Here is the beat to resonate with. Here is the beat of your heart. Here is the beat that will begin the journey. And what will you hear it say? It will say:

Fuck 'em. Fuck 'em all.

Day Two

Public Experiment #1 has begun. A rumble and acceleration of the hyperloop allowed me to fumble an awkward hand onto a stranger. You'd think in this day and age that we would've become closer as humans and that the New Age hippies from the turn of the century would have won out in the whole hug thy neighbour, plant a tree, oneness with the planet thing. But the current Martian faux pas of touching has made even the most conservative and tight-assed religious no-no's seem tame. Handshakes—limited to close friends and business associates—can make the boldest of individuals recoil in disgust as if you've placed a soiled palm in their face. Needless to say, the trips on the tube or other public transport is entertaining. And so, here we casually inject our first human test. An experiment that is a long time coming.

I have loathed the times spent on that damn locomotive heading for the subterranean factories and offices; piled in with so many others, all plugged into themselves rather than living fully alive on the Martian surface that surrounds their airtight homes. They should rather leave for the Moon colony than not experience this planet as it continues its transition from the deep orange reds to the turquoise and green patches spreading from the south. But the search for the perfect individual necessitated the most banal of activities—the daily commute. And although I prefer the freedom of my own two feet to that iron tube, I did enjoy studying the expressionless faces for clues of thoughts, emotions, and signposts, as to where they were in their lives. How happy are they really and what would they be doing differently right now if they knew what was ahead? But that is all romantic ideology. Anyone with a gun in their face is forced to re-evaluate their current life—or lack thereof—and if not, the bullet does the trick.

Preferring the ticking time-bomb to the lead capsule, we now can sit on the tube, breathing mask packed away, and take notes, compare data, and analyse the changes that the test subject will go through in the next few weeks. After much debate and to-ing and fro-ing we settled on (amidst sexual prejudices) a female subject. Points raised included the obvious physical makeup that could be analysed from a distance and the significance of the reproductive organs and their 'exposure'.

Although we are aware of the initial changes that will present themselves, this has never been tried before, so we can't, repeat, can't assume anything. That will only sway the experiment's results—and P00104 has made it clear that our intensions and focus on the desired results will only conspire to create those pre-desired results. Total physical meltdown may well be preferable, but how it is achieved is the key to phase one.

But in order to keep the data as extensive and precise as possible, I have made detailed notes on today's events. Here is a brief summary:

With the human dermasvirus#32 applied the evening before, I took a light, test shower (robustness of the virus needs to be fully tested, but let's not fuck around with a technical delay like accidentally rinsing it off on the day). Left my apartment at 07:28 and took a refreshing walk to the nearby tube station. Almost immediately I was engulfed in the stream of people heading down the mouth of the stairwell and into the humid stench past the turnstiles. So crowded yet not a push or shove in sight. Freaks.

As previously noted, and with exceptional efficiency, the locomotive came to a near-silent stop at 07:40. Personal spaces were subconsciously cordoned off, sideways glances completed, and then into their respective zones we began our journey.

07:44, we slowed gently to a stop at the subject's station (Station #S00205) and amidst the hoards, our subject emerged and planted herself on one of the few vacant seats on the side of the carriage. Subject's physical description: 32 years of age (ascertained after physical contact with her), unmarried, Caucasian, dark brown (near black) wavy shoulder-length hair. Fair skin. Weighing 81.4 kgs and 1.58 metres in height. Slightly rounded shoulders and stooped posture. As with most of the passengers she keeps to herself and doesn't make eye-contact. Fortunately, the temperature in the transport necessitates the removal of her gloves and the loosening of her brightly coloured scarf. The dermasvirus needs to contact the skin to be effective (especially for this initial experiment). The thick coat and long pants that she wears in the current climate makes it more difficult to implement any close contact—but this was considered.

After a few minutes of observation from a few metres (approx. 4 metres), I proceeded to edge closer to the subject—making it appear as though I were ready for my destination stop. She was standing with her right shoulder facing me (but I was slightly behind her) and as the transport made a switchover and the carriage rocked, I fell forward and proceeded to (heaven forbid) grab her hand. Although it appeared to be an instinctive reaction it took a few moments for her to acknowledge the cultural fuck up and rip her hand back and into her gloves. I apologised and proceeded to hide my face (seemingly embarrassed but more out of being inconspicuous). And so, it was done.

P00104 has indicated that he will be on the afternoon tube to take any visual information of the subject—although it will be too soon to see anything.

Sure, people need access rights or passwords to give and receive/accept data—but the virus circumvents all this. If only the on-planet government could get hold of that tech they'd have a fucking field day as far as personal rights go. And now we wait.

Day Three

Thieving bastards! If there was a trace of your DNA left on me I'd melt your faces, your bank accounts, and your social networking pages in an instant. Fuckers took my comm-unit right from under my goddamn nose. Need to learn from them as far as entering someone's personal space (let alone their pockets) to grab what's not fucking theirs.

So, all the tiniest details and notes from today's tube ride—watching our subject—are probably being wiped clean as we speak to make it sellable on the open-bloody-market! Damn, I knew I should've copied it via dermasdna before pocketing it.

Today's report was therefore processed straight from the good old-fashioned grey matter. Nothing of significance to report (as with P00104's afternoon observations). Far too early.

And here I sit, wracking my brain about who or what was near me during and after the journey. Long gone, I'm sure, but it's going to eat at me anyway. I'm the goddamn thief here. You don't steal from the stealer! Now I've got to watch my back as well as the experiment. How ridiculous is that?

The news coverage on the latest DNA developments is becoming more interesting by the day. Everyone seems to be fanatically enthusiastic about even the slightest tweak that some lab-rat can make to the current systems. Well, they've all got their heads up their bums if they are relying on scientists who follow their paycheques. Passion. That's what it's all lacking nowadays. Passion drives progress. Real progress I mean.

Need to get P00104 to develop a 'melt-face-on-site' DNA virus when this current experiment is completed. Expose on touch! And I don't want it to rely on the chance of only dermas contact (let's evolve from dermasdata and head straight to anything-goes-data).

Moving swiftly on...

I was up and down my climate-controlled apartment unit last night, with about two hours sleep, thinking about what we would see today. Staring out at the red-black night, I tried to imagine the future, my mind racing like a madman through all the different scenarios that might appear in the next few weeks, and even the 'final' result. I'm both excited and unnerved by the possibilities. There are so many variables and permutations of how the virus will express itself. Although it's a fairly exact science, in our experience chaos does reign and reigns supreme. But we set our goal and hold true to the formulae and calculations.

I do need to get my shit together and not let today's events affect how I function with something as important as this. After all, things are going to get a lot more intense and a lot more brazen than some petty train theft.

We've got our weekly meeting coming up and I'm sure security (and theft) are conveniently going to be raised, addressed, and workshopped to fucking death. As long as we remain focused on the goal, I'll take the flack that is due to me.

Eyes peeled. Skin crawling with anticipation.

Day Four

Every twitch and scratch that our 'subject' makes sends my pulse racing. An 8-minute ride on the hyperloop ends up being more nerve-wracking than any VR thriller I've ever watched. Added to the fact that there still aren't any visible signs that we can identify—again, it is still too early in the projected timeline. I'm spending the entire trip hanging on her every move. And I've got to remain inconspicuous.

Fellow passengers seem to keep even their glances to themselves, but anonymity is the key. I even removed my hair add-ons and donned the most uninspired clothing to blend in with the proverbial wallpaper. Every pore of my body is oozing and squirming in this conformist chamber— like a diver with the bends having to decompress in a dense, soundless vacuum—the air is thick around me and I want to throw-up but know I'll be left to rot in my own filth if I do.

Picked up my replacement comm-unit on the way home from the station. We have to deal with the lowest tech concerning these things—cheap and nasty and as far off the system as things will allow. Already ran the serial-wiper to rid the device of its tracking system. The randomiser seems to be running just fine in the event of anyone trying to identify the device on connection—runs a new comm-ID and GPS location each time.

God, I love having hacks at my fingertips.

Incoming comm...
Auto Transcriber Activated...
Names edited...

DNA PIRATE: 'Yes?'
UNKNOWN: 'Bro. What the fuck?'
DNA PIRATE: 'What you mean, P00102?'
UNKNOWN: 'Have to pull you off hyperloop duty for now. Your comm-unit problem.'
DNA PIRATE: 'Fuck, I knew it!'
UNKNOWN: 'Exactly, so don't get pissy when you saw this coming.'
DNA PIRATE: 'Nobody's pissy, I didn't think it was a big deal. It's all unconnected.'
UNKNOWN: 'Unconnected now, but when we're looking back in hindsight, we've got to make sure that we covered our tracks.'
DNA PIRATE: 'So why allow this morning's session?'
UNKNOWN: 'There were some back-and-forths over the issue and considering the amount of time we've all taken in grooming you and P00104 it was a hard call.'
DNA PIRATE: 'Who's in tomorrow, then?'
UNKNOWN: 'P00108.'
DNA PIRATE: 'She's not ready, damnit!'
UNKNOWN: 'It took a day, but she'll be just fine. Besides, we cannot assume that anyone is irreplaceable—no matter where we sit in the food-chain.'
DNA PIRATE: 'Whatever. I've got shit to organise, so I've got plenty to occupy my time.'
UNKNOWN: 'Exactly.'
DNA PIRATE: 'Send me the updates.'
UNKNOWN: 'As always. We still on for the meeting?'
DNA PIRATE: 'Naturally.'
Damnit.
I'll find ways to occupy my mornings. Need to gather information from the various broadcasts and news agencies

anyway. Plus, P00109 says that he's nearly through into the security and law enforcement agency systems. Fun when you just tell your code what to hack and it does all the hard work for you. That will, firstly, give us an eagle eye on any future investigations that may arise; and secondly, allow for a few manipulations.

And then, like a giant digital chessboard, the games will really begin.

Day Five

Stumbled on this interesting newscast from a few weeks back: *'Taking everything that is spewed from the gutters of The Fringe Magnet, this caster has just to mention up front that the following information may be somewhat tainted by their reputation. Nevertheless, an item that seem to be recurring on their casts is the possible infiltration of some sort of technical virus on a DNA-scale. Maybe it comes across on the surface as somewhat sensational, this caster does believe that there is an ounce of truth in the most banal and trite statements that anyone may deliver. But from a journalistic point of view it does smack of the 2075 attempt at distributing what was supposed to be a "planetwide annihilation of the vanity of the human race," to quote the Anti-Bio-Earthist-Conspirators. We all know how humiliating and self-destructive their little experiment ended up being, but it did give the relevant health and security organisations pause for thought.*

'And here we are, present day, with snifflings of another viral campaign of 'terror' by the Earthist movement. Yes, I may be over-dramatising. That's my job. But just to put it out there that maybe someone has been tinkering away at some little nasty virus thingy that, to all intents and purposes, could deliver on the original mandate of the ABEC crazies.

'The Fringe Magnet reports that the settlement city of EFP0023 has what is called a group of individuals that are One in mind. "Their operation is apparently leaps ahead of the current known technology that we the public are aware of (and possibly those so-called leading scientists involved in the most cutting-edge research in the field of DNA manipulation and storage)."

Journal of a DNA Pirate

'I don't want to be one of those post-apocalyptic I-Told-You-So's, but let's simply keep our eyes and ears open. One Mars.'

Where do these crackpots get their info? Nothing to worry about, I'm sure—anyone with half a brain could assume that there are those that refuse to buy into the vanity of the majority. Hopefully there *are* more like us out there. And if there are, let the best man annihilate!

Day Six

I decided to take a walk today. Regular exposure to the Martian climate is vital.

I walked onto my street as that early morning chill was dissipating like the sleep from my bones. The streets were busying, and the noise of the day had begun.

I came down the hill, and through the gaps in the low buildings I could see the manmade river—bringer of commerce and trade—snaking like a salesman through city I've come to know and love for the past few years. A feeling of disconnectedness briefly filled me remembering where I've come from. But this could be any city, on any planet, but only originating from one Earth.

I love my birth-planet. I love my origin-planet. I love this city. I love the touch of the red soil and the promise of its dust. But I hate the people. I hate the builders. I hate the government. I hate the rulers. And I hate the mess.

I stopped at the bridge bending its back over the glowing green river and I looked at the monuments, even the cathedrals, the stubby buildings no more than a few stories high, and the tourist gimmicks for visiting Earthers. But most of all I looked at the masked, faceless people: the people who built them; the people who use them; and most of all: the people who are really oblivious to them. The everyday people who go about their shit totally unaware of the monstrosity that they've helped create. The systems and structures and aerial views of their city—their supposed home—their cage that they've constructed to fit themselves into, comfortably. A mishmash of lanes and dreams and compromise and complacency. Only venturing outside when they absolutely must.

I long for the fresh air that the industrial digital age can't breathe into me. To be the rustic, earthbound troglodyte in his primitive cave in awe of his fire and the shadows that dance on his rough wall. He holds more value to me than the feel of my comm-unit in my pocket and the breather on my face: the weight of an age that feels like it's going to drag me down with it.

I had to take it out my pocket, so that I could breathe. I looked at the comm-units floating by—attached to faces—grey and dull and totally disconnected. Am I the only one who thinks like this?

I'm the freak—I think.

I think.

I long for the fresh air. I need a trip to Earth. The great outdoors. Fuck! I thought this *was* the great outdoors. Space. Go figure.

I had to rest against the thick stone slabs of the bridge. I needed to catch my breath. What am I doing here? What am I doing?

I think I'd see normal people if I went out tonight. Halloween seems so natural now. Let's celebrate the dead while they're still alive.

I noticed something after finishing this entry.

Everything begins with 'I'.

Me.

Day Seven: Signs and Wonders

Our subject has started to show signs of the virus. Although pretty arbitrary to the average Joe Shmoe, it's there and it's exciting. It's like watching a baby being born; the crimson sunrise on a brand-new day.

P00108's report shows that although not noticeably run-down, she doesn't look like the perkiest flower in the vase (my words). Every now and again she reaches into her scarf to scratch the tender skin around her neck. Sign number one. Then, with her arms folded, she twists and turns her wrists inside her jacket and gloves. Sign number two. The next few days will expose the raw and vulnerable skin to the elements—further aggravating the surface area.

Her discomfort is just beginning. In a way, I feel a tingle in my skin imagining what it must feel like, then a shiver, and finally a warm safe feeling envelopes me. After all, P00104's DNA vaccine was implemented within the entire group a week beforehand, so we're all safe and snug in our cocoons of wellness. But still, it is very humbling to know how close we are to the full-blown virus. Humbling and empowering.

But let's wait and see how it all unfolds. I feel totally exhilarated.

At midnight, we all meet.

Day Eight

Here follows this morning's midnight meeting:

DNA Pirate: Before we begin any formal structure here, I'd like to firstly apologise for the comm-unit theft—out of my hands so to speak. But secondly that we need to foresee these kinds of things happening and what's the point of going to all the trouble of getting serials wiped and randomisers installed if we then get pulled from our assignments when we hit a snag? Right. Let's begin.

P00101: Thanks for that. I don't think we need to get into that debate right now. The reports that P00108 and P00104 have been providing are beneficial to the project and the ongoing work. Thanks guys. We do seem on track for the final stage, but the reports are vital for the various stages and their possible symptoms.

P00104: I'd like to add that the research, the data collecting, and the technical knowledge of the entire dermasvirus team have created a marvel that should be respected on every level.

DNA Pirate: Are the symptoms of the subject in any way in line with what you'd projected? I want to know if there's any deviation from the goal here?

P00104: So far it is all on track. You can never fully predict, but we're strong.

DNA Pirate: Excellent. I'd also like us to consider moving our initiation date forward a week.

P00109: What?

P00104: We can't deviate-

DNA Pirate: I don't see how it would change the-

P00109: This is crazy. We need to know what we're dealing with here first.

DNA Pirate: We know what we're going to be dealing with.

P00104: 90% sure at this stage. 10% unknown.

DNA Pirate: I thought you said-

P00104: There's always a margin of error or deviation.

P00109: Deviation from the plan. We agreed!

P00101: Can we keep it ordered here? The focus remains. The plan remains. There is no deviation. The only deviation allowed for is the dermasvirus itself and any contingency plans that we've drafted.

DNA Pirate: Just a suggestion. It shouldn't make any difference if we're going to set it in motion no matter what. It's just the level of effect that's going to vary, surely.

P00109: I still don't think that we should do anything more than what we're doing to this subject and her family or colleagues. The message will be clear enough.

DNA Pirate: People have a low attention span. After a week, it will be in the gutters of the media and a side note in a conspiracy theorist's networking page.

P00109: Fuck. Whatever.

P00101: Again, back to the draft contingency plans. You'll each receive a copy. I'm not going to go through it tonight. But I want your thoughts and suggestions ASAP.

DNA Pirate: (the usual points were raised, and tedious admin dealt with).

P00101: P00108 has her early morning tomorrow so we're going to adjourn. As always, these meetings are to raise issues—briefly—to address anything that may come up late in the week, and to meet face to face: to remind each of us that we still remain a unified group. The faces before you are those that we trust and respect for what we can bring to this campaign.

Day Nine

I still don't get it: P00109 still insists on raising his concern for the level at which we are distributing the DNAvirus. For some reason, he thinks that a 'firm message' needs to be sent rather than the destruction that we plan.

'Oh, please Joe Shmoe, please don't manipulate your DNA to make you a better person. Please don't warp what evolution has taken billions of years to perfect. Please don't turn yourself into an egocentric megalomaniac.'

We've been harping on these issues for over a decade. We've protested. We've boycotted. We've terrorised. Now is the time to pull the pin on the grenade that they are willingly holding in their hands; the grenade that they've been daring nature to fight back with. Well, nature's about to get a friendly hand. And like the grenade, it's all going to blow up in their faces and there's bugger-all they can do about it. Blow their noses off to spite their faces.

Killing one person for the cause is a smudge on the tarmac. Killing a group of people causes a traffic jam—questions, answers, contingency plans, and paranoia. Kill a city and there's global awareness in half a day. Kill a planet and the worlds go mental. That's a message! Not a couple of post-it notes slapped onto the foreheads of passers-by. Small-time wastes Time. Time with a capital T-N-T!

The 1st Martian War is about to be declared and it's not between legacy countries from off-world. It's between the people that think they hold the power and the ones that *really* hold the power. There's no one to retaliate against. There's no one to aim their missiles at. And best of all, there's no borders to invade. Who do they stop when it's all begun?

They've said long ago that the death of the human race will not come from within, but from without. Viruses evolve. Viruses get stronger. Viruses come back at ya.

We've just put our own two cents worth into the mix for good measure.

Let's see what brews.

Day Ten

Been prepping for the next phase.

Although not being implemented just yet, the necessary plans need to be carefully laid out, locations confirmed, and contacts double-checked.

I'll be crossing zones, meeting new, like-minded people. A few planet-wide hyperloop rides, and a bicycle or two, will enable the safe dispersion of the global dermasvirus—the final strain! Once that has been successfully completed it's just a matter of waiting for the date to arrive. The greatest event that anyone has ever witnessed on such a scale. Millions of people will be watching it unfold across the planet. Possibly even those on Earth. No one will be immune. No class, no race. Just a select few.

Those select few will bring the stability that the world so dearly craves. Subconsciously man is yearning for this rebirth. They just don't know it.

Stephen Embleton

It will be like the dawning of the Iron Age. All the tools will be available to us, but we will set the standards up front. For the betterment of the species and quality of life on Mars—the wholeness of the planet considered. Not a prettier species, or the massaging of a superiority complex.

Down to Earth. Up with the planet.

Day Eleven

We're nearly at the stage of buying the various transportation tickets and hire-cars. I've gone over my checklist of personal items, clothing, and other travel necessities that I'm going to need.

Feeling somewhat detached from the group as I mentally prepare for this part of the journey. Being from another part of the planet I'm seen as the foreigner, the roamer. They're all attached to their city, their homes, and their safe environments. I left that long ago and escaped to a new life. I arrived here with minimal baggage—a small backpack and personal ghosts. They've got their lives weighing them down and they don't even know it. I wonder how easy it's going to be for them when the time comes and there's no turning back. Are they going to snivel and whimper at fate's feet? Is there going to be guilt and remorse flying around? Or are they going to step up and drop the shit?

In a way, it's like they are using me to distance themselves from the mission. Distance themselves from the very human emotion that genocide brings up in the pit of your stomach.

Nobody else rose to the occasion. I felt the stares and looks of judgment when I took the task. As if they all thought I was the callous one, the heartless freak.

Only a week or so of traveling and then I'm back. Back to reality and back to the group. They can all envy me as I tell them of the final days of each city; one of the last of our group to go where the virus will soon wreak havoc.

I'm feeling a bit humbled by the honour. Never thought that would happen. Not like I give a shit about the empires we've built, or the magnitude of man's reach on this planet and outer space. But to be the one instrumental in bringing it all down: God that feels good.

Crack! and our concrete idols crumble.

Bang! and our world dies.

Journal of a DNA Pirate

Day Twelve

Transport tickets have been bought. Vehicles at various areas have been booked and paid for upfront: all with anonymous business accounts.

A few days till the real journey begins. My bag is packed. Travel light.

The team will keep me posted on our subject while I'm on the road. I'll likewise be sending them daily summaries. I haven't had any contact with them today. I think they are filling their respective lavatories and receptacles with bile and diced carrots.

I won't lie, I've felt the urge to dry heave my conscience. But that's all it was, dry. No substance.

I must say this journal has been rather cathartic. Seeing my intentions, goals and purpose laid out in black and white makes me aware of the enormity of the task before us. Before me.

Before me?

After me?

What then?

A world of possibilities.

I expect the next few reports on our subject are going to be revealing. There is going to be a dramatic shift. One that will *not* go unnoticed.

Soon we will need access to her social online connections, doctor, and lab results. But that's already set up and accessed. Our penetration is more than just dermal. We are diving through the rotting surface of the world, into its writhing bloody cancerous mass, and pulling hard.

Day Thirteen

Just settled into my seat on the first part of my journey. On an encrypted data-link. Pinging my online system's security as I upload this entry.

All seems good. If it's not people hacking your network and accessing your data, it's people hacking your DNA. Ha!

Your immune system is no firewall against a breach on your DNA.

Depart in 20 minutes. Heading SW. 10 hours overnight. Arrive 09:15.

Today dragged on. Had my last meal at home for a while. Cleaned up. Took one last look at the stacks of hardcopy books in the hallway and living room. Most I'm carrying digitally anyway, but they'll be missed. It's the one luxury-personal-attachment I give myself in this world. They can be given away when the time comes and more collected wherever I find myself living. They are not allowed to hold me down. My backpack is bad enough.

I once took a trip across country, two hours there, two hours back. It was for a meeting in the other city. I took my jacket, mobile, and my pad. No carry-on luggage. No baggage to check in. I walked on and walked off. For some reason that was the most liberating feeling I've ever had in my life—if you don't count taking a piss in the wilderness without clothes on. No hands required.

The wheels are in motion: did the dermasvirus transfer onto the lady handing out our drinks orders. I think she thought I was coming on to her. Yeah, likely!

We have officially passed the point of no return.

I've sent a message to the others.

No damn response.

I'm just going to let the passing lights and gentle thrum of the transport drift me off to sleep.

Day Fourteen

Woke up about 5 minutes ago to the announcer cackling on about the next stop. My stop.

Ordered coffee. Hopefully it will be waiting for me by the time I'm finished here in the toilet. Then I'll grab a bite to eat and catch up on the news feeds. Still no goddamn word from those useless pricks. I get the distinct impression that I'm being left out in the cold. Whatever the case, our mission—my mission—is on track.

The same waitress from yesterday handed me my coffee. Ha! I think I freaked her out even more today. She stretched over to place my cup and saucer down on the table. I leaned in quickly, grabbing her hand and stared straight into her eyes. Deep blue. Flawless—for now. Didn't notice anything yet, other than a twinkle of fear and anger. 'Sir!' she had said and flicked my hand off hers. Totally unaware that I'm part of her already. Well, the dermasvirus anyway.

An hour till we disembark. Breakfast time.

Seriously, do me a favour. Message from the team reads:
Subject #1 has left work early.
That's it? Nothing else?
If they aren't going to furnish me with any more particulars, then I'm just going to have to hack her social networks. See if she goes crying to mommy about how she's feeling.
10 minutes to the main terminal. No problem.

Her online life has revealed little. No parents alive to speak of. Therefore, no snivelling. No recent posts. Dare I say no one to give a crap.
This is my stop.

I can't breathe! What the fuck just happened? P00104 that piece of shit traitor. How the fuck did we, I, not see it?

MESSAGE: P00102
You ignorant morons. What the hell is going on? Your comms have been practically non-existent. Now I get off at my stop at $@^# and guess who is there to greet me with a blank stare, that now says so much in hindsight? None other than P00104. Yes! That fucker Guillaume. And fuck protocol before you start preaching about using real names here. Because if what he says is true then it's all flushed down the toilet.
He calmly invited me for a cup of coffee as if he just wanted to catch up and talk about the goddamned weather. Like him being at $@^# was the most normal thing in the world.
My face must have said everything because I didn't utter a 'what the fuck', 'who the fuck', nothing and he smirked his 'Hi, Treycin. We need to talk.'
And talk he did. I'd didn't say a word. I just listened to his tale. You may be interested in it.

1. Subject #1 will die. But not because of the virus. The virus will reverse itself. She will die an old lady in 70 or 80 years.
2. I, on the other hand, am Subject #2.
3. As is the rest of the team in completely random descending order.
4. Within 5 days we all will be dripping skin, fingers, organs, and liquid eyeballs.

5. Everyone that I have come into contact with will have a slight cold. Nothing life-altering.

Charming. If I didn't have this sick churning sensation in my gut right now, I would say he was talking shit. Then again, nerves will do that to the strongest of us. And why would he travel all that way as a practical joke or even an empty threat?

So, best you rocket scientists get into the DNA sequence and check what the fuck is going on. In the meantime, I am on the first direct ride back that I could get.

I will be taking a fucking sleeping tablet and hope this bullshit oozes out of my psyche by the time the last drop of whiskey drains from my glass.

END MESSAGE

Day Fifteen

Arrived back. Something is up. No response. About to step onto the train before Subject #1's stop.

Damnit! She just boarded. I was about to get up when she stepped through the doors. She's looking all rosy and peach fucking perfect. She made direct eye contact with me as she weaved her way through the other passengers towards my section of the transport. It's like she's a new person. More open.

Happy to be bloody alive.

This has all gone to shit.

I've gone to shit. There's a red patch forming on my right hand and there is a burning sensation around my neck. Those bastards better be pulling the piss.

Heading over to P00102's apartment to get to the bottom of this fiasco.

Will record everything on my comm-unit.

>>>>>>Recording:

>>>>>>Translating to English:

'Do you mind if I sit here?'

'Ah, sure. No, go ahead.'

'Thanks. Haven't I seen you on this line before?'

'No.'

'You sure? You look very familiar.'

'Wasn't me.'

'Sorry, I'm not usually forward, but I recently realised that you have to make the most of life. Never let opportunities slip through your hands. So, I had to ask.'

'No problem.'

'You don't sound like you are from around here?'

'No. Not from here.'

'I would like to travel. See the world. There is so much beauty out there. Look at all these beautiful people. Just like you and me.'

'Not really.'

'Oh, I think so. They are all keeping to themselves, too afraid to reach out beyond what they know. Wanting people to like them, to notice them. But without drawing attention to themselves. Blending in but not wanting to blend in.'

'Doing things to be like everyone else, you mean.'

'Yes. But to feel like they are part of something. Not feeling alone. It's all about being accepted.'

'No matter what.'

'Sometimes. The pressure to be loved is there from birth. Wanting a parent to love you and accept you for who you are. Not what they think you should be. That is where the cycle begins. What we see here is not one person trying to impress a stranger. It is a son or a daughter trying to impress their god. Their parent. Even the parent who loves them unconditionally, no matter what, unknowingly puts pressure on their child to never let them down. People running their lives to maintain approval from a superior being. God, mother, mentor. What is the difference?'

'Status is another god. Ego.'

'And when you bring someone down to that basic human need, it is no different to a baby crying in a crib wanting the comfort of another. A baby animal does not survive if it is not accepted by its mother. It is dead if the herd does not see it as an equal. Runts who are different to the rest die off, starved and abandoned.'

'Better to be different than go with a herd heading for the edge of a cliff.'

'Better to be the one to make a difference and turn the herd around. Would you rather stand back and watch as they plummet over the edge, or be the one to tell them where they are headed? Kindness has a way of working for everyone, not just the individual.'

'This is my stop.'

'It was really nice talking to someone willing to talk in this place.'

'Sure.'

'I hope you go out there and make a difference. Will I see you again?'

'I don't think so.'

'Are you okay? You are sweating, and it is freezing in here.'

'Bye.'

[Sound of doors sliding open.]

'What the hell is happening to me?' [Heavy breathing.] 'I need to get out of here.'

[Footsteps quicken. The sounds of people moving past.]

[The sounds of the underground fade as traffic noises fill the air.]

[A hooter sounds]

'Pedestrian walking, motherfucker!'

[Running feet and panting.]

'Nearly there.'

[Sound of knocking]

'Open the fuck up, Kaylin!'

[Banging on a door. The squeak of a door opening.]

'Anyone here? Kaylin, where the hell are you? Where's the goddamn light switch?'

[A noise from a nearby room]

'Kaylin?' A light switch clicks. 'What the fuck?'

[Someone says something inaudible.]

>>>>>>Stop

We set out with noble intentions. I want the world to know this. Things got twisted along the way. Some of our group got twisted along the way.

I righted a ship that was going to end us—the planet. I'm not expecting accolades or praise for something I was a part of to start with.

The preceding journal is there as proof of the experiment and the knots that arose in the majority of the team. The insights into my colleague's thoughts should plainly show these knots and how the plan so quickly unravelled. I couldn't allow it to go any further than what was originally intended. So, I made adjustments. Call it a fail-safe. Security.

Our target was given an expiry date on her dermasvirus. Lucky her. My team wasn't. My only hope is that this will be recognised as the warning it was originally intended to be.

Why was she chosen? Other than she was young and healthy: no other reason. If we could create this virus, anyone can. And you put your lives, your DNA, in the hands of geniuses like us every day. Wake up.

I have sacrificed my team, my friends, so that the message is loud and clear. Fuck with your DNA and you fuck with our humanity. Our flaws are what make us. To become some hybrid outside of the realm of evolution and natural selection puts the power of God in our hands. We barely have the right to exist as it is, never mind assuming Divine control in every waking moment of our lives. Evolution says we are perfect as we are, right now.

If this document is buried, it will resurface.

If this DNA fashion continues, there will be something more to come. Patience and compassion go so far for an obstinate child.

Today, people need access rights or passwords to give and receive/accept data via dermas-transfer—but our virus circumvents all this.

Take your DNA back. Take the evolution of your ancestors back. Next thing you know you'll all be giving your souls away for a moment, an extra day or month, of longevity.

We are all meant to die. We aren't more special than a fruit fly.

As my colleague came to see the destruction, the fruits of our labours, laid out before him in that apartment, my only hope is that he saw the pain that was coming for him. Was there an inkling of regret for what was once a concept and then was bloody real?

The genius must be prepared to experiment on himself. Otherwise walk away.

> > > > > >Recording:
'The protector serum?'
'I tampered with it. What you all assumed was stopping any infiltration was in reality exposing you to the virus from inception. But it was manipulated to fight the virus for a time, and eventually lose.'

'So, it took a while for the virus to manifest.' [Cough]

'Yes. But your bodies would've already used resource fighting so when it was theoretically programmed to surrender, to shut off as planned, the virus hit a weakened body harder and faster than before.

[Spitting] 'And the lab samples?'

'They would've self-destructed by now.'

'No backup.'

'None.'

'We wasted our lives. You fucked us.'

'The lives were not wasted. Call it a sacrifice for the greater good.'

'The greater good? Those egomaniac fucktards are the greater good?'

'They are. They just need to be guided every now and again.'

'And what if they don't take the hint?'

'I will make sure of that.'

'I never liked you.'

'I know.'

'How long are you keeping me here?'

'I'm not keeping you here. I'm waiting with you. You can't move yourself anywhere. There is no doctor who can help you. Not even a hacker like me.'

'Where's Kaylin?'

'Her body is in the other room. She stopped breathing about an hour ago.'

'Fuck.'

'I'm irritated I wasn't there when it happened. I was moving you in here.'

'I'm sure that [cough] will weigh heavily on your heart.'

[Long pause]

'What was our original intention with hijacking DNA?'

'Kill the world and start again.'

'No. That became *your* mission. The original intention was to take one or two lives. Lives that would be noticed. We wanted everyone to see the death. We wanted them to see the blood.'

'Like this?'

'Yes. So how is this outcome any different?'

'Because it's me. Us. You fucking backstabbing cocksucker!'

'Sure. But we can't have fanatics with so much control in the world.'

'Says the dick watching me die right in front of him.'

'Change comes with the price of pain. You happen to be the one feeling it today.'

'So, what now?'

'You die. The world moves on. Evolution continues, naturally.'

'The vain species lives on.'

'And an evolutionary line of superiority complex dies in this bed today.'

'I hope they hunt you down and make you bleed, slowly.'

'You know very well they will never find me. They will be too busy trying to secure the lives of their citizens to worry about where I am on this planet or the next.'

'They should be worried.' [Cough]

Stephen Embleton was born and lives in KwaZulu-Natal, South Africa. His background is Graphic Design, Creative Direction, and Film. His first short story was published in 2015 in the *Imagine Africa 500* speculative fiction anthology, and more followed since. He is a charter member of the African Speculative Fiction Society and its Nommo Awards initiative.

The Interplanetary Water Company

Masimba Musodza

The frozen wastes of Pód, spun away slowly beneath the *Chapungu II*. Its atmosphere reminded me of diluted milk, the upper part shimmering in the morning suns. From the ground, the action of the suns on the different layers of frozen to near-frozen air would be a spectacular kaleidoscope.

The chronometer's alarm sounded, cutting through my musings. I could hear Njike perform her morning toilet.

Fifteen minutes later, she floated into the cockpit, beaming eagerly, 'Good morning, Kalu.' She took her seat. 'Sounds like the Fundi plans to sleep through the landing.'

'I do not!' Dr Hanga said as he burst into the cockpit. His hair and beard looked even more deranged than usual, like an old brush. But his eyes were clear, even though he had barely slept during the three-month voyage from our station, Potero, in orbit around the gas giant Ve-Haqq.

Now, we were home.

It had been nearly one hundred and fifty Standard Years since the catastrophe that had dislodged planet Bvuku from its orbit, a freak collision with three giant comets, pushing it out of reach of the optimal warmth of the three suns, plunging it into a perpetual winter. Nearly the entire population, thirty million souls, perished. The only survivors were a team of scientists, support staff, and their families, exactly six hundred people on Space Station Kulinda VII. The Commonwealth of Worlds' Interplanetary Rescue Mission only found the space station by chance. With the rest of the Bvukians, the IRM could not even find the planet for nearly a Standard decade until astronomers began to note its effects on the orbits of several planetoids in the region. It would take another year to establish as fact that Bvuku was no longer the world of freshwater springs and vast lakes, but a barren wasteland of ice. It was now too far from the inner worlds for any sort of resettlement to be viable.

The Interplanetary Water Company

In anguish, Professor Mungwaru Zule, head of the space station Kulinda VII, renamed the planet Pód meaning cold, and Kulinda VII he dubbed Potero: refuge.

However, Interplanetary Law held that as there was still an indigenous Bvukian population, the frozen planet was not open to colonists and prospectors. This law was needlessly enforced by the fact that every mission to Pód, illegal or not, had been a failure. Furthermore, it was now widely understood that only Potero-sanctioned missions could be conducted without fear of violence out in open space. Potero, under Professor Zule's son, Chimba, became the de facto representative of Pód at the Commonwealth Assembly. The space-station sustained itself at first by selling water prospecting rights, and then investing the proceeds in interplanetary trade across the Commonwealth.

In the past twenty-years, a growing population, an ebb in applications for prospecting licences and a downturn in interplanetary trade had taken their toll on Potero. It was estimated that if there wasn't any money to pay for repairs, Potero would simply drop into Ve-Haqq in five years. The Pód & Potero Government was yet to make an official request to the Commonwealth for assistance, not while other solutions still seemed possible. Solutions that were not attended by the rattle and clanging of fetters. Such as the privately-communicated proposal by the Emperor of Renje that Potero join his realm. This precipitated threats, also privately communicated, by the other planets that they would see the space station blown up before they let it enter into political union with a rival.

It was then that the Commonwealth Secretariat decided to act. A line of credit was extended to Potero, enabling us to finance what was being described as the first exploratory mission in over forty Standard Years. *Chapungu I* was a robot mission, meant to conduct a more thorough study of Pód's climate with a view to finding that one place on the planet where man could begin to reclaim it from nature. We were the follow-up, *Chapungu II*.

That was the official version of events. Any planet intercepting *Chapungu I* and *II*'s transmissions would have deduced that we were in a serious predicament, as the entire planet was frozen. Such a planet would have gloated, convinced that we were too desperate now to refuse any offers of political union. An easy enough deduction to make, since they wouldn't have suspected Dr Hanga's presence aboard.

Dr Tambayi Hanga's grandfather, Jama, had worked on the development of technology to move massive objects, such as a planetoid. It was an experiment in this project that dislodged Bvuku from its orbit. Fearing that they would be charged with genocide, Jama Hanga hid the accumulated knowledge on the one place he was sure no one, even if they somehow learnt of its existence, would ever think to look. Planet Pód.

However, the real reason no one had ever thought to look was because the way in which our homeworld had been dislodged from its orbit remained a closely-guarded secret.

The data *Chapungu I* and *II* sent back was all fake, the careful efforts of about thirty graphics experts on Potero. The real objective, Prof. Jama Hanga's notes, was still down there among those frozen wastes. We were here to retrieve them.

'Fire laser,' I commanded.

'Laser-firing sequence initiated,' said Kalu, without taking her eyes off her monitor. She was tapping commands with her slim fingers. As the land below heated, a plume of steam erupted to receive the ship, cushioning it against crashing into the mountains of ice and guiding it in an arc towards the surface. It splashed into the lake that had appeared.

'Flues!' I said, frantically, as an alarm sounded. We had barely seconds to prepare before all the water froze, trapping us.

'Flues up!' said Njike.

Two tubes, like a snail's antennae, began to prod out of the *Chapungu II* and burn their way through the ice. At their heads were nuclear-powered pumps, to get the water out of the tunnel we were creating as we seared deeper into the ice. When it was time for us to leave, the water would be allowed to fill the tunnel again, raising the *Chapungu II* to the surface while the water froze behind us.

The alarm fell silent; so far so good. I turned my head to see how Dr Hanga was doing. The academic seemed alone with his thoughts. There was no time to ask him, but I am sure I could guess what they were. He was reflecting on the fact that his own parents had seen this planet with their own eyes. The planet his parents knew did not exist anymore. Except, I reflected further, he wasn't actually seeing this planet with his own eyes right now. None of us ever could. Rather, he was seated in a superheated metal shell that was literally burning its way through sheer ice. Our old world was new, waiting to be discovered.

Another alarm sounded as I guided the ship to a rest. Njike looked at me, her face filled with awe. 'We are here!' she said in a hushed voice.

'It is here!' I said.

For two weeks, our robots bored deeper into the ice. Njike worked them, repaired them, reprogrammed them. I worked the ship. Dr Hanga retreated to his lab. How the *Chapungu II* was bearing up under the conditions on Pód deviated slightly from the projections the Exploration Lab team had come up with during simulation runs. All this new data could be valuable if we hoped to revive our lucrative prospecting licences sales. Or if we hoped to make such expeditions more affordable in the future.

One hundred and forty-eight Standard Years, nearly to the day our planet was flung from the life-sustaining warmth of the Three Suns, we found Prof. Jama Hanga's notes, a ndarium-encased cube the size of a human fist. There was no time to celebrate the moment. The cube was programmed to collapse in twenty minutes once the temperature around it changed by just two degrees. I transmitted the ship's credentials, encrypted in what would seem to a casual scanner the random seismic vibrations of ice under pressure.

'It should be happening now,' said Njike, rising from her seat. I followed her to the lab. We paused outside for a moment. This was it, the recovery of our past that would take us to the future.

The door panel slid aside. Dr Hanga was not alone. Another man stood over him, a hologram, dressed in the attire of a planet-side Bvukian. The family resemblance was startling. 'About two hundred years ago, scientists at the Bvuku Astronomical Institute projected that the Commonwealth of Worlds would face an acute water shortage. The most viable option to confront this disaster lay in harnessing the comets. We were developing a Repulsor Beam that could move massive objects in space. So, the official version of history, that planet Bvuku was dislodged from its orbit when it was hit by three comets at the same time, plunging it into its perpetual winter, is partly true. We, a team of scientists in our bid to sustain the life of millions, are responsible for the death of millions.'

Professor Jama Hanga paused, as if waiting for the full impact of his words on his audience. 'I cannot predict what conditions my message will find you in. If there are security concerns, and interplanetary intrigue and ambition have escalated since my time, it is likely that you are left with no alternative but to apply the repulsor to military purposes. If that is the case, look upon this world, your world, and think long and hard about the power you would unleash onto the Commonwealth. I pray that you will see at once that a secure future for all lies in returning to our original goal in developing the beam.'

Again, Prof. Hanga paused, this time to change his tone, from that of a pedagogue to a demagogue. *'Our leaders'* vision was of the immense power we would wield by controlling the system's water supplies. The power to sustain a population whose growth would be inevitably precipitated by the creation of the Commonwealth.'

This time, the pause was longer, as if the ancient scientist had foreseen that we would need more time to process this ultimate vision. Then, he smiled. 'I do not know how long it has taken you to raise the funds for this mission. But I am sure that you have come back home, to your past, because your future depends on it now more than ever. I will now transmit to you all our knowledge of the Repulsor Beam. I will also reveal to you the location of the prototype that drew the comets close, and, alas, pushed our homeworld away. You will need it to defend the knowledge that you have now acquired. I leave you with a fervent prayer that the ancestors rise up to guide and protect you now! The millions who died here, the onus of ensuring that their deaths were not entirely for nothing is on you.'

Prof. Hanga leaned forward and made a motion with his right hand. The hologram winked out, leaving us in utter silence. 'Let's get started!' he said, heading to his workstation.

The Interplanetary Water Company

Njike's robots found the prototype Repulsor after a three-week search. There was enough scrap metal around it to build more bots to execute the engineering programme that she had written. The *Chapungu II* had been designed to take us back home. Now that our mission had been a success, however, we could modify it to become the first base of operations here, the saved fuel essential for our prolonged stay. Any of the interplanetary eavesdroppers monitoring our transmissions would learn that the *Chapungu II* met its end after a power failure, and its crew perished. Interest in Pód would wane for a period long enough for us to strengthen our presence.

I was in my quarters when Njike came in, breathless, to announce that a Renjeian ship of the Kodi class was now in orbit around this planet. We rushed to the cockpit. I turned on the transmitter. 'This is Space Lieutenant Kalu Loma of the Pód and Kalinda VII Space Force. Please be advised that you have illegally entered our territory.'

The response was immediate. 'That is a matter of formalities, which I have no time for, Loma. Soon, you will join the Empire and whatever it is you have down there will be the property of the Emperor!'

'My government has not informed me of any intention to join your Empire!' I said, my voice calm despite a rising anger. 'Until then, I am under orders to defend this planet.'

There was a mocking laugh at the other end. 'You and which army? This ship can locate you by the vibrations your equipment is making on that lump of ice and blow you away in seconds.'

It could, at that.

'The Rombesans would not like that, I am afraid. Come to think of it, neither would your Emperor.'

'What do the Rombesans have to do with anything?'

'Planet Rombesa is our first customer,' I said. 'They have ordered water from us. That is the purpose of this mission, to obtain water from Pód and transport it to Rombesa. You will find that it was properly documented with the Commonwealth Secretariat.'

The transmitter went off. No doubt a little conference was being held aboard the Kodi. Minutes later, the transmitter came back to life. 'What if we just came down there and took over this operation? I am sure the Rombesans do not mind who is selling them the water as long as the delivery is made.'

Spoken like a typical Renjeian functionary. I glanced at Njike. 'Ten minutes,' she mouthed.

'You have less than ten minutes to do all that,' I said, my voice more confident. 'Because I am about to send you somewhere very far away. Thank you very much for stopping by, but we have work to do right now.'

I cut the transmission, and we waited for the Renjeians to come into range of the repulsor.

Masimba Musodza was born and raised in Zimbabwe but has lived most of his adult life in the United Kingdom. He has been published in Zimbabwe, the US, the UK, Jamaica and online. He has pioneered speculative fiction in his native language, ChiShona. masimbamusodza.co.uk

Safari Nyota: A Prologue

Dilman Dila

The humans were asleep. Not dead, or preserved corpses, which his Adaptive Memory identified as the right technical terms. Asleep, his Base Memory insisted they were asleep. Since B-Mem guided his operating system, it overrode the prejudices of A-Mem, so he saw them as asleep. With their eyes closed, their faces peaceful, their naked bodies floating in cryogenic tanks as though they were embryos in wombs, that is what it looked like. Asleep. But, his A-Mem was built to give him consciousness, to make him think and behave like his human doppelganger—who was in one of the five hundred and sixty-three tanks in this chamber, aptly named the Womb-Tomb—and the A-Mem had images of his *father* in a coffin. His baba had looked like this, seemingly asleep.

Polar error #985785185385.

Blink twice to autocorrect. Blink once to ignore.

Caution: Some programs may not function if you ignore a polar error.

He blinked twice.

Autocorrect kicked in.

They were on a journey across the stars to a planet called Ensi, which was blue and believed able to sustain life.

Humans could not make the journey alive for it would take a thousand Earth years, so they went into a long sleep, to reawaken upon arrival. Not like in the classical folk tale where a prince kissed a beauty to rouse her from a hundred years of sleep. Not like in the horror book where a scientist resurrected a mummy from a thousand years of death. Not like in Frankenstein where another scientist sewed up pieces of different corpses and gave the monster life. It would be very much like Lazarus, though in this case a machine, and not a god, would perform the resurrection, and the dead bodies would have been meticulously preserved for a thousand years, not just four days. It would be very much like hibernation, only that the heart had to be stopped for it could not beat for a thousand years and remain functioning. The Lazarus Machine would revive the heart while the corpse is still in the cryogenic tank, and then ease the reanimated human out of the tank just as though it were plucking a baby from a womb. Like newborn babies, upon awaking, the humans would have no memories. They would have to learn everything, including how to be themselves, from their android doppelgangers.

As part of autocorrect, Otim-droid floated down the Womb-Tomb to the seventh column of the twelfth row, where Otim-man lay in a fluid that made his beard look as though it was smeared with flour. This is an out-of-body-experience, his B-Mem instructed his A-Mem as he looked at his body in the tank. When the right time comes, I'll return to it, byte by byte, until I'm my old self again, back in my flesh and blood and bone body, in a new world, eleven light-years away from home.

But as he watched his face, as he looked at that all-white beard, which looked like a white flame, the resemblance to his father became so strong that it dragged up memories of his baba in a coffin of bark cloth. It seemed then that Baba's beard had grown a lot bigger and he had wondered if the mortician had added artificial hair to beautify the dead face? Possibly. His father had died in a boating accident. He had overstayed in the lake during a fishing expedition and the lake became angry. They found his body after five days. Maybe it was so grotesque that the mortician had to make it human, and so added a lot of facial hair.

Otim-man had wanted to look like that. He did not want to let go of the last image he had of his father, and he wanted this image to be the first thing he saw when he woke up in the new world. So, Otim-man did not shave for two years, from the day he became an astronaut. His beard grew wild and he bleached it white, until the resemblance to his father was so strong that some people, on seeing their photographs side-by-side, mistook them for twins.

Now, as Otim-droid watched his own face in the tank, he saw his baba's face wrapped in bark-cloth. Dead. Asleep, the B-Mem chimed in, like a parrot that had learned a word whose meaning it could not fathom. Dead, his A-Mem whispered. Asleep. Asleep. Asleep. Asleep. Asleep. Dead. Asleep. Dead.

Polar error #985785185385.

Blink twice to autocorrect. Blink once to ignore.

Caution: Some programs may not function if you ignore a polar error.

He did not blink. Otim-man should not have shown him that photo, the last one taken of Baba, but Otim-man had thought it very important.

'I can't be me without the memory of my father,' he had said. 'You must know about my father and teach my future self to treasure him as I have.'

They had spent countless hours talking about Baba, until Otim-droid could recreate the emotions the memories dragged up. They talked about Baba more than they talked about Nyakwe, even though Nyakwe's rejection had compelled him to become an astronaut and volunteer to crew the one-way ship. He had loved her with all his heart. He had wanted nothing but to be with her all his life. Alas! She was in love with another man. He could not live with that. He could not live on the same planet, not even in the same solar-system, where she was in another man's bed. He signed up for the call to pioneer the journey out into the galaxy, knowing he would never return, that he would die, and awake a thousand years later. He did not want to remember her when he awoke on the other side. He never showed his droid-doppelganger her photos, he never talked about her much. During the Memory-Transfer-Period, the one year before the journey when he lived with a droid so that the droid could learn to be him, he instructed it to ignore anything related to her. To dump it in the TrashDrive and to never bring it up in the reverse Memory-Transfer-Period, when the droid would teach him how to be himself again. He wanted to forget her.

Not Baba. He could not forget Baba.

Otim-man had shown his droid the photo album that told the history of his family. Pictures of his father as a little boy, playing on the shores of the lake, learning to fish. Baba with his first catch, a tiny tilapia, with his first boat, a small dug-out canoe, with the first house he built from selling fish, a mud-walled structure with iron-sheet roofing. Photos of Baba with his first love, who he married and was Otim-man's mother. Then there were photos of Otim-man as an infant, only that at that time he was just Otim, a little boy without a droid-doppelganger, relishing in the happiness of growing up the only child of a fisherman. There were sad photos, of when Otim-man's mother fell sick, of the long time it took her to die, of Otim-man and Baba sharing a beer at home after her funeral, of Otim-man crying and Baba holding him to comfort him. Then Otim-man joining the army, and a sense of happiness returning to the family. There were several pages missing, which Otim-droid suspected related to Nyakwe coming into Otim-man's life. The final pictures were from Baba's funeral, with the last photo being of Baba in a bark-cloth coffin, just before they lowered him into a grave, looking very much as Otim-man did now in the cryogenic tank.

Dead. Asleep. Asleep. Asleep. Asleep. Dead.

Polar error #985785185385.

Blink twice to autocorrect. Blink once to ignore.

Caution: Some programs may not function if you ignore a polar error.

The error dialog box hung in his eye sight like a picture frame, blinking like a neon light advertising waragi by making viewers tipsy.

He blinked once.

He floated away from his human doppelganger's tank, to the end of the womb-tomb where a bank of switches glowed. He initiated the key program, and a key protruded from his little finger. He inserted it into a lock and the glass panel protecting the bank of switches slid open. If he pressed the master switch, it would cut power supply to the womb-tomb, automatically turning off all the cyrotanks and immediately stopping the preservation of the bodies. This would save the three remaining batteries.

They were running out of power. A meteor storm had knocked out their lightsails. Though the photonic thruster still worked, the mirrors on the lightsails could not bounce light back to it so it could power itself in a cyclic system, nor could the thin film of panels generate power to charge the batteries. They were drifting. They had drained their backups in repairing the sails, and they had stopped the repairs for they were too far away from starlight to recharge.

They had to save power until they drifted into range of the nearest star, Alpha Magara.

Turn it off!

System error #885885778774

He could not. His programming was to ensure the sleeping humans reached Ensi and awoke successfully. If he cut power to the womb-tomb, the bodies would turn into shrivelled mummies. There would be no reawakening. But if he did not turn it off the batteries would drain before they reached Alpha Magara, and then the womb-tomb would shut down anyway. He, the last droid standing, would not have any power to keep his systems running. He had to shut down the womb-tomb.

They are asleep. Shutting down will kill them.

They are dead. Why transport dead bodies across eleven light years to a planet that might not support life?

Even if Ensi turned out to be exactly like home, the resurrection process might not work. No one had successfully resurrected a body after a hundred years in a cyrotank. Before the accident they were scheduled to reach Ensi in a thousand and three hundred Earth years. No one knew if a body revived after such a long period would function normally. Some projections said they would suffer from severe old age syndrome for the cells would have grown too old to be revived efficiently. It might have been better to clone them, but no one wanted to start a human colony with clones. The other option was frozen sperm and eggs, which were kept in special vats that did not need power to run, but no one was certain if they would be fertile after a thousand years.

The accident slowed them down. It would take much longer to reach Ensi, maybe an extra two thousand years. At their current drift speed, it would take three hundred Earth years to reach Alpha Magara for recharging. By then, all batteries would have run out.

He had to save power.

His A-Mem guided his hand toward the switch, but just as his fingers were about to touch it, B-Mem overrode the command. His hand fell so suddenly and slapped against his thigh that the bang echoed all over the womb-tomb.

System error #885885778774

They are asleep. Do not turn off the power.

Safari Nyota: A Prologue

After the accident, he had advised the captain that they must cut down on power consumption to save the ship. The captain had disagreed. Other droids had disagreed. Cutting down power consumption would involve, among other things, putting a lot of droids to sleep. Droids consumed half of the ship's power. They needed constant recharging, their parts needed constant servicing. Stowing them away would be tantamount to a death sentence for their parts would waste away in a long period of idleness. No droid agreed. They did not have self-destruct in their programming. Otim-droid's A-Mem would not have evolved to reason like this if Otim-man had not shown him the photo, but he had seen the photo, and he knew what death looked like.

He saw mutiny as the only way to save the ship.

He was a soldier, just like his human doppelganger had been while on Earth, in charge of the ship's defence. He wrote a program and emailed it to the captain as a security drill. His B-Mem and the WhiteCell.s security program would never allow him to write malicious software targeting the captain, so he wrote it as a drill. Even then, knowing his thoughts, WhiteCell.s prevented him from writing the program, until he activated a protocol which stipulated that WhiteCell.s had to allow him one security drill in the trip. The captain was suspicious, but her protocol demanded that she respond to any email from the Chief of Defence, drill or not. She opened it. The program shut her down and transferred the Cap.r file, which gave her authority over the ship, to him, as it would have happened in a real crisis. Being a drill, his B-Mem waited for the captain to reboot so it could transfer the file back to her. She did not awake. He had smuggled in code that would keep her turned off until someone manually powered her back on. After thirty minutes, his B-Mem decided she was permanently off, and so it allowed him to use the Cap.r file. He became captain. His first decision was to instruct all five hundred and sixty-three droids to shut down and then he used the service robots to stow them in the Garage.

Now, he could save the ship's batteries. He turned off the gravity simulator and other power-consuming features until he was left with two, the heater and the womb-tomb. One had to shut down to ensure the batteries would last to

Alpha Magara. If he shut down the heater the ship would freeze. Its chips would malfunction, and some parts would eventually break apart. The ship was their world. He had to keep it warm. There was even a high chance that many droids would reboot successfully if the ship stayed warm. He had to keep the heater running.

But the womb-tomb...

System error #885885778774

He could not do it with B-Mem in charge. He had to shut down and reboot with A-Mem as the default system memory. And yet, B-Mem would not allow that to happen.

He floated out of the womb-tomb to the Garage, where all droids were asleep, suspended on hooks in the ceiling. He stopped in front of his captain and touched a button on her chest, powering her up. Then, he shut down Cap.r, and B-Mem interpreted that as intention to relinquish captainship. To do that he would have to reboot. As Shutdown started, WhiteCell.s shutdown for five seconds. That was all the time A-Mem needed to write and launch a boot-virus that infected B-Mem. At restart, WhiteCell.s momentarily transferred the file Sys.r to A-Mem so that it could clean up B-Mem. The moment it did, A-Mem changed the file's attribute, making it the owner, and thus the default system memory.

The captain was awake. Her eyes, glowing red with anger, fixed on his left shoulder where a green light blinked to indicate that A-Mem was in charge of his systems.

'What have you done,' she said. Her voice sounded strangled, hoarse with a severe thirst, which is how the voice of her human doppelganger sounded when she was under a lot of stress.

'I'm saving us,' Otim-droid said. He punched her power button, shutting her down.

He whistled a song as he floated back to the womb-tomb, his hands working an invisible oar. Baba had taught him that song when he was only a little boy. It brought memories of the chilly air in the lake, of birds on the shore, the perfume of fish on his skin. When he cut power to the cyrotanks, it was just as if he were a janitor turning off unnecessary lights after everyone has gone to sleep. He hoped other droids would forgive him once they saw that his actions had actually saved their lives. He would show them the log, which would prove that if he had not shut down womb-tomb, the batteries would have run out long before they reached Alpha Magara and they would have all died.

'Row, row, row your boat, gently into the lake,' he hummed as he floated out of the dark tomb, using his night vision to avoid running into the dead in their tanks. 'Hmmph, Hmmph, Hmmph, life is not a cake.'

TO BE CONTINUED...

'Safari Nyota' is a multimedia project featuring prose, a graphic novel, interactive fiction for both mobile apps and web browsers, and a web film series.

The story is a little different in each media.

For updates, visit dilstories.com/safari-nyota.

Support the project at patreon.com/dilstories.

Watch the films when they come out by subscribing to our channel youtube.com/dilstories.

Dilman Dila is a writer, filmmaker, all-round storyteller, and author of *A Killing in the Sun*. Among his many accolades, he was shortlisted for the Commonwealth Short Story Prize and nominated in the Nommo Awards for Best Novella. He received an Iowa Writer's Fellowship in 2017. More of his life and works is at his website dilmandila.com.

Parental Control

Mazi Nwonwu

Prologue

The olive-green clock with large, luminous digital hands strapped to his arm chimed the final seconds of ten o'clock when Captain Dadzie breathed his last. Captain Dadzie, a fine officer, a gentleman, had led the Tin Island Braves for two years, and everyone, allies and foes alike, agreed that he was a formidable leader and a fearless fighter. Two days before, he had meticulously planned the charging of the Cattle Dung Hill. While most officers would be content overseeing the action from a rear vantage point, Captain Dadzie, as is his wont, was in the fore, swinging this way and that to relieve any of his men hard pressed by the enemy.

'Ahoy there!' he had screamed when he and the band routed the battlements of Cattle Dung Hill and linked up with their allies, the Six Jones Battalion. Awed by the tall dark dude with subtle war paints only discernible close-up, the Six Jones Platoon Leader shook his head and backed away two paces. It was better not to confront *The Dadzy* when bloodlust coloured his eyes.

Captain Dadzie died just as he wanted, with an empty gun in hand and dead enemies sprawled around him.

As his troops, the fraction that remained, moved in to carry their leader away from the fouled battlefield most of them had Nzeogwu's last stand in mind—this was because The Dadzy used to regale them of the exploits of his hero, Major Nzeogwu, and while this last stand didn't exactly mirror that of Nzeogwu, it was far grander for they were witnesses.

'Did you mark the time?' Sergeant Bulls Eye asked Constable Lee.

Constable Lee, an unusually tall Korean, looked at his blonde and thickset Sergeant for a bit before answering. 'Yeah I did,' wisely refraining from adding that he also confirmed the demise of Lieutenant Davids, Corporal Buckley, and Staff Sergeant Cowley, making Bulls Eye the ranking Tin Island Brave alive. As he looked at his fallen Captain, he was one of the few Braves with promotion in mind. It would be well-deserved. This is a battle meant for the history books, he thought as he bent to get better purchase of the late Captain Dadzie's legs.

Finally, the surviving Tin Island Braves reached their headquarters, bearing their dead and wounded on stretchers. A solemn procession it was that shuffled into the Braves' headquarters deep in Merit Wood. Fifty Braves had left that morning to meet an advancing rebel army from the outlands, only fifteen made it back whole. Of the twenty wounded, only nine could ever hope to fight again.

Woodkeeper Alice, whose job it was to nurse the wounded and see that the nutrient needs of the healthy were sated, looked on as the soldiers made their way across the booby-trapped approach.

She knew, without being told, that the Tin Island Braves had lost their leader. Dadzie would have been in the vanguard of the returning Braves, injury or not, and they would've been singing, win or lose.

Alice did not ask about the gaps in the marching troop or offer sympathy when her eyes met with that of the men. It was war, and everyone knew the price. She directed the wounded to the infirmary and pulled on her gloves as she rushed in to start the first aid that would mean life or death for the more seriously injured Braves.

'Did anyone remember to punch-out the deceased?' she shouted from within the white tent.

'Shit,' Sergeant Bulls Eye exclaimed, worrying about the big shoes he would have to fill and the soldiers he had to find replacements for, he had forgotten to punch-out the men they had lost.

It was a very serious error and one that would mean their sacrifice and victory was all for nothing.

'I punched-out, Sir,' Constable Lee intoned. 'Did it as soon as The Dadzy hit the earth. He is out, all the way out.'

Relief mingled with shame on the Sergeant's face. He shook his head, trying to shift the cobwebs.

'You know,' he said to Lee. 'I am very good at following orders. I am only as good as my commanding officer is. I can lead men and get the best out of them, but I do this by following precise orders, not thinking them up. Lee, I will need you to back me up on this, until whoever Dadzie is works his way back to the Island Braves.'

'You think he will come back?'

'I am positive he will be back, only we might never know it's him. One thing I know about him, he considered the Braves family. He will be back,' Bulls Eye said with a certainty that came from within.

Up in the sky, a skylark cried, and the gathered clouds were buffeted by a southerly wind that slowly but surely parted them to allow beams of sunlight to cleave the gloom over the collection of tents and wooden structures that served as headquarters for the Tin Island Braves. Far in the distance, other clusters of tents and wooden buildings sparkled as the sunlight caressed them.

1

Dadzie Maduka sniffed the food on his plate, shrugged and spooned some into his mouth. The food tasted okay, but he knew something was missing. He had never been able to put it to words, but he thought the problem with the food was that it was based on a generic menu that did not consider the inexact measurements of the Nigerian kitchen, where the size of a pinch of salt is proportional to the size of the individual cook's fingers, and where taste is also a matter of the idiosyncrasies of the human taste bud and acquired taste.

Dadzie liked his food spicy hot and slightly undercooked. He liked his greens barely cooked and his noodles dripping with sauce and his meat deep fried. At least, that was how he cooked it whenever he got the chance to prepare his own meal, which was rare as his mother cooked his meals and—because she doesn't sleep—he usually woke up to find a tray of steaming food on the old speaker box that doubled as his bedside stool and table.

'You do not like it?' His mother asked from the far end of the room.

'It's ok,' Dadzie said, not wanting to have an argument this early.

'"It is okay" is not exactly the same as liking it.'

Parental Control

'Please Mama, I can't do this right now. I am eating it, aren't I?'

'I bet it tastes great. I followed the instructions to the letter.' His mother pressed, ignoring the irritation in Dadzie's voice.

'I bet,' Dadzie said, scooping a chunk of brownish meat from the plate. 'Where did you get the ingredients?'

'I couldn't find the spices in the market, but the synthesiser did the magic.'

Dadzie dropped his spoon with a clatter. 'Synthesiser? You synthesised food?'

'Just the spices, I got the meat from the market. Dried though, but it hydrated well.'

She walked over to lean on the table and, appearing to ignore his hurt look, pinched a piece of meat he had spooned out and held it in front of her nose. 'See, the meat is natural,' she said.

Dadzie resumed eating, hating himself a little for allowing his irritation to get the better of him, especially as the spice appealed to him, and the meat though overcooked had a flavour that agreed with his growling stomach.

'I learnt you were killed yesterday,' his mother said, dropping the comment without warning.

'How did you hear?' Dadzie asked, feeling foolish as soon as the words left his mouth.

She laughed and rubbed his shoulder. He marvelled at how gentle her hand felt on his back and remembered how many times he had seen her bend steel with her hands or lift impossible weights as she cleaned around the house. He thought he should be used to it, she is his mother after all, but it continued to bug him. What if she forgot her control? It would only be for a moment, but with her, that would be enough time to crush every bone in his jaw, or whatever part of him she was grasping at that moment.

'They say you left in a blaze of glory. Everyone is talking about it. I think I am very proud. Dmtoo says you are now a legend and Estoo says her calculations point to your Braves winning the series on the strength of that victory alone. You should be happy Dadzie.'

'Everyone isn't your friend, Ma. What's there to be happy about? Even if the Tin Island Braves win, I won't be there to share in the glory, and though my banner will be there, it is not the same as being physically present.'

'You could go back you know. Trade in some of your points for a place in the Braves. I hear you lost a lot of soldiers on Cow Dung Hill, so the Braves will be shopping for soldiers soon,' his mother pointed out.

'You think I've not thought of that?' Dadzie asked with some heat.

'I know you have. Anyway, the game will be over in about a month. Why not take a trip instead? You could go to your father's.'

2

Dadzie had waited sixteen years to meet his father and as the plane taxied into the Abuja aerodrome he leaned back into his chair. He felt little need to hurry now that the day had arrived. He waited until the last passenger in his cabin was heading towards the door before, he stood up and pulled his knapsack from the overhead compartment. Travel light, his mother had said, a quirky way of telling him not to stay beyond the few days they had agreed. He smiled, thinking how much like a human his mother is. *She is more human than anyone I know.*

Dadzie's smile turned into a frown as he recalled how he had found out that she wasn't human.

Dadzie was seven-years-old and spent much of the time after school playing with friends at the tenement building they lived in then. It was late in the day and the kids were playing cops and robbers. Agile and fearless, even at that age, Dadzie, playing robber, had taken the fight to the 'police' and clearly shot Mark, who lived on the next block with his parents, several times. Mark had refused to fall as was the rule and an argument had ensued.

'I aint falling, cops are the good guys,' Mark had insisted

'It is wrong to say 'aint' and good guys only win when they are stronger,' Dadzie insisted.

'In the movies, cops win, in the end,' Sally, Mark's sister, who was supposed to be Dadzie's sidekick, offered.

'Well, this is not a movie and I shot Mark four times, he should be dead, or I am not playing again,' Dadzie said, turning to walk away.

Parental Control

'Who wants to play with you anyway? My father said we should stay away from you, that your mother is a mec, a robot. He says she makes all of them look bad at the plant, that she doesn't belong there. She's a mec, Dadzie's mother is a mec,' Mark threw at the retreating Dadzie.

Dadzie had continued walking, his head hanging lower and lower as what he thought was a victory turned into nightmarish defeat as the other kids took up the chant 'Dadzie's mother is mec! Dadzie's mother is a mec'.

Even at age seven, Dadzie, and all the other kids, had known what a mec was and how much people loathed them. They moved out of the tenement the next morning and into the suburbs where they had lived ever since. His mother made sure to hide her identity as well as she could, at least until the government introduced a law that banned discrimination against humanoid robots and androids.

It's almost ten years after, but Dadzie still smarts from those taunts and it was the fear of facing the same treatment that drove him into virtual reality and the escape it offered.

'Oh, you're still here, hope nothing is the matter?' an airhostess asked as she stepped into the cabin.

'No, nothing is wrong, was waiting for the rush to pass thanks,' he answered, wondering why she looked at him as if he was someone she knew.

Shouldering his knapsack, Dadzie stepped off the plane and was hit by a fierce blast of hot air. He had known Abuja would be hot, but not this hot. Strange, for someone coming from Las Vegas I should be used to heat, he thought, even though he knew it was the humidity factor: it was never this humid in Las Vegas.

Dadzie's Alincom, clasped on his right arm, buzzed and he tapped the patch behind his right ear to receive.

'You just got there,' his mother's voice said in his ear, 'Seen your father yet?'

Dadzie wondered if the electronic feel of her voice was greater than normal or if it was his imagination.

'Not yet, but I am walking towards the waiting area.'

'Okay, tell him I said aku.'

'Aku... What's that?' Dadzie asked.

'It's Fulfulde, your father will understand,' his mother replied with a laugh. He furrowed his brow, he had always wanted to tell her that she should have better control when she laughed, the higher octave seemed to ring too metallic, but he didn't want to hurt her feelings. Besides, she only laughed for him: part of her trying to 'bring him up like a normal human child' scheme. That scheme also included lessons on sex and sexuality when he turned thirteen, lessons that were beyond awkward.

'Do you still plan on staying three days?' she asked.

A tall man waving from the far end of the hall caught Dadzie's attention.

'I've only just got here Mum,' Dadzie complained, 'and I think James Maduka is here.'

'You need to learn to call him Dad you know,' she said.

'I don't. I don't think of him as my parent you know, not like you. He was never there. I know you told me about him and made sure I knew where he was and what he was doing. But it doesn't feel right to me.'

The tall man was walking towards him and he felt he needed to do the same.

'You know, Mum?' he said in a whisper, 'I thought when I finally get to meet him, I would run and hug him.'

'Like in the movies,' his mother said.

'Yeah, like in the movies,' Dadzie whispered.

3

Dadzie watched the athletic woman watch him as her husband, in a low voice, made the introductions. The woman had cold eyes, like a snake he thought. She had welcomed him with a cool stare, ignoring their greetings. He knew he wasn't welcome, that she hated him for some reason.

'Pelumi, this is my son. Dadzie, this is my wife, your stepmother.'

Dadzie had not expected her to hiss, but his raised eyebrow crawled higher when she ran her eyes from the top of the baseball cap he was wearing to his static charge shoes and back again before returning to the antique paperback she was reading.

Who still reads paperbacks, he wondered. He knew James Maduka was a green-nick, perhaps she was reading a paperback to annoy him.

'Dadzie, hand your bag to Jeremy, he will show you to your room. Jeremy will also give you a passcode and show you how to use the food dispenser in the kitchen. I will be in my study if you want me. Please feel at home,' James Maduka said, a sadness in his eyes colouring his voice.

Dadzie followed Jeremy, a second-generation house robot that lacked the fluidity and grace of later models. As they walked, Dadzie scanned the house, factoring in how different it was to the Spartan home he shared with his mother. The opulence was not strange to him. He had risen to the position of Minister of State in *Dictator 3* and the opulence of the minister's house was much more than this. *That was virtual reality, this is real,* he reminded himself. He wouldn't actually call the house opulent, it was mostly built from recycled material, but the workmanship was master craft quality.

'How long have you been working here?' Dadzie asked Jeremy as he followed him up a flight of stairs, trying but failing to ignore the rows of family pictures that lined the wall.

'99 years, 3 months, 4 weeks, 2 days, 12 hours, 59 minutes and 3 seconds, Master Maduka.'

'Eish, could you *not* go all roboty on me. Doesn't work on me. My mother is an android, so I know you lot are programmed to hold human-like conversations. And don't go calling me Master Maduka, I am Dadzie,' he said, laughing.

'Good to meet you, Dadzie,' Jeremy said, without turning, 'I've heard about you.'

'What did you hear about me?'

This time Jeremy turned, his metallic features bearing that fixed grin that freaked out many generation 2 owners. 'My record speaks of an android that did the impossible; give birth to a live human child,' Jeremy said, turning to his left as he reached the landing.

'Yeah, it will speak of that. The story of the human boy with an android mother is prominent in the AI chat rooms,' Dadzie said, unable to control the sarcasm.

'The record also speaks of a human boy that spends an awful lot of time in-virtual,' Jeremy said, as he stopped before a door and opened it. 'What are you running from, Dadzie Maduka?'

4

'What are you running from Dadzie Maduka?' his mother's voice asked, stopping Dadzie in midstride. In front of him, the traffic light walking man avatar beckoned him with its green pulsating light.

With his right foot caressing the first white bar of the zebra stripes across the road he was itching to cross, Dadzie turned towards the voice. There was no out of place feeling for him when he saw that the voice was coming from the humanoid traffic control robot leaning on a signpost.

Frowning, Dadzie tried to sniff back the blood that wouldn't stop flowing down his nose. He could tell from the numbness that his left eye was swollen. He stood, facing the robot, in a way that presented his right profile, defiant. He wasn't going back.

'What are you running from Dadzie Maduka?' His mother's voice asked again.

'They are mean Mama. They said I am a halfling, that my mother is not human,' Dadzie said. He meant to be brave, but the tears poured from his smarting eyes and he leaned into the metal and plastic body that offered comfort. 'I am not going back to that school, Mama.'

'Come home Dadzie,' his mother said from the speaker in the traffic robot's chest, 'come home my son.'

Dadzie did not go home, not immediately. He spent most of that afternoon playing truant, ignoring his mother's voice that came to him from the shuttle bay public address system, from the robot medic in the street ambulance that passed him in South Boulevard, from the Bus Rapid Transit shuttle and every cash point he passed.

He expected a lecture when he got home later that day, but his mother only pulled him close and started telling him about his father and how she had met him on a Mars bound research ship.

5

'What are you running from?' James Maduka asked Dadzie, who was leaning over a cyberseat fiddling with the straps of an I-Immersion headgear.

Dadzie didn't respond, he instead ran his eyes over the leather-bound cyberseat that bore the likeness of a dentist's couch. He gingerly thumbed the button at the base of the helmet and felt the steady buzz that told him the helmet was fired up and ready for an immersion.

For a moment, Dadzie forgot he was in the library of his father's house and that his father was leaning on the door frame. He pondered donning the helmet and escaping back into the world he had so unexpectedly been pulled from almost three weeks ago. He placed his right palm on his chest, recalling the searing pain he had felt as a blaster bolt tore through his armour and pierced his heart. Even before he heard the beep-beep that announced someone in his team had punched his code number into the system, declaring him dead, he knew there was no way he could have survived to continue to lead the Braves.

Three weeks out of the game, a game that held more meaning to him than what the real world offered. His mother said he was obviously itching to go back into the game, and that if he wanted it that bad, he should buy off one of the players still in the game. It was a tempting offer, one he had considered, but somewhere in his mind, a voice told him that it was something that addicts do and he wasn't an addict.

He had been with the Braves for three years, started off as a grunt but rose swiftly through the ranks. Two years, a year ago, he would have gone back without a second thought, but things have changed. Or rather, one thing changed. He had met his biological father for the first time in his sixteen years on Earth and ceased being a single-parent child.

'People who get addicted to in-virtual are most likely running away from something,' James Maduka said, bringing Dadzie back to the room.

'That's Benjamin Koons, right?' Dadzie said.

'Yeah, you read psychology? I didn't know that.'

'I needed to pass a psychology course to qualify as a team leader in a world game. Also learnt all there is to learn about first aid, map reading, and I bet I can drive or fly any automobile known to man.' Dadzie's sense of pride was not suppressed.

'Really, that must have taken an awful amount of time to learn. How long were you immersed?'

'Not really that long. The Editi system cuts all that real time talk of years ago by stimulating your brain. And you know you do things about four times faster in an i-IMMERSION.'

'i-IMMERSION? Isn't that military grade tech?'

'It is, or it should be, but since the army sends soldiers to take part in the world game, some of them shared the secret to advance the cause of their team.'

James Maduka shook his head slowly, awed at the teenager in front to him. How much of him was his own natural intelligence, how much was the influence of the android woman that raised him?

'Do you mean to go back to the game?' he asked, concerned.

Dadzie placed the helmet he was holding back on its cradle. 'I don't know, maybe I will, when I get home,' he said.

6

'What do you mean you want your son to live here?' Pelumi flung at her husband.

'The boy is okay, but I think he spends too much time in-virtual. He is just sixteen, and no matter how human his mother thinks she is, the truth is that she is a machine, something built to mimic. This child needs a subtle human touch, this child needs a mother, a human mother,' James Maduka reasoned in a whisper.

'I hope you are not saying what I think you are, James Maduka? First, I discover you have a bastard son, then you want me to be his mother. Do you take me for a fool?' Pelumi's voice was near screaming point now, and she looked like she would start flinging the fist-sized sculptures of Fulani maidens from the table near her.

'Calm down Pelumi. It's been months. I don't know how else to explain it to you. Yes, I slept with an android. Yes, the boy sleeping upstairs is my son. Yes, I still don't know how the android got pregnant, but I can't turn away from the fact that the boy carries my blood. I cannot let her raise him this way. You know the boy died last month? He was killed in Game World. He is fucking sixteen years old, but his life is spent more in-virtual than in real life. He is even contemplating selling his chips and going back into Game World,'

'And why do you think I should care about that?'

'Because the boy is my son, if you care for me like you say you do, then that should stand for something. You shock me Pelumi, you used to be so compassionate, what happened to you?'

'Your betrayal happened James Maduka, and any time I look at that boy I am reminded of the fact that I've been unable to give you a son,' Pelumi turned and ran from the room.

James Maduka watched his wife go. He understood the pain she was feeling, understood that she might never forgive him, but knowing did not make his decision any easier.

7

Dadzie pulled away from the door as soon as he heard Pelumi's footsteps approaching. He didn't think of her as a stepmother and any feeling of affinity that might have developed between them had been killed by the cold look in her eyes anytime their paths crossed. Hidden in the dark service robot recess in the space between the master bedroom and the study, Dadzie watched as she passed. He thought she looked very regal, with the way she appeared to glide across the polished floor, her chin in the air.

He thought about all he had heard and shivered. It wasn't fear.

He waited for the bang of her door closing before he ventured out of his hiding place. He walked on tiptoes, hearing the soft creaking of the shipping crate wood floorboards as loud cracks.

He paused in front of the door, half-turned towards the way he had come, and then he shook his head and rapped on the door, once, twice.

'Pelumi?' James Maduka inquired from within.

'No, Dadzie.'

'Come in.'

Dadzie pushed the antique aluminium door with his shoulder and stepped into the room.

At another time, the apparent sparseness of the room and the racks of books almost entirely covering one wall would have intrigued him, but his heart was too heavy for that.

'What is it Dadzie, you look forlorn?' James Maduka asked.

'I heard your quarrel with your wife, I am sorry I caused problems. I will leave in the morning,' Dadzie said. He spoke without feeling, as if he had pondered the situation and was taking a step that he considered practical.

James Maduka smiled. 'We didn't mean for you to hear. No, my problem with my wife started before you came. Yes, it is about you, your birth. We're working it out. Don't let it bother you,' he said, moving over to stand in front of the boy. 'About leaving, I don't think that is the right thing to do. I have spoken to your mother, but you officially became an adult on your last birthday and I think it is time you put away childish things and begin wearing the toga of an adult.'

Dadzie frowned. He took a step back, saying nothing.

'I know you, Dadzie. I have been watching you since you came, and I am beginning to think that that fierce uncompromising mien you carry is just a facade. I was in the army, I know a sixteen-year-old can't command an army if they are not super smart and resourceful. Enough with the invirtual. I agree that it has taught you about life, but if there is one marked difference between there and here, it is the fact that you don't get that many chances to try again. You have to learn to live in the real world,' James Maduka said, looking the boy square in the face.

'And you think I can learn that here?'

'Yes, but the choice is absolutely yours.'

'But your wife hates me.'

'I know Pelumi is very difficult to relate with at the moment, but I assure you that it will pass. She is a very sweet person when you get to know her.'

'I don't know what to say,' Dadzie said, pulling his gaze away from his father's.

'Don't say anything, just think about it. You can enrol in the space academy. I am sure that will give you a healthy dose of adventure, if you still want that. Or you can do anything you want. However, if you stay here, it means no invirtual, no World Games,' James Maduka said.

8

I don't want you here,' Pelumi said from behind Dadzie who was hunched over a cereal bowl in the dining area of the large kitchen.

Dadzie didn't look up. He nodded his head and continued to spoon the cereal into his mouth, saying nothing.

'Listen, I know it's not your fault. You didn't ask for any of this, but neither did I. I have struggled to accept you, and I guess I have accepted the fact of your existence, enough to say your name and allow you have a relationship with your father, but... I don't know... I really think I need more time to... you know... adjust appropriately,' Pelumi added, keeping her gaze on the boy who had stopped eating and was staring into his plate.

Dadzie looked up at last and his gaze was firm and his eyes dry when he brought them to level with hers. 'I understand, I will go before he comes back,' he said, clinching his jaw.

'Thank you,' Pelumi said and walked out of the room.

Dadzie watched her until she left the dining room then he nodded twice and tapped the patch behind his ear and hailed an air cab.

9

'James Maduka says I should come live with him and his wife says she doesn't want me around,' Dadzie said to his mother as he strode into the house.

'Welcome back, Dadzie,' she said, walking over to pick up the knapsack he had dropped by the door. 'You didn't say you were coming back today.'

'You are avoiding the question,' he accused.

'You didn't ask a question.'

'Ok... let's not debate human speech mannerisms now. What do you think about me living with James Maduka?'

'Dadzie, you know I don't think. You are an adult now and you can make you own choices. Your conception, birth, and upbringing were my purpose. I am what you may call the first attempt to have an android act as a surrogate for a human child. My purpose ended the day you turned sixteen.'

'Why are you telling me this now?'

'Because it would help you make the right decision, for you.'

'I have never questioned the right to call you mother, but I have always wondered how I was conceived. I know enough about human physiology to know I am human. I don't know if I am part android.'

'You are one hundred percent human. Your biological parents are James and Pelumi Maduka.'

'What?' Dadzie's eyes were as round as saucers.

'Yes, the egg was harvested from Pelumi Maduka.'

'But... you carried me in your tummy; I've seen the holo-gram of my birth.'

'Yes, I was designed to be able to carry a human child to term. That is the whole point of the technology creating an android surrogate. I am the first of many.'

Epilogue

The white military grade truck with a raggedy red cross painted on the sides lumbered into what had been no man's land a few hours ago. A tall youth stepped out of the passenger side and, medic bag in hand, ran across the gutted ground checking the pulses of the shot-up bodies of soldiers that gave their lives for what was essentially a worthless piece of earth.

'One is breathing here!' he called out, beckoning to his colleagues.

'What is your name and unit sir,' the medic asked the injured soldier as he cut off his combat fatigues to see how damaged he was.

'Dadzie, Captain Dadzie Maduka, Tin Island Braves,' the soldier murmured.

Mazi Nwonwu is the pen name of Chiagozie Nwonwu, a Lagos-based journalist and writer. While journalism and its demands take up much of his time, when he can, Mazi Nwonwu writes speculative fiction, which he believes is a vehicle through which he can transport Africa's diverse culture to the future. He is a co-founder of *Omenana*, an African-centrist speculative fiction magazine, and a Senior Broadcast Journalist with BBC Igbo service. His work has appeared in *Lagos 2060* (Nigeria's first Science Fiction anthology), *AfroSFv1* (first Pan-African Science Fiction Anthology), *Sentinel Nigeria*, *Saraba Magazine*, and *It Wasn't Exactly Love*, an anthology on sex and sexuality publish by Farafina in 2015.

Inhabitable

Andrew Dakalira

The smell of formaldehyde was faint, but Jumbe still caught a whiff as her eyelids fluttered open. Parted green curtains revealed streaks of a golden light she had not seen in a long time. Jumbe did not need the smooth, dark-skinned face staring at her to tell her where she was.

'Mukupeza bwanji?'

Jumbe ignored the inquiry into how she was feeling. 'When did I get here and how?'

The nurse smiled, revealing a set of pearl-white teeth; a perfect model in her uniform. 'The hospital? You were brought here yesterday. The farmer who brought you in says someone must have thrown you out of a moving f-car, because you fell straight into his aeroharvester.'

'Aeroharvester? Where exactly am I?'

'You're in Balaka, Malawi. Bwanji, are you alright?'

The district hospital's corridors, usually filled with moans of pain and sorrow, were instead inundated by Jumbe's maniacal laughter.

I was home. The lush pasture, with cattle lazily nibbling on tiny shoots, minimally supervised by cantankerous herd-boys. Light rain pattering on iron sheets, creating the fresh-mud smell outside that always raised even the lowest of spirits. Roast goat, with the aroma of fresh Kambuzi pepper still lingering.

'Wake up.' A slap to the face. Kareen was looking at me. It had all been a dream. I was not home. I was still surrounded by glass; still a prisoner.

'How bad was it this time?' She helped me off the cold glass floor. 'Did you give it anything?'

'Yes, I did,' I shot back, still a little groggy. 'Some Manganje music and M'bona's decapitation.'

Inhabitable

Kareen is still laughing when another voice chimes in. 'Who the hell is M'bona?'

Toni is by far one of the most beautiful women to have ever walked in any galaxy. I have said this so many times that Bayo voiced what everyone else was probably thinking; that I was attracted to her. They all agreed with me, though. She was tall, with a bronze face and sculpted cheekbones, plus the healthy muscle tone of a soldier. It was hard not to like her.

'A legend from my country,' I say, suddenly disinterested. 'One of the greatest sorcerers to have ever lived. I'll tell you about him some time. Am I the last one back?'

'See for yourself, "O Captain! my Captain!" All you need to do is twirl.' Jakaya's words were as condescending as they were true. The glass cubicle serving as our cell, suspended five feet in the air and only linked to the other glass buildings by an escalator, was sparsely furnished. We each had a steel bench, covered with what felt like polystyrene, and nothing else. It was easy to see that everyone was back.

'How long until they give up, you think? By my calculation, we have been here for two and a half Earth months,' Jakaya continued.

Kareen's response was unenthusiastic. 'I don't think we want them to give up just yet. At least, I don't. I have a feeling these neuro-probes are the sole reason we are still alive. Whatever it is they are looking for, if they find it, or decide that it is longer important, then we're toast.'

Nobody could disagree with that logic. I turned to the rest of the party for input. 'What's the matter with you two? You're unusually quiet. Any ideas?'

Hossam and Bayo glanced at each other. 'With all due respect, Captain,' Hossam said, 'I do not see the point of this discussion.'

Bayo's smile was light and playful. 'I hate to agree with El-Hadary here, but he's right.' Hossam shot him an annoyed look, which Bayo acknowledged with a lewd gesture. 'Besides, it seems we have aroused their interest even more now. Someone is coming.'

Species: Human
Planetary origin: Earth
Planet location: Unknown

188

Andrew Dakalira

Known associates: Oliver Mtukudzi, Michael Jackson, M'bona, Simba.
Probe results: Inconclusive
Recommendation: Employ alternative tactics; delay anti-colonisation mission.

The thing that came to get me was no different from my other captors. It had one eye, a nostril, and a mouth that was really just a no-lips slit. There were three claws on each hand, long, slender and poking out from a large grey robe, scaled like the Chambo fish back home. Its eye seemed to dress me down like a disapproving mother-in-law. 'You. Come.'

In the glass corridor, surrounded by purple and yellow shrubbery, I was an animal; caged and put on display. They all stared up at me, my brown skin a distinct point of fascination, despite the blue worksuit that covered most of it. The uninterrupted light was also something I was not used to. It was a mystery to me how this species, whatever they were, managed to live without darkness.

We went past a room I was all too familiar with—a reminder of the probing I had recently undergone—into a cubicle I had not been to before. Its single occupant seemed out of place, dwarfed by the gigantic screens it was looking at. It was the same as the others, save for the gold robe it was wearing. The robe shimmered as the thing turned to face me.

'We have not yet met, Captain, purely by design. I was very confident that there would be no need for us to do so during your entire stay here.'

Its grasp of the English language was impeccable, something which astonished me. It noticed. 'I see you're surprised by my fluency in one of your languages. We have the neuro-probe sessions to thank for that. We may not have the information we need, but we were still able to extract a few essentials. Your names, for example.'

I remembered Kareen's words, *whatever it was they needed had not been found.* 'What information do you need from us? If it is our planet's location, then you can forget it. We would rather die than divulge such sensitive information to our captors.'

Inhabitable

Its mouth let out a few intermittent hisses, which I took as a sign of amusement. 'Death? Believe me, captain, I have no intention of killing you or your friends. I admit that our methods have been far from endearing, but we were not sure if you would accept our request. Now I fear we have no choice but to approach you directly.'

'Request? What request?'

'Well, you see, Captain, we need your help.'

'So, let me get this straight,' Toni began. 'These things damn-near paralyse us with their daily probes, now all of a sudden they ask for our help?'

'Yes,' I replied, slightly annoyed by the reproach in her voice. 'If we agree to help them, they will let us go.'

'Captain, are you out of your mind? We cannot trust anything that these things tell us. Are you so naïve or too incompetent that you would take the word of an unknown species that may just kill us at any moment?'

'That's enough, Jakaya,' Hossam spoke, diffusing what would have been a hostile exchange. He, however, was also not convinced. 'He is right, Captain. We cannot just take their word for it. What guarantee do we have that they will not execute us anyway if we do as they ask?'

'We don't,' I said, 'but it is better than just sitting in this glass box, getting our nerves fried until they decide to get rid of us. Besides, as soon as we get on the ship, we can disable any tracker they have installed and destroy any ship that tries to follow us. Once we hit hyperspace, you know they cannot find us.'

Kareen lightly tapped the glass she was leaning against. 'You know, J, the question these space cadets ought to be asking is, what exactly do they need our assistance with?'

Part of me was glad it was she who had asked. 'Actually, Kareen, they really need just three of us; Toni, Bayo, and yourself.'

Bayo did not flinch. 'A career soldier, a weapons expert, and a nuclear physicist. No need to guess what these ugly little mongrels want.'

'Weapons? I don't believe that,' Toni spoke again. 'Captain, you saw the guns they had when they captured us. They paralysed our systems, for Christ's sake. Why would they need our guns?'

'I know why,' Kareen answered. 'There are some types of weapons that they do not have. Like the ones in the ship's hull, for example.' She turned to me. 'That is what they are after, isn't it? The six little devils.'

I nodded. 'They need to know how to arm and fire them, or if it is possible to manufacture more on this planet. Once we help them with that, they will let us go.'

'And why would we do that, only for them to turn and fire the missiles on us?' Jakaya had asked the question I did not have the answer to.

'By the way, Captain,' Bayo chipped in. 'You didn't happen to make this deal with a cretin dressed in gold, did you?'

'Yes, I did. How did you know?'

'He's coming this way.'

It seemed in a hurry. 'Have you decided, Captain?'

I took a step forward and immediately three guards raised their guns. 'We cannot help you manufacture or handle weapons you can just as easily kill us with,' I said. 'We refuse.'

'I anticipated that answer,' it said with a slight hint of disappointment. 'You misunderstand our intentions, Captain. The weapons are not intended to harm you. I wish I could explain further, but since we are running out of time, perhaps it is only wise to show you.'

It held out its hands, six yellow pills nearly slipping from them. Hossam instinctively stepped forward.

'I assure you, Captain, that these pills will not kill you. These are history pills. All they will do is show you why we are badly in need of your assistance. Besides, had it been my intention to kill you, it would already have been done. Now, I'm afraid I have to insist. We are pressed for time.'

I did not know this species well, but it is not too hard to tell when anyone is being serious. I took one, and it had hardly stroked my tongue before the room disappeared.

It was the same planet; the green, purple, and yellow shrubbery, had clearly been around for a long while. However, it had a certain freshness which had been absent from my glass prison. There was only one building here and it was at least fifty feet tall. The glass had the lemon green colour that hid whatever entry point it had, which is why my body shivered as I inexplicably found myself inside.

Inhabitable

Of the four occupants, only one seemed out of place. His purple head was peppered with streaks of grey, with what looked like a small blue tomato where his nose was supposed to be. It was clear that they couldn't see me; no one moved.

'You do not stand a chance, Bajaji. You are aware of this,' the strange man spoke directly towards the thing I only knew as my captor. 'Surrender now and save your kind while you still can.'

My captor, dressed in gold as I had seen him before, was defiant. 'You already destroyed one planet, Mbalale, you mbuzi. We offered you and your kind a chance to live here as our brothers, but you would rather conquer us. We shall not yield.'

Mbalale's hostility oozed through the pleasantries. 'Look outside, old friend. We are built for war. Your kind will not survive.'

'Be that as it may, we are united, and despite our primitive weapons, we clearly outnumber you.' Bajaji stepped forward. 'Go back to that wretched planet you call a home and try to save what is left of it. Perhaps it is not too late to correct what you have so unintelligently destroyed.'

'You always were stubborn, Bajaji,' Mbalale began to say, but I was drifting out of the building and back into the odd vegetation. It was then that I noticed them; camouflaged among the trees, weapons unstrapped. I knew they were with Mbalale, and as I turned around to warn Bajaji, I saw the familiar purple heads of my captors.

It was similar to an ant colony, streaming behind the lone glass building and beyond. Their heads lined up like dominoes, unmoving, aware of their opponents. Inside the building, I saw Mbalale smile and lift his arms. My body was instantly hit by a flail of painful blue light.

I woke up with a taste of copper in my mouth. Bajaji was leaning over me, holding what looked like a salt shaker.

'Are you alright, Captain?'

'I'm fine,' I snapped. 'What the hell was that?'

'Electronically-engineered tablets. We gave you the nanobots infused with the memory of our first war. We have to destroy them after each session, though, before they multiply. Which is why I have this.' He held up the shaker. 'They have all been short-circuited.'

'And if that thing doesn't work?' Jakaya asked.

'The nanos are also equipped with trackers. Should we fail to neutralise them this way, we use more shocking alternatives.' Bajaji seemed pleased with himself.

'That technology was only a concept in the medical field when we left Earth,' Hossam said excitedly. 'How did you manage to perfect it, yet you cannot make your own advanced weapons?'

I was about to reprimand our doctor for spilling out information, but Bajaji spoke first. 'Priorities, Doctor al Jabari. We have always been a peaceful species, until this conflict began not long ago. By the way, Doctor, I have been meaning to ask you; why does one of your colleagues call you El-Hadary?'

'Famous Egyptian football player.'

'Doctor!'

Hossam realised what he had done and immediately stopped talking.

Our captor only smiled. 'We do not have much time, Captain. War is upon us. Will you and your kind assist us?'

'This is not our war,' I said. 'It does not matter what happened during the first war. We will not help you slaughter each other, so you can kill us now if you want.'

Bajaji's smile disappeared. 'That is quite unfortunate. You must understand, Captain, that the last time they came, half of my kind perished. Without your help, then we are destined for failure.' Then, turning go, it spoke again. 'I told you that I would not kill you. However, given the circumstances, I cannot guarantee your safety. If we die, then you and your men shall die with us.'

Toni spoke even before the reinforced glass doors had closed. 'Is it just me, or has that thing just subtly said that it is going to leave us here for that other group to kill us?'

Species: Human
Cooperation Status: Unwilling
Recommendation: Postpone Anti-colonisation mission
Interplanetary Conflict: Imminent

The African Union Academy had taught us many things. Exploration missions were tough, and we had to expect different scenarios, even different species. Four years we had

Inhabitable

travelled in the deep, dark expanse, with only countless un-inhabitable planets providing a refreshing distraction. The galaxy was as we were told; a never-ending canvas of darkness and spinning orbs. But our mission had been a failure, until now.

'The very first planet we find with signs of life, and it just had to be populated by bloodthirsty animals,' Jakaya said, staring directly at me. 'Talk about bad luck. Who forgot to visit their mother before leaving Earth?'

'He does not really intend to leave us out here in this glass thing unprotected, does he?' Kareen was beginning to turn a shade lighter. 'I am not an expert on war tactics, but won't that make us easy targets?'

'You're right, Kareen,' Bayo chipped in. 'Captain, maybe we should reconsider helping them, at least for now. It just might keep us alive for a few more hours.'

I shook my head. 'It was agreed only a few hours ago that we will not be the people that introduce this lot to nuclear weapons. Besides, what if they turn those missiles on us? Also, our mission is to find new planets, habitable ones, for colonisation. With those missiles, we could very well destroy this planet.'

Toni's hand lightly touched mine. 'J, right now I don't think we have a choice. If we don't do it, then we're dead anyway. Besides, you saw what happened to them the last time they faced these guys. I didn't exactly finish the memory, but...'

I had not seen it, either, but she was right. Even without the rest of the memory, it was clear that not many of them had survived. 'Alright,' I said. 'So, we help them. I just hope that we do not regret it.'

Species: Human
Cooperation Status: Voluntary
Recommendation: Initiate Anti-colonisation mission
Interplanetary Conflict: Imminent

We waited. Outside the multiple glass buildings, in the green and purple, all was quiet. I knew who lay there, terrified by the prospect of combat, but unwilling to just lie down and die. Beside me, Bajaji was calm, concentrating on one of the giant monitors in front of him.

Andrew Dakalira

I was not afraid. Granted, the idea of dying on another planet, in another galaxy, was unnerving, but actually dying, my body giving up, was not unwelcome. I looked around at my team, sans three, noticing their anxious stances.

Bajaji said something I did not fully understand, until his eye flicked away from the monitor and upwards. Against the planet's bright light, the numerous hexagon plates provided shade that reminded me of my home planet. They were about the size of a half-ton pickup truck, their charcoal-grey colour not reflecting much light.

Bajaji's eye closed for a split second, and at once there was movement in the shrubs outside. Then, almost simultaneously, ripples of thin yellow light shot to the sky and the little plates rocked, flames bursting from underneath them.

'Looks like your weapons work just fine,' I muttered under my breath, but Bajaji heard me. 'They are really not as effective as you think, Captain. Wait and see.'

Some of the plates were falling. They crashed into the purple undergrowth, bits of grey metal and red flame providing an unwelcome change of scenery. Bajaji was not even looking, but there was no mistaking his hand signal; retreat. I could hear a faint humming, and then it happened. The remaining plates fired from the air in unison, transforming the bushes into purple and red fire. I winced as the heat permeated the glass shielding us from the flames. Outside, they were not so lucky. Purple heads had a darker shade of slime, while others lay in the middle of the ash, a few charred bones the only significant remains.

'Lieutenant Vermeen,' I began to signal Kareen, but Bajaji raised his hand again. 'Not yet, captain.'

'Are you insane? Your people are being barbecued out there, and there's one of my own with them!'

'I know that, but we must wait for a while longer. They cannot know about our plan yet. Listen, Captain. Can you hear it?'

A few seconds passed, before the humming transformed into the sound of a thousand bees. It was not coming from the plates, which were now descending. It was something else; something much bigger.

With its angled wings and tapered, smooth, silver body, it reminded me of a flying fish. It glided over us, covering most of the buildings with its shadow. I turned to look at Bajaji, who was not even flinching, eye fixed on the giant monitor. 'It's here.'

Mbalale was exactly as the memory had shown me. Right ear half-sliced, solitary eye tinted black, with the grey-and-black frame dressed in red. From the monitor, Mbalale's triumphant demeanour was apparent.

'I shall make this simple. Yield your planet to us and destroy all your weapons. There is no need for us to annihilate you. After all, we were brothers once.'

'Go to Vetibra and die,' Bajaji replied. 'I told you before that never shall we ever be ruled by a tyrant. We shall die protecting our planet.'

'I had not finished, Bajaji. I have another condition. You have prisoners, visitors from another world. I want them publicly executed, and their ship destroyed.'

I heard myself gasp while Mbalale continued. 'It was foolish of you to think that I would not be aware of such an important event. Now, you know what we are capable of. Do this within the next ten quintines. If you do not,' one tinted eye moved faintly, and the hexagon plates opened up, 'Those will only be the genesis of your downfall.'

I did not wait. 'Bayo, get in here.' He was through the glass doors in seconds, his normally-pristine uniform covered in ash and smelling like kerosene. Half his face was covered in tiny gashes lathered with black slime. 'I heard,' he said.

'The others are all set. After what that thing just said, I do not want you out there. He wants us dead in ten quintines, which is five Earth minutes, and I don't trust our current allies not to turn on us and act on it.' I turned to Bajaji. 'We need to act now.'

'Yes, we do, captain. You may go.'

The others were waiting. Jakaya was pacing around, speaking to no one in particular, while Kareen sat in her chair, unmoving. 'We have about three minutes. Does everyone remember what we have to do?'

'Yes, Captain,' Hossam replied. 'I already collected the samples we need, so the rest is up to all of you.'

I was about to bark everyone into their positions, when I heard the distinct crooning of Toni.

Andrew Dakalira

Ni nde undirije mwana
Yo gacaracara
Yo gacana injishi
Akenyegeza ibisabo
Wirira wihogora
Nkwihorcsc

'What are you singing?'

'My mother used to sing it to me when I was a child,' Toni replied. 'Something like, 'who made my child cry, don't throw a fit, I will calm you down' and all. She always sung it when I was troubled. Seemed appropriate.'

'I like it,' I said, and she looked into my eyes and gave me one of her disarming smiles. 'Time's up. We should get the signal anytime now.'

The signal came in the form of a giant plume of smoke; Bajaji's men had taken down two of the plates. Even as we rose, we could see the two sides' ground troops firing on each other in the charred underbrush. I knew what we had to do. 'Shoot at the little plates first. That ought to get that big fish's attention.'

It did. Toni and Bayo concentrated their machine gun fire on the hexagon plates, and at once the underbelly of the big ship began to move. It was repositioning, getting ready to fire, just as Bajaji had predicted.

'Now is your chance, Captain,' Bajaji's voice materialised from within the ship. 'We are counting on you. Also, if you miss, you die along with the rest of us.'

'It would help if you shut him up, Captain,' Bayo interrupted. 'Concentration is hard enough already without his bullshit.'

'Yes, Captain, that would be wise,' Toni echoed. Then, directing her gaze at Kareen, 'Are you sure these things are okay?'

'Yes, dammit, now fire!'

Simultaneously, two thermonuclear missiles were fired at the large vessel. I stared, waiting for impact. There was none. Kareen sat still and only spoke one word; 'Wait.'

'Wait for what? That thing is about to vaporise us!'

The big ship's stomach rumbled, and cracks began to show, bleeding out molten flame. We watched as, like melting plastic, parts began to disintegrate. The hexagon plates also began to fall, crushing unfortunate troops on the ground beneath them.

'We did not think things all the way through,' Toni disrupted the unusually silent bridge. 'Those troops down there are going to get crushed by all those falling dishes.'

'I anticipated that, which is why I recalibrated the nuclear cores in the missiles to melt the pieces, not just tear them apart,' Kareen said, her eyes betraying excitement and satisfaction. 'At least it won't be as bad. Isn't it time we left, J?'

I agreed. We had kept our end of the agreement. 'That was the plan. Are we okay, Jakaya?'

'We will all be better if we get the hell out of here, Captain.'

We had just passed the melting monstrosity when a familiar voice filtered through the ship again. 'Leaving so soon, Captain?'

I had expected this. 'We have done our part, Bajaji. Now, as per our agreement, we are free to go. I'd rather not wait, lest you change your mind.'

'We still have a war on our hands, Captain. It would be unfortunate if...'

'It would be unfortunate if you forgot that I still have more missiles aboard this ship,' I interrupted. 'Now, I have taken out your biggest threat, even some of the little ones. You can do the rest. I told you before that this is not our war.'

Bajaji's hologram came onto the bridge, his mouth straining into what I'm sure was an attempt at a smile. 'Very well, Captain. I truly am grateful to you. We shall not be colonised in the near future, thanks to you and your technology. Perhaps we shall meet again one day.' Then it was gone.

'Meet again. God forbid,' Bayo exclaimed, cracking his knuckles. 'You did sweep this whole thing, didn't you, Gufuli?'

'Yes, I did, while your face was getting roasted, and don't call me that,' Jakaya fumed.

'Okay, everyone, relax,' I managed to say, trying to control my laughter. 'We found a new planet, the Doc collected the samples he wanted, and most important of all, we survived intergalactic imprisonment and kicked some alien ass. We accomplished what we came for, now let's go home.'

Andrew Dakalira

Something was following us. Jakaya noticed it first. It was a simple speckle on the radar, but when we were so close to home, such a thing was a major risk.

'Pirates?' Toni asked.

'Don't be daft, Kagame,' Bayo chimed in. 'Those are a myth. Besides, we haven't encountered anyone since we left the planet of whatshisname a couple of months ago.'

Something about what Bayo said made me think. 'How long until we have visual, Jakaya?'

The man did not answer, but instead pointed at something to my left. I turned and immediately wished I hadn't. There was one hexagon plate heading straight for us. The pilot was all too familiar; I had seen the gold apparel a few times before.

Kareen's scream brought me back to the ship. Bayo was slamming a skinny man against the aluminium floor. 'I asked you if you checked this place for trackers and you said you had! How the hell did that thing find us?'

'I checked the entire ship, I swear! I have no idea how he followed us here!' Jakaya was now being lifted off the ground.

I knew there was little time to do anything, least of all figure out how he had found us. The re-entry sequence had been initiated.

'Fire the remaining missiles,' Toni suggested.

'Don't do that!' Kareen snapped. 'We are attempting re-entry. You'll kill us too.'

There was only one thing to do. 'Warn ground control and strap in! There is nothing else we can do now. He timed this, and he timed this very well'

It still bothered me as we swept past the red heat, slowly approaching home. Despite our differences, I trusted Jakaya; he was competent. And if he was right about the ship being clean, how had Bajaji found us? And if he had been following us the entire time, why hadn't he killed us?

Bajaji fired when we hit Mesosphere. I tried to reassure myself that it was turbulence, but the explosion soon ripped through the ship's hull. Toni was saying something to me, and then she was gone. The last thing I thought of was how close we had come. Now, death was literally at Earth's doorstep and we had brought it there.

Inhabitable

'So, tell us, Captain,' one of the two men finally spoke to Jumbe, the mockery in his tone unmistakable. 'Do you really expect us to believe this wild story?'

'You have to, if you want to live,' Jumbe replied, tugging nervously at her hospital gown. 'Those things are out there, and now they know our location.'

'Which is, by your own admission, your fault,' said the other man. He had stood by the room's large French windows while Jumbe narrated her story. 'How exactly did they achieve that?'

Jumbe looked at her two visitors, well-built men in expensive suits. 'I have told you before; the history pills. They had inbuilt trackers so that they could be short-circuited afterwards. Clearly, we were tricked into thinking that they had been destroyed.'

The two men were apparently unconvinced. 'Look, Captain,' the man by the window began. 'Your ship was destroyed, your entire crew is dead, and all the samples you claim to have collected have not been found.' He was looking directly at her; Jumbe looked away. 'Worse still, you claim that an alien ship shot you down, something which was not detected by any of our advanced satellites.'

Jumbe had nothing to say. She felt drained. All the years spent travelling, searching for a new planet, and she had found one. They had endured prison, and then they had fought alongside their captors in order to earn their freedom, only to return to death and an untrusting world.

As the men left her, she remembered Bajaji's words. They would never be colonised. And what better way to ensure that than to destroy the only other intelligent species they knew?

The sun shone brightly on the freshly-mown grass outside the hospital. The skies were happy, the clouds playfully chasing each other. Beyond them, thousands of miles away, little hexagon plates, recently commandeered, lightly floated, waiting to fire upon an unsuspecting planet. Inside the hospital, in a room on the fifth floor, a solitary occupant softly sang to herself.

Andrew Dakalira

Ni nde undirije mwana
Yo gacaracara
Yo gacana injishi
Akenyegeza ibisabo
Wirira wihogora

Nkwihoreze

Andrew C. Dakalira draws his inspiration from the people, places and events happening around him. His stories have been published by *Brittle Paper*, Africa Book Club, *The Kalahari Review* and *Africanwriter.com*. His debut novella, *VIII*, appears in *AfroSFv2*. Andrew won Malawi's 2014 Dede Kamkondo Short Reads Contest. His story, 'The (Un)lucky Ones', was shortlisted for the 2017 Writivism Short Story Prize. He lives in Malawi's capital city, Lilongwe.

Ogotemmeli's Song

Mame Bougouma Diene

To Marie Therese Diene and her undying love.

The ChinaCorp's planetary-harvesting ship, the *Kublai Khan* decelerated over Mùxīng's moon, Mù-wèi-sān, the gas giant's gravitational pull stabilising the ship synchronously with the moon. As it spun to a halt the ship's reflective surface blended with the empty space around it, catching flashes of the Jovian world's tempests of resources and the large moon's shining frozen surface.

Standing by the glass panel in the Control Room, her black, red and blue uniform sending heat into her body against the effects of cryo-sleep, Captain Wu looked down on her mission's target. The layered gases, broken by the Great Red Spot reminded Wu of the vegetables her mother would blend with eggs into pies.

She missed carrots—most of her crew had no idea what they were.

'Lieutenant Arnaudeau,' She commed into her wristband.

'Yes Captain,' The 1st Lieutenant responded, his French accent breaking through his Canto-Mandarin.

'Has the Harvesting Crew recovered from cryo-sleep?'

Arnaudeau laughed. 'As well as could be expected. Still a little sluggish, but they're excited.'

'Perfect. We'll need a few more hours to lower the Great Khan into the upper atmosphere.' She didn't know why she had taken to calling the ship that. Perhaps because this was the first step to uniting the Solar System since the Western Chinese Empire's Han Industries and the Eastern Chinese Republic's ChinaCorp had agreed on the merger that ended the war.

Ogotemmeli's Song

Captain Wu shivered, unsure if she was still weary from the bone-deep cold of six months in cryo-sleep, or in apprehension of the responsibility she carried.

She retired to her quarters while the ship's computer guided the *Kublai Khan* within harvesting range of a patch of hydrogen floating on the planet's upper atmosphere.

If the corporations had merged only two hundred years ago, they could have been here much earlier; perhaps she would have known what an organic orange tasted like.

Lieutenant Arnaudeau chimed in on the com-line. 'We're in position, Captain.'

'Good. Have the harvesting crew connect the pumps to the outer hull. No leaks, I hate helium on the air, and what we breathe is recycled shit already.'

'Yes, Captain. Beginning Planetary-Harvesting now.'

Wu took her position in the ship's Control Room. This close, the planet's curve was invisible, only an endless sea of brown and beige gases and micro-storms merging and dissolving in peevish bursts.

The pumps spread their hungry black tentacles down from the ship, disappearing into the swirling atmosphere.

And that was it.

Six months of cryo-sleep, years of training to operate the equipment, more years of building the prototype, and now all she had to do was wait. She would have to make something up. No one would want to hear about how dull the process was.

'The tanks are full, Captain.' Arnaudeau informed her.

Already? Well...damn. 'Well done, 1st Lieutenant,' she said, thinking about the next ice-cold plunge into cryo-sleep. 'Have the crew check the pressure on the tanks. I'll supervise from the Control Room.'

'Of course, Captain.'

Wu turned on the screens to the storage containers. The football field-sized tanks swirled with the colours of Mùxīng, mingling freely until the crew floating around them inserted suction pumps, pulling the different gases apart, and storing them.

'Captain,' Harvesting Sergeant Rahman, commed. 'We have a minor leak, it was expected, but we're losing hydrogen and helium, and...'

Mame Bougouma Diene

His voice drifted as a cloud of brownish-red gas hissed from the canister, passed in front of one of the screens, pulled itself together into a fist, and smashed into the face panel on Rahman's suit.

The young sergeant gasped, tendrils of hydrogen and helium pouring into his throat and nose. The arm elongated, the gas formed a shoulder, neck, the outline of a face, and then smiled at the camera, Rahman's corpse floating behind it.

The tanks exploded. Hundreds of gaseous beings swarmed the remaining team, tearing through their suits and bodies. Their miasmic forms changed dynamically, limbs without bodies, heads floating in shifting colours, anthropomorphic elements appearing and disappearing in a flurry of violence. More of the beings made their way into the ship's filters, and soon Captain Wu began to feel light-headed from helium.

She scrambled for the hyper-space transmitter, '*Kublai Khan* to Earth! *Kublai Khan* to Earth!'

Major Perng's familiar face appeared on the screen. 'Captain Wu!' He smiled, 'Congratulations! We were expecting you to-' His smile faded.

Wu looked behind her.

A tall, humanoid shape towered over her, its eyes an image of the Great Red Dot, its body the swirl of gases of the planet, and launched a fist into her throat.

She felt the oxygen sucked out of her, her lungs burning dry, held mid-air by the creature, and thought, *Now,* this *is a story*, and died.

Major Perng watched Wu's body fall through the being as it marched towards the transmitter. It looked directly at him, its face firmed, forming features with a broad nose, thick lips, and almond shaped eyes. It grinned at Perng and said: 'We were expecting you sooner.'

"*One thing that worried me, was that all the books that I read about astronomy, whenever they mentioned the history of the subject, there was always one part missing. It was the participation of Africans in astronomy,*" who said these words?'

Teacher Rakoteli pointed at the floating letters of blue-purple argon drawn against the yellow sky and the smouldering grounds of Fida. Impervious to the blinding gusts of superheated sulphur billowing through the children of her clan they shot their hands up to answer her question.

'Thebe Medupe!' a little girl answered, her hair glowing red and gold with neon while her body shifted in tones of brown dust broken by faint traces of water vapour.

'Very good Seynabu,' Rakoteli answered, though her eyes glowing a moment of purple reprove, her body and hair a uniform brown of dust held together with opaque traces of carbon, 'but you spoke out of turn. No points for you.'

She pointed at a distracted young boy, dissolving into the storm and rebuilding himself of random elements billowed by the wind, a little lava mixed with greenish-blue gas mélanges.

'Olumele!' she snapped.

'Yes, Teacher!'

'Does what Thebe Medupe said matter anymore?'

'No, Teacher!'

'And why is that?'

'Because,' he said, dissolving completely, his voice floating over the class 'now, we're everywhere-'

'Apparently, it still matters,' a melodious baritone interrupted Olumele, who reappeared in a blast of nitrate. The voice came from a being of pure flame, emanating waves of intense cold, an ice cube dancing in his eyes.

He ran his hands through the boy's flickering hair, the mix of gases crepitating to the flame, looking at Rakoteli who bowed her head. 'Why humble yourself, Rakoteli?' he asked. 'You are Okyin Afi. Fida is yours to rule, I'm just a passer-by on your humid planet.'

'You're always welcome, Ogotemmeli,' she said smiling. 'Fida isn't humid. Feel the static on the storm. Don't you miss the tremor of wind on your ball of ice and flame?' she teased, dismissing the giggling children who disappeared in puffs of vapour.

'I wouldn't have it any other way,' he said, letting her wrap her gases around his ice-cold flame, freezing and melting over him. 'The duality of Awukuda is the duality of life,' he responded, laying a hand on her floating waist, absorbing some of the storm to sustain him on the planet.

'Why are you here?' she asked. 'You seldom come anymore. Our drumbeats sound empty without your song.'

'I'm sure others have come to perform here,' he said.

'Yes,' she said, smiling faintly. 'And you haven't answered me.'

'Ha! I wish it were to make children laugh and parents cry, but I'm on official duty.' He'd missed Fida he realised. It was a world to his liking. Warm and angry. He had missed her too, fleeting though her form may be. 'What Medupe said six hundred years ago, might still matter.' He exhaled deeply, crystallising the air before him. 'The Okyin Yaw has called all the High Griots to discuss the intrusion on Yawda.'

'I know this.' Rakoteli said, smiling faintly.

'Yes. That's why I waited for your High Griot to leave. I shouldn't be here, but...' he hesitated, they knew each other from old, and his heart didn't lie. He was a storyteller, and he would tell her any tale she wished. 'It's one of my... instincts.'

'The Xam you rant about?' she laughed. 'Ever since you'd trail your father peddling arcane tales, you've had these hunches. Well, out with it.'

Ogotemmeli smiled. Xam was always his burden. His and the other griots. 'The Osrane are venturing into space.'

Rakoteli's body shifted colours, gaining and losing elements—grey to green, to grey to blue, to a dark black, raging like the storm around them.

'But the Benadan have deflected their probes for a century... No matter, they can't harm us anymore,' she said firmly, though betrayed by her shifting body.

'Perhaps,' he said, changing to warm ice, flames dancing in his eyes, soothing her with his heat. 'We shall see what the Yawdan say.'

He turned back into flame. 'I have to hurry. I'll return on my way back to Awukuda, with stories for the children.' The flame burned stronger, sucking all the cold into itself, shrunk to the size of a pebble dancing on the gales, and shot into space.

Where the hell do they land? Chief Technical Officer Kiania Hui Bon Hua-Figuerido thought, watching the black-breasted grouses fly by the windows of her company helithopter. The birds' hazel wings blended with the dusty air swirling around the aircraft, the clouds filtering the sun's bright rays to mud, only the vibrant red of the grouses' combs marked them against the streaking particles.

The birds were from the forests of Upper Yangtze, but there were probably more trees and ponds in Beijing than anywhere in the Republic. It was hard to believe there were any left at all.

One of them slammed into her window, its face splattering against the glass. The darkened window reflected her slanted green eyes over her light-brown skin, and the bird's blood seemed to stain her teeth. She looked a killer—she felt like one, even though she wasn't, yet.

'We'll be landing in ten minutes, CTO, lots of dust in the air.' The pilot's voice rang through the speakers.

The thopter broke through the clouds and over Beijing.

Metal and concrete spurted from the soil. Buildings twisting and screeching like angry lianas, barring the earthy sunrays from the streets. Two-hundred and fifty million people living like roaches, and roaches living like kings. The avenues spreading from hundreds of circular plazas disappeared into a horizon barely a few blocks away.

She could see small parks, rare, tiny bursts of greenish-brown, with sickly veins of dark blue water, out of place in the ravenous beast of sewers and sweat.

The merger had gone ChinaCorp's way, but she missed her home and the old Han Industries Headquarters in Rio, the city's hills, and the headless Christ, his arms open over the industrial bay.

'Landing, CTO.'

The thopter hovered above ChinaCorp HQ—three square miles of dragon-shaped spires and smooth, slanted, reflective walls; inviting the monster of the city to look itself in the eye—and landed on the central helipad, marked中國公司 of China Corporation in a cartouche.

A junior executive came to greet her as she stepped down from the machine to heavy gusts from the thopter's wings. 'CTO Figuerido!' he screamed over the beating wings. 'CEO Hans Chang would like to hear your report immediately! He'll meet you in your lab!'

Kiania's lab embarrassed her, but Chang walked in before she could clean off the dozens of vials and diagrams covering every unoccupied surface.

'Always up to something, CTO.'

'The war doesn't wait, Sir.'

'Never been righter, Kiania,' he said heavily, looking around at the clutter. 'Did your research dig out anything we can use? Fifty years, CTO. We can't afford another loss. You know this better than most.'

Indeed, she thought.

'So, what do you have for me?'

Kiania pressed a button on a console in front of her, opening a panel on a balcony overlooking a soccer field-sized glass box containing a large lump of gold under a thin cannon attached to the ceiling. She hit dials on the console, and the cannon shot a narrow beam of red matter into the metal.

'See?' she said, 'When you ionise the beam, it vaporises the metal...'

The metal bubbled and exploded into small to microscopic particles, until it was undistinguishable from the air in the box.

'Check the screen CEO. The gold is actually still there and when the beam vanishes...'

The beam snapped back, and the gold reformed itself.

'That's what we use for satellite mining. But now, if I modify the gravity pull by just this margin...'

She pushed a small button.

The beam hit the gold. The lump bubbled again, but as it exploded it shot up directly into the beam, the screen on the console registering no trace of Au in the box at all. Chang smiled.

'I need a few more days to finish the prototype and work on the red matter. I need to enhance it, and-'

'I think a field test is in order, don't you?' he asked rhetorically. 'What would be your suggested target?'

'Well. It's something for your Chief Military Officers to decide, but Jīnxīng will be in closer orbit than it will be for two years. We should move fast, CEO.'

'So? They're sending their fleet to Fida?' a voice boomed from a being of pure methane, icy smoke flowing down his neck in a boubou. 'They have sent warships to every planet in the system for fifty years... Every year was another Yawda.'

'It's a very large fleet, Karamata,' Djenaba, the Okyin Amene, interjected, interrupting her High Griot, her methane smoke body broken along her neck by icy ammonia forming intricate necklace patterns down to her waist. 'Perhaps we should send troops to Fida.'

Sitting on the floor, Ogotemmeli watched the exchange silently. In the fifty years since the intrusion on Yawda, the Osrane had lost millions of lives, their best technology consistently overcome. Yet he felt the weariness brought on by Xam, the tug of the previous lives passed on to him, and the holes in his memory. Something was off, but he couldn't name it.

He let his mind grow blank, looking at the palace Djenaba had called to life on the rings of Menmeneda, drawing together the dust and debris into a hut of blues and browns, colourful bits of stones forming each of the dignitaries' home worlds spinning along the walls. A courtesy for visitors from non-gaseous worlds, even the ice giants of Yaada and Aabada appreciated it, looming over the room like massive pillars of living ice.

'I agree with Kara,' Abeba, the ruler of Yaada said proudly, her indigo head looming over the circle, delicate braids of methane hydrate reaching into it. 'Rakoteli's a relative on my mother's side. If she needed our help, I'd have heard it first. She didn't bother to send her High Griot, I wouldn't worry.'

The attendees nodded, they would call on relatives first, but again Ogotemmeli had doubts.

'What can the Osrane do to us that they haven't done before?' Tiwonge, the Okyin Bena and angry ruler of Benada, said dismissively. 'ChinaCorp tried to kill us once and look at us now. They tried to drain Yawda and would probably do worse to the other worlds. Four hundred and fifty years. They'll never learn. They can only make us even more powerful. If they attack Fida they'll be crushed. We should let their wave smash and go on the offensive.'

'They can always kill half of us again,' Ogotemmeli heard himself say out loud. 'Then half of what's left.'

Tiwonge threw him a glare, her reddish, dusty skin pulling together into a rocky carapace.

Ishimwe, Awukuda's Okyin Aku, laid an icy hand on the flame of his shoulder, melting and dousing each other in a blur. 'You're the oldest among us here, Ogotemmeli. Speak your mind.'

'Easy to speak when Awukuda is too close to Akwesida for the Osrane to reach,' the Okyin Bena snapped.

'It's interesting that since the conflict started the Akwesidan have not made their presence known.' Ogotemmeli said. 'They've... changed, since becoming pure energy. Perhaps there is something they see that we don't.'

'Further proof that we've nothing to fear,' the Okyin Yaa said.

'Or not,' Ogotemmeli said and rose. 'I'll seek their council, with your permission.'

Ishimwe nodded. 'You have mine,' she said.

Djenaba nodded as well, while Abeba shook her braids, and said: 'Why not? I trust my cousin. The Akwesidan advice couldn't hurt.'

Tiwonge fumed.

'I'll return shortly. On my way, I can observe the Osrane fleet. If anything's amiss I'll contact the soldiers on Benada, with your permission Okyin Bena,' said Ogotemmeli.

Tiwonge nodded grudgingly.

Ogotemmeli pushed his head to Okyin's and vanished from the hut.

Ogotemmeli paddled his fishing boat of space dust along the solar winds. He liked the boat; the motion of the paddle soothed his mind. It was meant for the open seas, and there was no wider sea than this.

There was something horribly off about this war. The Osrane were foolish, but perhaps his people had been too, before the red matter had shot from the satellites and modified their ancestors' cells. Perhaps when they were trapped in flesh, they'd had bigger dreams and smaller hearts.

And yet, here they were. The other planets owed Benada a debt for keeping the Osrane subtly at bay, but if they destroyed Earth, they would turn their backs on everything they'd stood for. They'd changed so much already.

Ogotemmeli's Song

There was a piece of his father that had been passed on to Ogotemmeli when he'd dissolved into the universe. His mother had followed soon after. He was the finger and she the string, and just as many times the opposite. Their atoms had needed each other. Perhaps he didn't let himself get close to Rakoteli for that reason. Perhaps he was a coward.

Some of the memories must still be there, all those who'd died when the sky had burned red, those who'd been scorched into the ground. Xam.

He drifted closer to Earth's moon. He was almost a hundred now, his cells wouldn't last much longer, fifty years maybe, but the planet had decayed since he'd seen it as a child. The heavily colonised moon, with its protective iridescent dome, artificial lake, and intricately connected towers, shone in stark contrast with the scars seared into its mother planet. The large expanses of blue were gone, shrunk to gigantic lakes, barely visible through the brownish vortexes, open air mines, and tentacular stretches of urban metal.

They'd been wise to leave. There were other worlds out there.

Ogotemmeli felt a pang of sympathy at their mad rush to pillage the rest of the system. What would he do? But something was missing. Not the water, not the ice caps, not the... *the Fleet!*

He let the fishing boat dissolve, and melted, bouncing from atom to atom in a mad dash to Fida.

The last of ChinaCorp's fleet appeared, but the battle already raged. A dozen battleships were falling from orbit towards Fida, burning against its outer atmosphere. Geysers of lava reached out of others, disaggregating and reforming in space dust. The Fidan army was fighting, but they weren't winning.

Hundreds of battleships blasted red rays at the swarming darts of rock and gas, and every time they hit the Fidan, their particles stood apart, shrunk, and vanished.

The red matter? What have they built, they're... killing *them.* In fifty years, his people hadn't suffered a single casualty.

Five destroyers lay hidden in clusters of battleships. Ogotemmeli sensed a sharp increase in energy, and one of the destroyers fired. A thick ray of red matter shot towards

Fida, boring through the golden atmosphere into the planetary core.

Ogotemmeli roared. *Rakoteli!* His voice echoed soundlessly, his cells burned with rage, and gathered space dust in thousand-mile towers.

ChinaCorp. Feel the bite of your dragons!

The towers turned into giant, winged snakes, their jaws growing and crashing into the ChinaCorp ships.

His own cells stretched and strained with effort. A few exploded. He gathered more space dust to compensate, welding random atoms into his own.

ChinaCorp ships exploded and went out. The Fidan warriors saw help and redoubled their efforts, slipping into engines, and draining them before melting the ships' hulls.

Ogotemmeli took out dozens more. The serpentine shapes closing in on the four destroyers getting ready to fire. He cut through the first two, then the third, the battleships disappearing into the energy propelling his dragons.

The last destroyer fired.

The thick red ray connected with the first cracking the planet's surface into ten thousand puzzle pieces momentarily glued together with magma like a purulent wound and, exploded.

The shockwave sent a ripple through the surrounding fleet, vaporising it instantaneously. Ogotemmeli dissolved, allowing the wave through him, the release of gravity replenishing him. He would feel the other Fidan doing the same soon and hear them laughing at the Osrane.

But the void was silent. Rakoteli's voice was nowhere to be found, her students were gone. The daring little boy and peevish girl. They were gone. All of them.

His shape snapped back, the flame and ice wrestling against each other for control. His people could kill all the Osrane anytime and occupy that drying dirtball. Was it sympathy he'd felt for them?

What have you done?! His weakened elements screamed at the disintegrated fleet.

He saw the few remaining Fidan warriors staring at the stony void hurling comets into space, their eyes wet with traces of water. They turned to salute him, then dived as one into the planet's core before the lava melted away, binding it together with themselves, spinning and spinning until it vibrated, and their cells disappeared into a brontide and sorrowful drumbeat, beating forever where Fida once spun.

'No to the war with the Elementals! No to the war with the Gods! No to the war with the Elementals! No to the war with the Gods!'

C^2-Police thopters hovered between the five-hundred story skyscrapers over the crowd of Elemental Cultists, machine guns gleaming, powerful wings beating the dusty air into a dome over the demonstration.

'You are part of an illegal demonstration!' voice enhancers boomed from the thopters. 'You are summoned to withdraw from the streets or we will open fire! You will be given a ten second warning! Remember to rely on ChinaCorp for your every need! Ten, Nine, Eight...'

The hundred thousand in the crowd resumed their chanting, shaking their fists at the thin streaks of sky between buildings. Others opened their coats, revealing localised seismic charges.

'...One.'

The thopters unloaded into the screaming crowd, machine gun fire rattling down the avenue like jack-hammers. The cultists hit the triggers, ripping the streets open with sewage-filled fissures, taking the city block down with them, the thopters, and the nine hundred thousand souls in residence in a screaming storm of concrete hail and bloody dust.

The shockwave spread without further damage through central Beijing. A few blocks away, Kiania braced herself for what she thought was an after-shock from the freak earthquake that'd followed the victory against the Elementals on Jīnxīng, a few days earlier.

Her driver deactivated the shock-absorbers, restarting the engine. 'No worries, CTO,' the driver said. 'Blasted cultists again. They'll never get the point.'

'No,' she said, looking out the window at the cloud of debris spreading over the city. 'But after fifty years of riots, they keep converting people, and the earthquake made things worse.'

'Pff... The Elementals aren't Gods. No matter what Wu's hyper-space message showed. Thanks to you, we know they can die, CTO.'

'And if I'd failed would you be driving me, or would you have joined the cultists?' He shot her a dark glance. 'I'm sorry. That was unfair, but what they are doesn't matter, Benyamin. They were on the defensive all along, will they attack now? Can we fight a war against them, and against ourselves?'

The merger between ChinaCorp and Han Industries seemed useless now. Planetary-Harvesting was on halt, and the planet's dwindling resources were swallowed in a conflict larger than the hundred-year battles between the hemispheres' corporate giants. And now there were earthquakes. They'd spread from Central Africa, a 9.3 on the Lǐ shì guīmó, ripping through deep-sea mining operations, covering a third of Australia under water. 139 light seconds after destroying Jīnxīng, the exact distance between the two worlds at the time.

There has to be a correlation.

Her car slid underground a few blocks from ChinaCorp's Headquarters, stopping after the security holoscan registered her vehicle and its passengers. She thanked Benyamin, and walked into the elevator, heading to her executive meeting on the top floor.

'Ha! CTO,' CEO Chang said, from the front of the table. CTOs and Chief Financial Officers from every regional branch of ChinaCorp were present, including her old Han Industries colleagues. 'We were expecting the delay. Damned Cultists.'

'Traffic delayed me, CEO,' she answered. 'It's getting worse with the influx of population from the after-shocks.'

'Don't we all know it? But you have found a way to end this war. We can resume Planetary-Harvesting soon.'

'Not if we destroy the planet again,' CFO Balamaci intervened. 'It did absorb the Elementals, but also cost us our fleet, and the few destroyers we had reverse-engineered with CTO Hui Bon Hua-Figuerido's enhanced red matter.'

'We've lost a lot of lives, but made definite progress, Balamaci,' CEO Chang countered. 'If we can keep casualties to a minimum, we can afford to destroy our next target. There's nothing for us on Huǒxīng.'

Except maybe another earthquake. 'We're making rapid progress, CEO.' Kiania answered instead. 'But your schedule might be too fast for us. I'd also like to examine the freak earthquakes we registered after Jīnxīng; they affect all the areas where we've used red matter for satellite-mining.'

'Yes, well...' he replied, waving a dismissive hand. 'We'll have to build better shock-absorbers around strategic areas. But my own CTOs are certain it's a consequence of red matter's lingering effects on the core. They will stabilise.'

'It's been four hundred years, CEO,' Kiania insisted. 'I doubt any of this has to do with the primitive red matter developed at the time.'

'And what do you suggest? The vengeful wrath of dead spirits?' The rest of the room snickered. 'You sound like a cultist. I need you focused, CTO.'

'Of course, CEO,' she said calmly. 'Even if it was the red matter, it would have little to do with Jīnxīng. But the riots, CEO. The Cult spreads rumours that we're paying the price of killing Elementals, for what was done to the places that were mined. Better investigate and squash the rumours for good.'

'Ha! I'm glad you're not giving into Cultish delusions,' he answered, convinced. 'And you're right—we need to show the population that we'll keep them safe. Investigate, as long as you don't delay your work. Now,' a hologram of Huǒxīng appeared in the centre of the room, 'on to our next campaign...'

'Destroy them now!' Ogotemmeli yelled at the Akwesidan occupying the sun, the dark streaks of plasma trapped in the magnetic fields of the corona forming a face of orange and black flame, smiling placidly at him, while he almost tore apart with Rakoteli's death.

How many songs could they have shared over the years? Those dead children could've been theirs, chasing after them, as he'd chased his parents and she'd chased him. She would've said he'd chased her. She'd favoured neon back then, bright reds and yellows—she'd been impossible to miss. She'd become more sombre later, but she'd always been too free-spirited for her heritage. They'd been just perfect for each other.

'Have you forgotten where you're from?' he asked, exhausted and furious.

The sun laughed, solar flares exhaling from its mouth. 'I wish any of us could forget anything anymore. And remember other things...' the Akwesidan calling himself Ngai answered.

Ogotemmeli wished they wouldn't do that. The Akwesidan had become so detached they hardly made sense. They had no Griots, no Okyin. They stayed warm at the heart of their star, naming themselves after old gods, oblivious to the universe.

They had forced him closer than even his Awukuda-bred cells could sustain for long, and they refused to fight. The Benadan were right, they had to go on the offensive, couldn't the Akwesidan see that?

'You have,' said Ogotemmeli flatly, 'you have forgotten everything. Xam, your friends, and family. They've destroyed Fida, they won't stop until they destroy us and themselves! Send your solar flares. Just one would end the war forever! There'll be life again! Time is immaterial to you, remember your people!'

'Do you remember yours? Xam has guided you here, should you doubt it now? Let yourself feel, Ogotemmeli.'

'I feel too much already... and you want me to search myself for more pain?'

'Yes, more pain. There's always more pain. How much more can you handle?'

A massive solar flare hit Ogotemmeli in the chest, melting his iced core, tying his atoms together with quantum voids, forcing him to break through the strata of agony, and into memory.

Nyadzayo looked over to the hills surrounding the gold mines in the plains and laid the last stone of the towers of Dzimba-Hwe. The sun shone high above him, his sweat drying on the stones like lacquer, and gleaming like the two distant rivers of the Gokomere.

The shining white robes of the Kilwa delegation appeared at the far end of the valley—come to trade in gold—just in time to admire the Gokomere's triumph.

'Daddy!' his son's high-pitched voice called, reaching all the way up the stone tower.

217

Ogotemmeli's Song

Shingirayi would be a builder just like himself, and his dead grandfather whose name he carried.

'Careful boy!' Nyasha, his wife, admonished their son. 'You'll scare him, and he might fall.'

She knew it wasn't true, but that wouldn't get in the way of her raising Shingirayi.

He took out his knife, and carved their names—his wife, his son's, and his father's—into the last stone.'

'Run Ahmadou!'

They should have expected the Yoruba to attack them in turn. Malam wouldn't tell her what happened on the coast. But she had heard of things. Boats larger than palaces and deep dark holes in rock where people disappeared.

She turned and punched a short, stocky, man in the face. He reeled back, surprised at how much strength she hid under her delicate features.

Her bald head caught him in the nose, sending blood into her eyes, blinding her just as she stumbled back and a sling wrapped around Ahmadou's legs, sending him face down into the long grass.

'Don't worry Haweeyo,' Abuubakar told his sister from the payphone. 'I have enough savings to last. I tear down walls every day, but you only get married once.'

Truth was he was heavily indebted anyway, but what did it matter?

'They pay well in Canada, huh?' Haweeyo asked. 'Must be for the heating bills.'

'Yes, and long-distance calls to Somalian villages. Gotta go, I'll send the money in a few hours.'

He hung up, zipped his blue Northface all the way over his nose, shoved his hands into his pockets and walked away.

When he finally got his visa, he'd been worried about the culture shock—where he'd pray, all that funny French, and he'd heard there was pork in everything. He'd looked forward to tasting pork. He should've worried about the climate shock. They called it 'Frette'. What they meant was -40c.

He missed Aden, even the pollution, and didn't see the crowbar coming as he rounded the corner.

Mame Bougouma Diene

'Pran lajan l'rapid,' someone said.
His left shoulder was dislocated, but he swung a hammer all day with his right. He grabbed one of the two hoods by the neck, pinning him against the wall, but his left arm was useless.
The crowbar hit again, and again, until he passed out.

'After a long delay, and believe me, no one is more excited than I am...' President Dambudzo Marechera said to the crowd of United Nations delegates assembled at the African Union Headquarters in Asmara.
It was a day most had never wanted to see, none less than the CEOs of ChinaCorp and Han Industries overlooking the hall.
The Eastern Chinese Republic extended tentacles into South and Central Asia and had anchors through ChinaCorp throughout Europe and the Middle East, while the Western Chinese Empire had grown since Taiwan bought the USA's debt and seized control of the NAFTA free trade zone and the Caribbean with Han Industries. It reached almost to Bolivia, through a loose network of protectorates and corporate buy-outs.
They would go to war. And both wanted a slice of the continent.
They'd called subsidising African farmers and manufacturers unfair competition, had accused the AU of harbouring terrorists when the Massina-Sokoto Caliphate cut access to uranium mines in the Sahara. Visa restrictions had backfired. The embargos had done nothing.
'...so with no further delay, I am proud to announce, that Africa is now entirely self-sustainable in renewable energy!'
Both CEOs stormed out of the room, to half-hearted applause.
'Why did we listen to the Caliphate?'
The black vortex of clouds dominated the horizons, swirling red, high up in the atmosphere, wrecking the towers of Lagos in a shower of lightning storms.
Chinelo could hear the screams from the streets, such things happened when twenty million voices screamed at once.

Ogotemmeli's Song

Chiagozie's hand landed on her shoulder. 'Because they were right.' he said, shutting the window but failing to block out the pain. 'There was no choosing between the Republic and the Empire.'

'We could've fought,' she said. Looking out the window to the city drowned in magenta hues, the shadows of fleeing millions outlined against the burning buildings like waves of bubbling tar, crashing into each other, fighting to gain more ground.

'We should've fought them,' *she finished, pointing at the sky.*

'We'll fight them again, my love.'

Something cracked over the city, followed by a large suction, a single, deep bass note, and then an avalanche of red energy, crushing like stones through shattering glass into the heart of Lagos.

'I love you,' they said, turning towards the window and the incoming ray, which swallowed block after block in evaporating waves of stone and bone. Hand in hand they pulled down the blinds and let the heat take them away.

Ogotemmeli stood alone, skin of dark brown, deep blue eyes peering out into a stormy wasteland, broken by chains of mountains and smouldering rivers of lava under a blue sky.

So that's what's left of our homes...

The oxygen-rich air flooded his brain with dizziness. He was cold, and weaker than he had ever been.

Where are the Osrane? Why aren't they attacking me?

He saw himself floating over Fida, hurling dragons at ChinaCorp. Damn you, *he thought at the Akwesidan.* Again? Why?

He saw himself reaching, the planet overheating and cracking, as a rumble threw him off his feet, and the ground waved and split beneath him, sending ripples into the ocean bottoms.

The cracks released the hint of a broken melody, strings that vibrated there and elsewhen, the bits of now and here to the bits of then and there, just beyond the limits of his body. It battered his emotions more strongly than music had before. It was his song, he knew the notes, but they broke against his vocal chords.

He tried to pull strength out of the air. He tried to expand. He was trapped in flesh, and the anger almost ripped his mind apart. He saw the universe, and Rakoteli dying, a faint trace of argon and neon battling each other for her last wisp, it was right there, but he couldn't reach it. Was that their pain? Always an atom away from eternity? A DNA strain away from knowing the void? He had to fill his life with everything he could take, to fill that emptiness, no matter the cost, no matter who...

No. *He closed his mind to the pain and looked back on where he'd been. It wasn't pain that tied them together...*

'Do you see now?'
The voice burned Ogotemmeli blind and tore him out of the world.

Akwesida bloomed ahead of him, Ngai drew back the flare leaving Ogotemmeli depleted, caught in the fevers of the lives he'd touched. Xam.

'I do. But what do I do now?' he whispered.

'You? You finish the song. There is a heart that always beats Ogotemmeli. It beats like the drums of dead Fida. It beats for home.'

The song was the key. To the war and to their exile.

'Perhaps I can make the Okyin Council see...' He hesitated, his cells too weak for him to think. 'Tell me, Ngai, what were you before Akwesida?'

Ngai smiled. 'I can barely remember the sound of my cows, or the taste of their milk, but I had many, and I tended them well...' His smile faded and disappeared into the sun.

Kiania barged into CEO Chang's office. The sky through the window overlooking Beijing was black with reinforcements for the Huǒxīng Campaign, and another minor quake felt like her stomach was sent lurching into her spine.

Hans Chang looked up from a pile of progress reports, his eyes red from sleeplessness. Six months into the Huǒxīng Campaign and ChinaCorp had scored impressive victories, but the elementals kept coming, running through their ships like strings of firecrackers.

She was certain now, it wasn't tectonic; the elementals *were* the quakes...

'You're tiresome, CTO.' He yawned. 'What now?'

Ogotemmeli's Song

She hesitated. The Board of Executives had implied several times that her suggestions were treacherously cultish.

'My apologies, CEO. I know how stressful times are. But I'm certain now. I've been comparing tactical reports against the seismic data. They're a perfect match. I must've missed some, but the margin of error...'

'Tactical reports...' he mocked. 'I've had a dozen meetings with our best seismologists, and guess what? They agree with you. Destroying the planet would have been easier, but the campaign drags on, one elemental at a time...'

'Yes, sir. But they always start in Africa. All of them. I honestly think that...'

Hans Chang rose from his chair and walked around his desk towards the CTO ignoring her. '...As for you, I'm afraid that, no matter how ground-breaking your contributions to the company, I have to ask you to step down, and turn in all your research immediately.'

She froze in shock.

'You're too erratic. I cannot have instability among my senior staff,' the CEO went on. 'Return to your office-lab and prepare the handover files. You'll receive full severance pay and a comfortable pension for your silence.'

He held out his hand.

He knows... she thought *...they all know... One genocide wasn't enough for them yet... even if it becomes our own...*

The corporations had been around for so long, they couldn't conceive of a future they didn't rule.

'I'm sorry I've let you down CEO.' she said.

'We all have our limits,' he said curtly, turning back towards his desk. 'Remember to rely on ChinaCorp for your every need.'

'He's waking up.'

Ogotemmeli heard the voices, still caught in the hum of Xam, and felt the slab of stone he was laying on slowly freezing with nightfall. He opened his eyes to Akwesida dropping beneath the horizon. A meddling mountain range reflecting the last of the rays from its frosty peaks. He had to fix the melody before the others retaliated.

'What happened?' he asked, looking into the concerned flame in Ishimwe's eyes.

'The marabouts have been binding elements into you for days,' Ishimwe snorted. 'We found what was left of you drifting towards Awukuda. The few Fidan alive told us what you did. You can't push yourself so, Ogotemmeli, none of us can. You-'

'I have to talk to the other Okyin and griots,' he said. 'What I saw...'

'The Yaadan troops are about to turn Earth into a snowball, a delegation is on its way now. The Okyin is delirious with pain. The Benadan are fanning the flames. Whatever you've seen won't make much of a difference. I'm of a mind to launch an attack as well. We all respect you Ogotemmeli, but this new red matter is too dangerous.'

The Yaadan chose that moment to land around them in a ring of frozen gases.

The Okyin Yaa looked around her, and then at him.

'Night is my favourite time to visit your world Ishimwe. I am happy to see your High Griot is alive and back from his foolish mission, but I don't see your troops—I was expecting thousands of warriors, not healers and citizens.'

Ishimwe snorted. 'Awukudan are all warriors,' she said. 'You best remember that Adeba, outnumbered and far from home.'

'Foolishness seems evenly shared,' Ogotemmeli said.

The Okyin Yaa's opened her mouth to speak, but he stepped in.

'I loved her,' he said. 'Since we were children, we'd been inseparable. Don't you think I want revenge? I was there when she died. You counselled against intervening, and now you counsel an assault? You want to destroy another world? Where our ancestors are still burnt into the ground? That will kill us all, on every world, and then what?'

'The Akwesidan told you those things?' Adeba said, ignoring his taunts. 'Those exact words—destroying the Earth will destroy us too?'

That's what the melody told him, but they hadn't said it. Some said storytelling was a lie. So, he lied. 'Yes,' he said, looking into her eyes. 'Those exact words.'

She paused. The Akwesidan were the oldest of them all. Ogotemmeli watched her face strain between her emotions, her traditions, and her own mind.

'The Osrane are already attacking Benada, we're taking losses. The planet is safe for now, but...' She sighed, turning to Ishimwe. 'He has to tell the Okyin Bena himself. I will not attack... yet, but only if he joins the fight on Benada. If we are to risk the planet then his life should be on the line as well.'

Ishimwe looked at him. He was still weak, but her honour depended on this as well.

'He will leave with you for Benada,' she said, turning towards Ogotemmeli. 'You loved her, it wasn't meant to be, but you did. We cannot take your pain for granted, but if Benada suffers the same fate as Fida, then the Earth is gone. I will land on it myself and set it on fire.'

'ID Please.' The officer's eyes popped at the rank on the ID bearer's card. How did a girl of twenty-four become CTO? And what was she doing at a cult fair? But it wasn't his place to ask, so Kiania stepped into the crowd of cultists gathered on New Tiananmen square.

Letting her keep her ID as a courtesy had been a bad idea, as was letting her access her lab before leaving.

She shoved her way towards the chaotic central stage where various cult leaders and agitators took turns insulting each other for their followers' amusement.

She stepped on stage unnoticed and did the one thing she knew would catch everybody's eyes. She stripped off her clothes and held up a syringe of red matter.

The air was warm against her chest, but the intake of breath by the crowd sucked it away, leaving her in cold silence.

Was she supposed to say something? She hadn't planned anything beyond the theatrics.

'Drop the needle or we will open fire!' a voice rang out from the security thopters. 'You have a five second warning. Remember to rely on ChinaCorp for your every need! Five...'

She slammed the needle into her buttock.

This has to work, this has to...

Her insides took fire at once. She felt her liver melt, then her right lung, then her left, and her stomach. She dropped to her knees, her hands glowing, leaving molten imprints in the metal of the stage. She tried to scream but couldn't, her open mouth blooming red with her vocal chords burning.

Her brown hair crackled and flew off, her eyes melting down her face. *No, no, no, no!* And the last of her synapses exploded. The red matter ran through her, gorging each of her veins for the world's cameras to see.

The glow shrank until only a blood-red tear floated on the breeze and disappeared.

The crowd was silent. The thopter had stopped its countdown. The air tingled with static, and a slew of raindrops hit the stage in a single line, echoing like rapid-fire, and took the shape of a translucent, naked woman, floating inches above the stage.

It worked! she thought, barely remembering the agony of the previous moments. The thopters opened fire, bullets passing through her, ricocheting on the stage and into the crowd.

Instinctively, she pulled heat out of the air, dousing the thopters in flames.

She drew the elements upon herself, becoming a single drop of water, and floated upwards into the atmosphere, while the crowd poured out of the plaza, rampaging through Beijing to another tremor.

'It's snowing on the ship, Captain!'

Captain Niimi-Feng had seen strange things since being dispatched to Huǒxīng on the Ming Destroyer; but snow falling in space was the strangest.

'Get ready to fire!' he commed back to his 2nd Lieutenant.

'It's too volatile, sir!' Panic registered in the lieutenant's voice. They knew what came after snow. 'If we wait until it solidifies...'

That's the point, the Captain thought.

'Start loading the weapon! Keep it aimed at where the snow blows thickest!' he barked. *We'll have a second, maybe less.*

The snow coagulated with a crunch, and an icy-blue being materialised, looming over the Ming, billowing frozen winds at the ship.

'Now!' Captain Niimi-Feng screamed as the giant brought down two destroyer-sized hands on the ship.

225

Ogotemmeli's Song

The red matter blasted the creature in the chest, just as its hands were about to smash the ship, and it dissolved into the ray.

His crew exulted on the com-lines.

I'm not dying today, he thought, just as a baritone note rang against the Ming's outer hull. *Oh no...* the walls around his cabin dissolved, the note vibrating him out of existence.

Ogotemmeli sat above the battle, playing the strings on a Kora drawn from the rusty Benadan dirt, while an ice giant disappeared to coordinated blasts of red matter.

A small note of space dust rose from his instrument, and sped towards the Osrane destroyer, gaining size and momentum, and crashed into the ship, turning all its particles and crew to vapor.

'They're getting better,' the Okyin Bena's voice rang over his shoulder.

Benadan warriors rained from their planet in clouds of magenta dust, consolidating around ships and turning to stone, crushing them to diamonds. But far too many were cut down by the red matter.

'The Osrane don't care how much they lose. And they hardly stand a chance,' Ogotemmeli said. 'They're unrelenting. Perhaps there's something to learn in that.'

'Have the Akwesidan grown addlebrained?' she asked. 'Or do they just not care?'

A hundred gaseous rhinos in brown and beige shades, charged down the plane of the elliptic, dodging blasts of red matter that hit other Osrane battleships, disintegrating them.

'Perhaps there is something to learn in *that*,' the Okyin Bena retorted.

The beasts melted into the ships, poisoning the crew, and reforming outside as the ships collapsed to Benada's pull.

'Well, we can certainly destroy them,' she said, rising, her hair a cluster of tiny golden meteorites in a halo behind her head. Something drew her attention.

'Ogotemmeli. You've seen stranger things than I. What is that?' she asked, pointing at a swirling mass closing in on Benada.

Ogotemmeli didn't recognise the pattern of elements. It approached slowly, a swirling mist of browns, greens, and blues, a flurry of minerals reminiscent of...

'Osrane!' the Okyin Bena growled, launching herself at the being.

Of course! Ogotemmeli thought, shooting after the enraged Benadan queen.

Why would an Osrane do that? Was it a trap?

If he had known the flesh, perhaps an Osrane had made the opposite choice.

He released his energies, trapping the Okyin Bena in a ring of ice and fire just as she struck at the intruder.

The essence of former human, Kiania Hui Bon Hua-Figuerido drifted towards Huǒxīng. The memories of trees and lakes, the few holograms of falling snow she'd held on to since childhood, all drifted away from her in minute particles of H_2O, chloroplast, and silica.

Her consciousness tugged her towards Earth, no matter how hard she tried to pull together.

ChinaCorp pacifier jets speckled the skies, dropping payload after payload on civilian areas. Rio was on fire. Had it only been less than a day?

A glimmer caught her eye above the planet's curve. A full fleet of Destroyers was preparing for translation to Huǒxīng.

If the people couldn't stand up to the company's war machine, perhaps the strange elementals could.

Strange? Is that what I am?

Huǒxīng glowed ahead, but a storm rose from its orbit, wrapped in a golden aura, coming straight for her.

Whatever it was, she hoped it would listen first, she thought, before losing consciousness.

'We should kill it.'

The Okyin Yaa wasn't the first to suggest it. The death of thousands of Yaadan had left her wary, and the mix of elements floating in the plasma bubble was an easy target for their exhaustion.

Ogotemmeli felt drawn to the bubble. The swirl of matter hummed to him. It was hard to keep his flame burning; it wanted to change, to become wood, grass, gasoline...

Ogotemmeli's Song

He placed a hand against the bubble, and dissolved into a pure cold flame, the elements inside pulling closer to him, pushing against the translucent plasma.

He drew all the heat under the dome to him.

The plasma bubble exploded.

The Osrane burst through, pulling herself together in a flurry of blended hues, and hit the ground panting.

Kiania looked up, her jaw dropping, letting little puffs of oxygen into the Huǒxīng air.

They were all different, a chaotic mix of elements held together into ice giants, gaseous ghosts, rocky armours wrecked with storms of gas. But she was right, it was there in their shifting features, in the dress and ornaments, Luba and Oromo, Berber and Nuer, Wolof, Ndebele, and others. Those who'd survived the corporate satellite-mining, and now they had her.

'They're coming,' she said desperately. 'They're coming.'

'That's a warning,' Ogotemmeli said, turning into flame-lit ice. He reached his hand out to Kiania. Their elements mingled, his warm ice turning her traces of auric powder to gold melting on the floor, and they merged into one. A giant of bubbling water, waterfalls in its eyes, and the breath of a forest after the rain.

Do you hear me? he thought at the Osrane girl. He didn't know her name, but he knew *her*.

Yes. She answered him. She felt her own weakness in the blizzard of the man's power, in how solid he felt, grounded in his worlds, while she was one sneeze away from vanishing. *And there is also a tune. What is it?*

Salvation. Or I'm a complete idiot. Why would you do this to yourself?

It's my technology you're fighting. None of us knew what you were. We have nothing left, we needed the resources. I understood who we were fighting, worse, the CEOs knew all along. I had to do something. I made things worse. ChinaCorp is losing it.

What happened to us? The red matter changed our ancestors somehow. Why is it killing us now?

I don't know. Everything we mine leaves an imprint. I don't know for sure, but the elements recognise each other, and then they vanish. Jīnxīng... *What do you call the second planet from the sun?*

Fida.

Fida was just a test, I didn't know the planet wouldn't take it, then the earthquakes started. We... She felt a change in his emotions and paused, letting his feelings for Rakoteli envelop her. *I'm sorry for your loss, I truly am, but we'd been losing people for half a century. All I ever knew was the war, my father died before my birth, my mother on one of the destroyers. I guess we all try to make up for something. But what about you? You can kill us anytime, why don't you?*

The song you're hearing? I heard it whole. I heard what your mathematics showed you. If you hadn't killed my only love, I wouldn't have convinced the others. You'd be dead and so would we.

The melody aligned suddenly, and they saw Earth, gleaming, blue, green, brown, and then it was gone.

Did you see-

Yes, he interrupted. *Yes, I did... I think I know what to do. I will need you, but...*

But we might not make it?

We won't *make it. Not in that sense.*

She thought back on the carnage she'd caused and the future she'd seen and nodded.

They separated, and the humming stopped.

Ogotemmeli turned towards his people, standing stunned.

'For a moment, you had us all in a bind,' Ewaso the Aabadan Griot said, his icy features twisted. 'And... I heard something...'

'What you heard is what the Akwesidan showed me. It ties us to them and them to us. We can't let this war go on, we have to *return* somehow, we left the continent when it was broken, we have to return to heal it.'

'Our ancestors sought elsewhere what was stolen from them. It's when they dug their heels into what was theirs that we became an inspiration to others, and a threat to the corporations.'

'Some of us must return, and find what we have left, only then can we leave this system, and become all that we can.'

The Okyin Bena laughed, a genuine smile lighting her eyes.

Ogotemmeli's Song

'We'll take care of the fleet,' she said, the other Okyin acquiescing with resolute grunts. 'You heal that dying planet if you can, but if we can no longer hold before you have, we will attack.'

'If you fail so do we,' Ogotemmeli said, turning to the other High Griot.

'Xam,' Karamata said.

The others chorused approval and knelt, placing their foreheads at their Okyin's feet.

'Your tales will be missed,' Ishimwe told Ogotemmeli.

'I've been told that once.'

'Sing when you get there, for all of us.'

He smiled faintly and turned towards Kiania. 'What is your name by the way?'

'Kiania Hui Bon Hua-Figuerido.'

He moved his lips soundlessly.

'Can't pronounce that,' he said. 'Are you ready?'

'I shot myself in the ass in public for this.'

Ogotemmeli laughed. 'You would make a fine griot.'

They merged.

'Gather your forces!' the Okyin Bena yelled at the other Okyin, the ground cracking beneath her feet. 'We're gonna give the Osrane what they're coming for.'

'Take out as many ships as you can,' Kiania commanded.

Six massive forces blew through the ChinaCorp fleet, slamming ships into each other, exploding bubbles of red matter absorbing industrial and organic matter alike.

Ogotemmeli heard new voices on the song, and Earth appeared in the distance. He remembered the stone towers built so many years ago.

That's where they'd land.

They broke through the clouds over the earth.

'Stop the carnage,' he told the others. 'Neutralise all ChinaCorp operations, their military and industrial bases, leave nothing, then join me.'

They broke off, and Ogotemmeli landed.

The land looked like a writhing snake, valleys and canyons of lacerations, like a slave beaten by a thousand overseers.

A dozen ChinaCorp pacifiers hit Mach 3 overhead. Kiania took over and scrambled the magnetic field around the jets.

They fell spinning and slammed their watery fist through the ground in a wide circle.

Water bubbled through the gritty soil, brown and muddy at first but the water washed out the mud. A small pond, and a few withering reeds. A start. But they would need the others.

Karamata and Afalkay, the Griot of Benada, landed and looked approvingly at the circle of Pacifiers.

'The skies are clean,' Karamata said, grinning.

'So are the streets,' added Waysira of Yaa, landing with the impact of a glacier along with Ewaso of Aabada.

'Knocked 'em cold,' Ewaso said, pounding an icy fist into his hand.

Maitera of Yawda landed last.

'I might have polluted the 'seas' a little...' he said, shaking his head at the blasted lands, '...nothing worse than what they were doing to themselves.'

The earth shook.

'The battle has started,' Ogotemmeli said letting drops of water flow away from their body, forming a liquid Kora and sat stringing an aqua-melodic note. 'We know what to do.'

Waysira and Ewaso called their ice djembe and balafon, pounding deep bass, and light notes.

Another minor tremor shook.

Afalkay called a kalimba of red dirt, dissonant keys, twanging over the bass and ringing balafon.

A shekere appeared in Karamata's hands, beads rattling a hip-shaking groove.

Maitera let his algaita appear from his breath, blowing a deep monotone in the thin tube.

They sat, the ground rising and falling in wavelets around them.

And they played.

The ground shook, and they dreamt of their families and their homes, and they played.

The melody shifted through rhythms before there were kings. Ogotemmeli hammered at the liquid strings, his voice gliding over the changing tones, trying to fall in line with all the broken notes of broken epochs.

Focus. Kiania thought. *They are only one song.*

He kept playing.

Ogotemmeli's Song

I am not going to last much longer, she said, feeling the last of her energy riding the tide of keys. *I'm almost there. Hold on. I'm close. Just a moment,* he answered,

He saw themselves play. A cascade playing a cascade, and dived back into his body, strong with his own soul and Kiania's, and the waterfall peeled away from the head of a bald man in a blue boubou with brown skin and deep-blue almond shaped eyes, playing a kora of bones and strings of streaming blood.

They were riding the melody now, the rising ground wasn't random at all, the streaming clouds overhead did so because they sang, and they sang because they streamed.

A halo of all their forces enveloped the griots. The earthquakes stopped. Kiania disappeared.

They all looked at each other, one with the vibration.

'The battle is won,' Ogotemmeli said. 'We can go now.'

They vanished into the atmosphere.

The ice giants melted into the ground, plunging through the cracks in the rocks, where they bubbled into a geyser, crashing to the ground, and spreading towards the dried-out ocean floors and filling them.

Afalkay, Maitera, and Karamata, merged into each other, creating matter and minerals that dispersed on the air, and where the geyser landed, small seeds grew into bushes, ferns, and lianas. Their combined elements drawing from the air and the ground the substance that would renew all that had been destroyed.

Ogotemmeli's eyes danced with all the elements of the universe, neither flesh nor soul, just music.

He struck a final chord and let the bones fall to the ground. He sung one final note, and let his arms and legs dig roots, his chest and neck thicken and elongate, the crown on his head turn into a thousand, thousand branches, and a baobab stood where Ogotemmeli's song ended.

'You need another Griot, Ishimwe,' Tiwonge said, looking at the Earth change before their eyes.

'So do you,' Ishimwe retorted.

'Do I?' she asked. 'And have a man argue my decisions in rhymes? No, thank you.'

Just as she said so, an Akwesidan appeared in a solar flare, radiating mid-summer warmth.

'You're late for the fight Eshu,' the Okyin Yaa said disapprovingly.

'You wouldn't want us to join, believe me,' he answered with a grin. '

Where will you be going? We'll keep watch here, as we have before.'

The Okyin looked at a star glowing brightly beyond the solar system.

'Sigui Tolo.' She said. 'We used to believe we came from there once. Well, we'll make it our home now.'

And just like that, they were gone.

Mame Bougouma Diene is a Senegalese-American humanitarian living in Brooklyn, and the francophone/US spokesperson for the African Speculative Fiction Society. His collection of novellas *Dark Moons Rising on a Starless Night* came out August 2018 at Clash Books. Google him, he's got some fun stuff out there.

CPSIA information can be obtained
at www.ICGtesting.com
Printed in the USA
FSHW011512301118
54150FS